TÉRÉSA
AND OTHER
WOMEN

TÉRÉSA
AND OTHER
WOMEN

SHORT STORIES

ALBERT MEMMI

Translated from the French by Stephen Wilson

The Book Guild Ltd

First published in Great Britain in 2023 by
The Book Guild Ltd
Unit E2 Airfield Business Park,
Harrison Road, Market Harborough,
Leicestershire. LE16 7UL
Tel: 0116 2792299
www.bookguild.co.uk
Email: info@bookguild.co.uk
Twitter: @bookguild

Copyright © 2023 Stephen Wilson

The right of Stephen Wilson to be identified as the author of this
work has been asserted by them in accordance with the
Copyright, Design and Patents Act 1988.

© for the original publisher Les Éditions du Félin 7 rue du Faubourg-Poissoniére 75009
Paris, 2004
Title of the original publication:
Térésa et autres femmes
(Éditions du Félin, Paris)

All rights reserved. No part of this publication may be
reproduced, transmitted, or stored in a retrieval system, in any form or by any means,
without permission in writing from the publisher, nor be otherwise circulated in
any form of binding or cover other than that in which it is published and without
a similar condition being imposed on the subsequent purchaser.

This work is entirely fictitious and bears no resemblance to any persons living or dead.

Typeset in 12pt Adobe Jenson Pro

Printed and bound in Great Britain by 4edge Limited

ISBN 978 191560 3159

British Library Cataloguing in Publication Data.
A catalogue record for this book is available from the British Library.

To Térésa
and even to Nathalie.

Contents

We were finishing our dinner   ix

The rose in the desert	1
Térésa	10
A taste of paradise or the last chance	22
Julibellule or the devil's darning needle	39
The grit in the shoe or the virtual child	60
The Sonotone	76
The ogress	91
The whore goddess	100
The Buddha's smile or love's good fortune	115
The Seine's castaway or love's misfortune	120
The double secret	125
A true friend	134
The two spoons	145
My neighbour's dog	149
A Kurdish passion	161
The swing of the pendulum	171
The carnivorous rabbit	176

The marvellous night   *219*

We were finishing our dinner

We were finishing our annual old boys dinner from the top class of the lycée Carnot, in a special room set aside by La Pérouse, that excellent restaurant on the Quai des Grands-Augustins.

There was a ritual we all understood, dictating that each of us had to tell a story, one experienced by himself or someone close, or as a last resort made up, but they all had to be on the same theme, chosen in advance by common agreement.

What do men talk about among themselves after a good meal when they get out their cigars and pipes? Hunting, war or women, nearly always the same subjects. That year's theme concerned our relationships with partners, despite the presence of a priest who, like everyone else, was smiling whilst waiting his turn.

I will refrain from giving the names of the different diners, some of whom now occupy public positions. I'll simply say that apart from the Abbé and our waiter, there was a high-ranking Corsican civil servant, proud of his conquests, small in stature and nervy like the goats of his native country; a public works engineer, two doctors, one of whom, a distinguished gynaecologist, took pride in the authority acquired through the exercise of his profession; the literary director of a Parisian publishing house, whose speech was typical of those fond of aphorisms; a writer who would have been quite pleasant if he wasn't perpetually sarcastic, a business executive, the columnist for a weekly art magazine and even the director of a marriage bureau… It can *easily be seen that "The two spoons" and "The marvellous night" are the Abbé's contribution, the triptych on solitude, that of the director of Matrimonia; I leave the supplementary pleasure of guessing the respective authors of the other stories, which I have done my best to recount accurately.*

Everybody has a different opinion on such a serious topic, and not always sympathetic, it would be unfair of me to attribute the authorship of all the stories. For my part, if the company of women has not rendered me blind to their faults, it has reconciled me to the human condition. I share this sentiment with most of my comrades: in the end, if we don't quite know how to live with them, we cannot live without them. As our literary director concluded, if the joy of loving is always precarious, it's a misfortune never to have loved.

The rose in the desert

Gilles Lourson had only written one book titled *Music and Literature: Correspondences*. Having vaguely dreamt in his distant adolescence of becoming a pianist, he was fonder of music than literature, but the work stimulated interest and gained him the post of artistic adviser in a publishing house. He demonstrated qualities of flair and judgement which secured his position, and that was enough to satisfy his ambition. From then on he thought no more of writing and limited himself to publishing other people's books; not without the occasional pang of nostalgia, but lacking bitterness, he sincerely enjoyed the success of his protégés.

He lived on the Rue Georges-Berger in the 17th *arrondissement*, but for a long time the area had become totally alien to him. He occupied an apartment left to him by his parents, where he was born, had grown up, married, and spent the two short years of his conjugal existence. Incapable of making the weighty decision to move, he continued to reside there as if it were a dormitory imposed by fate.

His life unfolded quietly around the Church of Saint-Germain-des-Prés, between his office on Rue des Saints-Pères and, at a few hundred yards distance, the Cafe Le Saint-Claude, where he usually ended his evenings, fixed his meetings with friends and ate a "mixed salad" accompanied by a glass of Beaujolais, before going home.

Come winter or summer he could be seen, sometimes on the right-hand pavement, sometimes on the left, where he bought the same weekly magazine in a kiosk situated near La Faculté de Médecine, walking toward Le Saint-Claude or coming back from Saint-Claude, always clad in a small hat made of English tweed and a jacket of the same material worn over thick beige corduroy trousers. When it was very cold, he added a reversible raincoat from the same manufacturer, without ever ceasing to suck on his pipe, most often not alight.

On this particular day, as he'd left his office and crossed the road to buy his weekly magazine, which had just come out, he found himself behind an attractive young woman, who had a large chignon of silky black hair, held in place by the elastic band from a yoghurt pot, according to the casual fashion of the time. He couldn't overtake her straight away due to the narrowness of the pavement and the heavy traffic on the road. Gilles Lourson, although not a fast walker, was like those car drivers who, having attained their habitual speed, harrumph if they're obliged to slow down and panic if you're on their tail. The young woman seemed in no hurry, stopping in front of every shop window, sometimes just to look at herself, but noticing his impatience she stepped aside to let him pass. Lourson discovered a brunette, actually very young, a fusion of the whole Mediterranean, large almond-shaped black eyes, hair of an opaque opulence set off by some loose curls, the probable shadow of a future moustache, waist likely to expand – he wouldn't be there to observe that decline – but for the time being an elegant, attractive young woman, as only certain girls from the South know how to be. He thanked her with a smile for having given way and having turned out to be so pretty; she smiled back very naturally.

But scarcely had he taken a few steps in front of her than he reached a junction and had to stop at a red light, which permitted the young lady walker to catch up with him, so they found themselves side by side on the kerb. He smiled again and this time addressed her, as if they already knew each other, which, in a way, was true. He apologised for his previous impatience:

'It wouldn't have mattered, despite your kindness… I'm not in a hurry.'

She gracefully replied that it was quite understandable; since the traffic was always heavy round there and he couldn't step into the road…

'Ah! You come from round here?' he asked.

'No… no… but I've passed by four times in the last two days, and there have always been the same number of cars.'

'Four times… for me maybe a thousand! But, forgive my indiscretion, why that number? Is it simply chance or is it intentional? Or is it just your favourite number?'

She smiled, white teeth:

'Neither one, nor the other, I'm taking an examination nearby.'

'In what? If that's not too indiscreet.'

The light changed to green; they crossed together.

'Public works.'

He thought he'd misunderstood:

'Public works? To become what?'

'An engineer, in Telecom.'

'Oh!' he said, genuinely surprised. So, women put themselves forward to become engineers… 'I admire that, truly.'

'Why? Did you think that women couldn't do it?'

'No… at least, yes. The two images, woman and engineer, don't go together in my head.'

'Well then,' she said in a challenging tone, 'they'll have to work hard at it.'

'I'm going to try, I promise you… to gain pardon, would you like to have a drink? You must be tired.'

She replied with the simplicity of the younger generation, or so Lourson imagined.

'Yes, and I'm thirsty! I haven't drunk since 8 o'clock this morning, it was hot in the examination room... but I haven't got much time: I have to be at Cachan at two o'clock for the rest of the exam.'

He looked at his watch.

'My God! But it's 12.45! You won't even have time to eat!'

'I'll have a sandwich... I'm used to it.'

'I'll buy you one with your drink, come on.'

He took her along with him toward Le Saint-Claude which wasn't very far, he explained, and which had the advantage of being near the *métro*. They sat on the terrace, from where one could see both the centuries old church, still intact, and La Rhumerie, where the same customers had imbibed alcohol for twenty years. Luckily, Lourson thought, he couldn't take strong alcohol, otherwise he'd probably have been sitting opposite and wouldn't have been able to view that marvellous monument, with undiminished admiration. Paris is astonishing, he thought, the way it blends a cathedral and a bistro together so naturally.

The waiter was slow in coming, Lourson went to look for him. His young guest ordered a potted meat sandwich and a mint drink with water; he had a kir.

'Aren't you eating anything,' she asked politely, in the tone of a mistress of the house addressing herself to an anorexic guest.

'No, I have to eat very soon with... you know for business... I'm sorry you're obliged to satisfy yourself with a sandwich... I hope we might eat together another time, really... but,' he hazarded, 'when would you be able to?'

'I couldn't right now. I'm with friends this evening, to celebrate the end of the exams. Tomorrow I'm catching an early train.'

'Where is your train for?'

'For my place, my parents' house.'

'Meaning?'

'You want to know where I come from? Where I live?'

He bit his lip, this time he really had lacked discretion, but he didn't discern any ironic nuance in the young woman, just as she hadn't shown any recoil from his invitation to a future meal. She was a scientist, a positivistic mind: she wanted him to be more precise in order to better respond.

'Toulouse.'

'Now, I realise; actually, you have a slight accent.'

She laughed cheerfully.

'It's true, I have an accent… my friends tease me about it…'

'But I'm not laughing at you!'

'I know, anyhow when someone gets at me, I thump them.'

'You thump them? How do you mean? You thump your friends?'

'Yes, with both hands, like this.'

'I'm sure you really do them harm.'

'Be careful, now you are laughing at me!'

'No, no, I hope you're not going to thump me…'

They laughed together, as if they were the same age, Lourson thought with satisfaction.

'I can understand your friends, you know, you're charming, accent notwithstanding, you laugh with your eyes, I like that a lot.'

'What do you mean! People say I have sad eyes.'

'Not at all! You have laughing eyes; do an experiment, hide the bottom of your face, look at yourself in the mirror: you'll see that they're laughing on their own.'

She seemed very pleased that he liked her eyes so much. He noticed and continued:

'They're very unusual: they're almond, as so often in the South, but in addition, yours are half-moons, at the corners… people must have told you… you must surely have some Nordic invader among your ancestors, a Mongol perhaps…'

The waiter placed the drinks on the table and the sandwich, which was enormous; Saint-Claude clients must often have lunched on a sandwich.

The young girl swallowed a large swig of mint, then attacked the half-baguette at one end. Lourson took it from her hands paternally, broke it in two, without pressing hard so as not to make the meat squirt out, and gave her back a half:
'Otherwise, you'll poke my eyes out.'
She laughed with her mouth full.
Lourson was playing at cleaning his pipe while watching her eat; he scarcely ever smoked since he discovered it gave him little pleasure. As for women, he contented himself with rare encounters in the neighbourhood.
'So? When will I see you again? If you're leaving tomorrow...'
'Oh! If I pass, I'll be here all next year.'
She seemed quite sincere; it wasn't some ruse to put off a too-forward old man. Or was it? He couldn't be sure; in any case he was happy with that information, which held the future open.
'How nice! May heaven and your examiners make sure you pass! But you will! You've got the head of a good *candidat*.'
'*Candidate*!'
'Yes, sorry, lady candidate; you've got the head of a future engineer.'
He hesitated, slightly worried, ran his hand over the surface of the table.
'I'm touching wood, and if, by some bad luck, you don't pass... can I send you a card?'
'Yes, of course.'
'How?'
'You mean you haven't got my address?'
'Er... yes, here's mine.'
He gave her his business card with the publishing house heading, that was his real address. She read it carefully.
'You're a writer?'
'No, not exactly, I work for a publisher.'
'So, you're a kind of literary civil servant...'

He looked at her a little shocked, but she was right, wasn't that exactly what he was? She added:

'Like me, I'm going to be a public servant for Engineering Works.'

'When you come back, you must let me know if you'd like to receive some books, from among those we publish of course.'

'Oh, I don't have much time to read… with all the technical stuff I have to take in!'

Apparently, she didn't miss literature.

'But I don't have a card,' she remarked. 'Hang on.'

She pulled out a yellow sheet from her bag, part of her examination paper, and carefully calligraphed her name and address in printing. She was called Josiane Bouisson and lived on the avenue des Remparts in Toulouse. She even added her telephone number.

'There you are.'

Then she picked up her bread which she bit into with the same relish.

'How old are you?'

'Twenty-one.'

He sighed.

'God you're young, Madam Engineer!'

The superb half-mooned black almond eyes laughed back all on their own, her mouth being occupied.

Lourson hadn't just wanted to pay a compliment; his remark derived from melancholy, also a little guilt: wasn't he in the process of trying to pick up a twenty-one-year-old girl? Soon he'd be running after female babies in their cradles… but then hey! At twenty-one years, one is a woman. How many times had his own mother proudly told him that at twenty she already had two children! When he got married to Monique, she was only twenty-two and he twenty-four; now he remembered very well, he'd never have thought at that age that he wasn't responsible for his life and his decisions. It's true that if he'd treated Monique more like a woman, she wouldn't have left. He knew now what he should have done; it was too late, but he knew... he could have at least pretended, for example given compliments, as you might to a kid...

'You've got a pretty dress, it suits you very well.'

'It's an exception, I usually wear jeans.'

He thought, without saying anything, that she was wrong; jeans only suited formless creatures. Thank God, Josiane wasn't lacking in that department. Anyhow, he had a horror of those asexual clothes, which prevented one from recognising a female bottom at first glance.

The sandwich had totally disappeared; she finished the last drop of her mint. He looked at his watch; not that he was in a hurry, editorial lunch hours were elastic enough and overflowed into the afternoon, but he felt responsibilities toward his new and so young friend.

'You'll have to be quick, you know, if you're going to get to Cachan...'

She glanced at her own watch.

'That's true, I'm going to be late!'

She put down her glass and got up. He got up too, hesitated.

'You're promising to let me know if you come back here aren't you?'

'Promise.'

'I can also send a card, to your place?'

'Yes, yes, of course, I told you.'

She reassured him almost maternally.

'You could come to Toulouse.'

'I don't really travel much nowadays...'

'Why not?'

'Because Paris is enough for me... it's a world, you know, one never finishes exploring it.'

'Ah.'

She seemed surprised that the whole world could be reduced to a single city, even such a prestigious one.

He accompanied her to the entrance of the *métro* where they said goodbye, see you soon. Fearing he might ruin it all, after having raised his small publisher's hat, he decided to plant a light kiss on the young girl's fingers. She smiled at him and rapidly descended the stairway. He watched her disappear, saying to himself he'd probably never see her again. But it made no difference. He felt an inexplicable sense of wellbeing, then became aware of the reason: as long as young women like Josiane existed, who'd continue to devour a sandwich in his company with such healthy appetite, all was not lost, he'd never be completely alone. One rose in the desert was good enough.

Térésa

Once a year the Paris PEN Club organises a sale of signed books to raise money for good causes. Jean Le Guillochet enjoyed great success as a writer. He had a faithful public, which confidently purchased each of his new works. Now, the PEN Club by preference called upon authors who could fill their coffers, Le Guillochet was regularly in demand.

So he found himself once again in the Musée des Monuments Français, flanked by two women about town tasked with helping him in his heavy duty, surrounded by a humming swarm of fans as well as the simply curious, come to verify the existence in the flesh of their favourite writers or current literary stars. For his radiant and eager selling assistants, it was clearly a big day. Their jobs were often acquired through fierce competition, in fact the author of their heart's desire was frequently sought by another person and that led to dramas.

'I said to the president, for me it has to be Jean Le Guillochet or nothing,' declared his companion on the left unabashedly.

The writer was as much embarrassed as flattered by her forwardness. Luckily the brouhaha stopped him from hearing the other assistant who was placed close to his bad ear! What was that grey-haired sexagenarian with hair cut à la tomboy, dressed in a Neuilly school uniform — lacy blouse over a kilt, trying to confide to him?

'Last year,' his first assistant continued, 'I was only a hostess, I bought one of yours, do you remember? I adored *Le Battoir d'argent*, like everything you've written!'

No, he didn't remember, he participated in several book signings in both Paris and the provinces every year. He murmured some vague thanks. However she was a tall, beautiful woman, a Viking type with slightly rough features, nose perhaps a touch too large but that was only apparent from the side and didn't look out of place in proportion to her face. Her tan, carefully maintained but drying out a bit, added to the impression of health, to the charm that changed according to the frequent and lively movement of her head. A large red cape was hanging on the back of her chair, "For which bull?", Le Guillochet thought, amused that her vitality extended to her choice of garment. Highly voluble, she would have reduced the other seller to silence if Le Guillochet hadn't felt obliged, out of courtesy, to drop the occasional word to his right, which immediately triggered a long speech of which he heard only the odd fragment. On the other hand he learned from his neighbour on the left, sequentially, that apart from the fact that he himself was vigorously in demand, she lived in Geneva although originally from Zurich (it's true, she spoke Vaudois with a Germanic accent), because her husband had chosen the Vaud capital as more suitable for his business. He makes a lot of money, she explained, with the simple admiration of Lutherans for those who succeed economically. But as a result, he works long hours and travels a lot, which didn't seem to bother her too much. She had her own life, hence her charitable activities, for example in the Geneva section of PEN, which had kind of loaned her to the Paris section, to promote an event which honoured all French speakers, etc. She talked excitedly and unceasingly, only stopping to reply to visitors, to receive the price of a book and give change.

The afternoon was exhausting but, as usual, a financial and social success. When the crowd eventually thinned out and the receipts had to be counted, the other seller, claiming a headache, perhaps put out at having been neglected, disappeared. Térésa – she was called Térésa – pulled out a calculator from her bag and set to work conscientiously. The result was flattering for Le Guillochet, she congratulated him warmly, he had "made a lot" for himself and for PEN, she noted in her light Genevan sing-song. She was glad to have been a part of it. He thanked her for her help, for her dedication to PEN, but it was difficult for him to explain that financially his gains were negligible. Like most readers, she thought that authors pocketed a large percentage: 50%? 40%? Less? That's not possible! 12%, it can't be true! Her husband also worked with books, he sold bargain editions of world literary masterpieces, principally in third-world countries... he made "lots and lots of money!" That insistence on what he *made* and on her husband's skill in making it, needled the writer. Wearied by the noise and incessant movement of the crowd, he was getting ready to part from Térésa when she declared with the same direct simplicity:

'I'm coming back to Paris next Wednesday, I'd be happy to talk it all over with you, we could lunch together...'

Le Guillochet wasn't lacking in natural seductive powers but he knew all too well that his true passport with women was his writer's aura. Flattered nonetheless, and out of tiredness, lacking the strength to refuse, he accepted. Térésa asked him to meet her at the restaurant in the Hilton, where she usually stayed. The following week, after an excellent and copious lunch, she suggested they have a coffee in her room. They became lovers.

From then on Térésa came to Paris every Wednesday. She arrived by a morning plane, Le Guillochet was forbidden to look for or find out the exact time. He had suggested meeting her at the airport, rather feebly to be honest, with the egoism, or the egotism of most creators, he was jealous of his time, even when he had nothing in particular to do. She refused, point-blank. She wanted to spend her morning in Paris without him ever knowing what she was doing. But she would always telephone him the night before to confirm their programme together for the following day, which invariably began in the Hilton restaurant. Could he have her Geneva telephone number, in case? No, to what purpose? As she would call him, she, always. If, by chance, she didn't call, he'd know that the meeting was off. It was childish, he could have been informed at the post office or at PEN, but Térésa insisted on her arrangements. He respected them.

To save appearances, he also expressed concern over the regularity of their meetings: didn't it risk awakening her husband's curiosity? No, she didn't interfere with his business and he didn't interfere with hers. She was only accountable to her mother, to whom she told everything. "Everything?" exclaimed the writer. Yes, everything, it's indispensable, she replied, with no additional comment. Furthermore, she added hesitantly, in case of absolute necessity, he could telephone her mother whose number, in contrast to her own, she confided to him. He didn't seek to find out more, at the end of the day he benefitted from Térésa's little mysteries which relieved him of all responsibility. Moreover, he too wasn't accountable to anyone, he was single, he had decided once and for all, he believed, to remain so. Not that he disdained loving interactions, on the contrary they were one of the most delicious resources of existence. But a writer, more than any other artist, he claimed, had to lead a life outside normal conventions, otherwise he would slumber in routine, which is to say boredom and mediocrity. He would deprive himself of the greatest part of the richness of the universe, indispensable for feeding and renewing his work. Well, with Térésa, it was precisely satisfied.

"The party" (it was her expression) began at midday on Wednesday. From the moment he walked through the revolving door of the Hilton, he found himself swept up by a whirlwind known as Térésa, whose exuberant vitality and inexhaustible curiosity showed itself immediately at the table. She had a healthy appetite, which wasn't astonishing for a woman of her size, but she was also willing to try anything, discover everything. She studied the menu at length, letting out little exclamations of pleasure, then she organised her meal, establishing hierarchies between dishes: the entrées, the desserts, those she just wanted to have a taste of and those she wanted to try out, regretfully postponing to the following week those it was impossible to consume at the time. She commanded "naturally" the maître d'hotel to always put the bill on her account. Le Guillochet protested, he refused to profit from her husband's money, but Térésa explained to him expressly, that it was not her husband's money but her own; she was in possession of a comfortable personal fortune that she could never spend, she added somewhat ruefully. Anyway, was he a misogynist? Why couldn't a woman pay for the food of those people she loved?

It was in bed that she astonished him most, he had to admit that in the whole of his well-furnished love life he had never known such a magnificent lover. After the coffee swallowed in her room according to the established ritual, she leapt on him. As with the money, at first he felt a recoil. Stupidity or masculine angst demands that the man should be in charge of the game, otherwise the woman is suspected of shamelessness or, worse, almost dangerous voracity. Feminine wiles, sensing this male pride or fear, ingeniously appear hesitant and shy in the face of a partner's advances. But Térésa seemed too carried away for such precautions, too much in a hurry to fake waiting for her lover to discover her and give her the hoped-for caresses. As at the table, she ordered the feast, acted and soliloquised, spelling out every move, which embarrassed Le Gouillochet who preferred to make love in silence. It was as if she wanted to be fully aware, and increase the intensity of the experience by doubling it in words. She promised herself other marvels for the following Wednesdays, just as she anticipated her forthcoming menus. She wore extravagant, brightly coloured underwear, transparent, edged in effervescent lace, which clashed with her Swiss-German married life – at least so Le Guillochet thought of the Zürchers and other German protestants. She probably picked them out of some specialist shop window in Pigalle, which she had combed through during her free time in the mornings. At first, caught between embarrassment and amusement to see that superb body tarted up, the writer abstained from all comment. It was Térésa who initiated it with sarcasm: was she going to so much trouble just to please him! Those naughty outfits, those indiscreet lacy things, were part of the play that she was intending to put on with her lover. From then on he made a point of complimenting her on each innovation… before it was removed, as she had to be undressed with teasing slowness, a practice she had no doubt discovered in some steamy page-turner. She openly explained what she expected of him: he had to follow a calculated order in undressing her, which culminated with her knickers, the centrepiece, which he haltingly slipped off, marking each portion of skin conquered and uncovered with caresses and kisses. The writer didn't know whether he was supposed to find all this ridiculous or touching; he had to recognise, however, that in obliging him to engage in these tortuous subtleties, Térésa had directed his attention to his own body, sometimes revealing pleasures he had never known, as a skilful musician draws out unexpected cadences from an ordinary instrument. Sometimes she led Le Guillochet's hands, exploring herself with them; sometimes, constraining him to immobility, she explored her lover's body with the same avidity; sometimes she made him join in a concerted effort which brought them to multiple orgasms at the same time. When she was satiated in this way, she reminded Le Guillochet that he also had a right, and duty, to act according to his desires, and do *anything*, anticipating new pleasures from the freedom finally conceded to her lover.

Sometimes, however, in the middle of that frenzy, like a tempest which suddenly gives way to complete calm, Térésa remained lying on her back, staring at the ceiling, head drowned in her hair spread out on the pillow, while tears ran down her cheeks. Le Guillochet noticed and put it down to excessive physical pleasure, abstaining from all movement himself. But soon, the enchantment ceased just as suddenly as it had begun; the inanimate doll came back to life wanting to resume their romps which he agreed to more and more gladly. Always excluding her breasts: "please not my breasts", she, a person so sure of what she wanted, seemed to be begging. At first Le Guillochet thought it was caprice – some women like to hold back their breasts in that way – it can even be an inverted invitation. She had a bust too imposing, too tempting to be ignored. But when he let himself go, against Térésa's wishes, allowed himself to massage those marvellous globes with some insistence, she let out a moan which he could well see was not of pleasure. Obviously he didn't insist and when he happened to forget that limitation, he could tell from her cry that she was suffering. He restricted himself to stroking their surface very gently. Le Guillochet ended up by abandoning his own will altogether and gladly submitting to that powerful femininity, which fascinated him and was more than enough.

And so every Wednesday, thanks to Térésa, he discovered paradise before the fall. What is it other than a perfect conjunction between Adam and Eve, between a man and a woman? He surprised himself by getting so high before the first cigarette and the coffee, singing to himself in the morning, waiting for the forthcoming Wednesday from the very next day, counting down the days which separated them: six, five, four, three… the night before, he could scarcely contain his impatience, till the moment when he was transported once more into a world without end, with no other bearing than that woman. Then, after those hours of drunkenness, in the true sense, when Le Guillochet no longer knew what was happening to him or where he was, when nothing in the world seemed more important, they got dressed and left by taxi in order not to waste the remaining time, to take tea elsewhere, at the waterside, in the woods or in town, in one of those luxurious establishments reserved for lovers of which Térésa had made a list, which she ticked off as and when required. It was the only time when Le Guillochet regained himself a little. He would gladly have stayed lying in the comfortable bed in the Hilton, prolonging his dream, listening to his mistress chat, whose sated body he unceasingly admired, caressing it lightly and intermittently, as one eats a cherry or a nut after a good meal. But she wouldn't hear of it; they were going ("We must go," she said) "to have some tea", her exact term and sing-song intonation. And in fact, whether it was in the Parc de Bagatelle, L'Orée du Bois, La Cascade; at Fouchon or La Maison de l'Afrique, and even once at Chez Gégène where they were refused service; between the little kisses given and taken on the fly which punctuated her continuous stream of words to the amused astonishment of the waiters, she succeeded in talking about everything except herself. Térésa ate, drank, and enjoyed.

When she undertook a systematic tour of "Les Passages", those astonishing dreamy manifestations of XIX-century bourgeois architecture, she added them in advance to her inventory. She insisted on going into every one of those surprising boutiques, delighting in every unusual object, stopping for something in every bistro, at every counter. She didn't omit the Musée Grévin, situated nearby, which Le Guillochet only discovered because she wanted them to experience things together. Stupefied, his muscles deliciously languished, Le Guillochet let himself be carried away by the vitality of his friend, except when it came to eating, when he excused himself. But she kept demanding more, "the speciality of the house", whether it be North African cakes dribbling with honey and melted sugar, or Corsican charcuterie, black as the face on the island's flag, and if there were no alimentary curiosities, she ordered treats such as plum or rhubarb tart.

'You want some?' she asked with her mouth full.
'No, thanks.'
'Why?'
'I'm not hungry.'
'You'll be hungry, later on.'
'Not me, you're enough for me.'
'You're making a mistake, this is good.'

She swallowed enormous pieces of cake, drank glass after glass of tea. Even though he said to himself that this important body had to be nourished, he was, all the same, astonished by such inexhaustible appetite. Térésa ate, as she spoke, as she made love, with excess and urgency, as if she wanted to exhaust everything as rapidly as possible.

Finally Le Guillochet accompanied her back to the Hilton, but that walk wasn't allowed to put an end to the party. She lingered in front of every shop window, admired the ingenuity of the designers, went into ecstasies over a "Parisian" detail. When, at last, they arrived in front of the hotel door, content with a sense of fulfilment he had rarely known, breathing more freely, he felt rejuvenated, he would have gladly followed his lover inside. But Térésa said her goodbyes on the pavement. Forbidden to go further. She preferred to sleep alone, even at home she added, and moreover she had to catch the first plane the following morning.

At first, he'd accepted this extra edict imposed by Térésa without demur. Satiated with her after those long afternoons, it would have been unpleasant to quarrel. He didn't like getting up early and he was thankful not to have to accompany her to the airport. Now he asked her with more and more insistence:

'Let's spend the night together.'
'No.'
'Why?'
'I can't.'
'You don't want to!'

She didn't reply, closed herself up. So he kissed her very quickly and left without turning back, already in expectation of the Tuesday telephone call.

Which, one day, didn't come. He'd had her number for a long time, but he had to respect her diktat. The telephone's silence also signified, she had explained from the beginning, and repeated over again, that she wouldn't be coming on Wednesday. The next day, the writer who fiercely protected his time, who'd made a kind of art of living out of it, found himself invaded by anguish. Without Térésa, it seemed, he couldn't get through the day. He couldn't work, he occupied himself with tidying, for him a definitive sign of upset. He tried to sort out various problems which had been hanging around, to reply to letters from editors or readers. In vain, nothing could distract him from that emptiness, from that lack of Térésa.

Could it be, contrary to all his convictions on the matter, that a single woman could advantageously replace all women? That just one particular woman could unlock the reality of passion?

When she telephoned him the following Tuesday he was still angry with her and only replied with yeses and noes. During the meal he remained silent and, whether she was responding to his sulkiness or whether she had some reason of her own, for once she scarcely said a word. As soon as they were in the bedroom, for coffee and what usually followed, before even touching Térésa, Le Guillochet announced in a commanding tone that he had never previously employed:

'This evening, I'm staying with you, we'll sleep together.'

'No, that's not possible, you know very well I get up early and—'

'I'll get up at the same time as you.'

'That'll annoy you,' she murmured feebly.

'No, it won't.'

And, to his own astonishment he heard himself declare:

'Moreover, you're going to get divorced and we're going to get married.'

She looked at him with what seemed like fear, it was the first time that he'd appeared angry with her.

'I can't bear this ridiculous state of affairs anymore, that you're away the whole week… and to only have what's left over,' he added bitterly.

She tried to stem the flow, she scolded him with feigned severity, as if he was a self-centred adolescent:

'And my children? Have you thought of them?'

She stammered:

'I… I don't want to be separated from them!'

Le Guillochet countered:

'They'll come to live with us.'

'They won't have their father.'

'I'll love them as I love you.'

'It's not the same thing, they'll miss him.'

But, this time, Le Guillochet wanted to corner her:

'How old are your children?'

'I've already told you, you weren't paying attention…'

'Now I'm going to pay attention, how old?'

'Fifteen and thirteen.'

'Good, in two years, they won't need you anymore, I can wait two years, ten years!'

Then, suddenly, she began to sob, without making any noise, without saying anything, like a desperate child who's given up hope of help and is going to sleep with its pain. And then, suddenly, at the same time, Guillochet understood to what extent he had become attached to this woman and, without knowing exactly why, that he was going to irrevocably lose her.

Never had he worked so well as in the last few months, with so much elation; he'd taken up an old project, deferred for a long time, written an upbeat, even comical book. But also, paradoxically, he seemed to have become distanced from his writing, which perhaps wasn't his only preoccupation. Life, perhaps, had more value than literature.

He held her in his arms, in a manner which sometimes happens with lovers, where tenderness prevails over pleasure and is mixed with pity.

'What's all this, my darling? Speak to me, tell me what's going on...'

She was still sobbing but not answering, only shaking her head to say no; without him discerning whether she could not or would not reply. But now he knew for certain that he had to protect her from some monstrous unknown. He cradled her against himself, his marvellous Viking became his suffering little girl. He noticed that she'd lost weight; her tan always so carefully maintained no longer hid her pallor. Believing it to be coquetry, dangerous to her health, he'd ticked her off jokingly and said that there'd been a misunderstanding between women and men who, nearly all, preferred rather "well-covered" women. She hadn't even smiled, hadn't found it funny.

For the first time, they made love badly; she allowed him to sleep with her, and the next day he accompanied her to the airport.

She didn't telephone the following Tuesday and didn't come on the Wednesday. But he'd expected it. Nothing happened the following week. He could have telephoned her, he didn't, not for fear of upsetting her but because he knew it would be useless.

Finally sometime afterwards he received a letter from her mother, who, it turned out, knew everything. Térésa had died, she hadn't come through the operation. The missive was ambiguous: Térésa's mother thanked Le Guillochet for what he'd done for her daughter during those difficult months, but perhaps for that very reason, because she hadn't paid sufficient attention to her illness, Térésa had waited too long to get her operation.

Le Guillochet thought of sending a word of condolence. To whom? To her husband! He didn't have her mother's address and there was no indication on the envelope. He could have found out, but to what end? Would it have brought Térésa back to life? Brought himself back to life?

A taste of paradise
or the last chance

In the taxi bringing us back from the cemetery, my old aunt was no longer crying, exhausted; I respected her silence. Then, to my surprise, I saw her dear wan face give birth to a smile, that of a naughty child, shameful and wicked, but not altogether repentant, a ray of sun coming through the clouds...

'He had,' she murmured, 'marvellous hands...'

I'd noticed those hands, they'd seemed more impressive than average, strong, a bit fat, with round fingers. I smiled back at my aunt, then she looked at me, this time sure we understood each other, and said:

'We had the best of him, come on!'

My aunt and her late husband we'd just buried, didn't have children and lived modestly on a single workman's salary, but they were happy, because their bed remained a festive occasion.

How many couples fail to understand that obvious fact, resumed Dr Jean-Baptiste Donnadieu, Head Physician in General Medicine at the Hôtel-Dieu. Professionally I've come across so many where I've noted misery and disillusion if not resentment and betrayal. I've rarely seen a married life remain a love life; more often I've observed a love life transform into a conjugal one. There you are, that's why I've remained single. Well actually I was married for eight months, enough to persuade me that I wouldn't have been any happier in marriage than most of my contemporaries; an affair here and there, yes, but a definitive and exclusive attachment, ah, no!

But let's leave generalities aside and my own modest person. I'll content myself with a single case, whose heroes I'm particularly familiar with since they became my friends; I even dined with them last week.

Several years ago, I received an emergency admission at the hospital, a woman accompanied by her husband who was quite a well-known painter, let's call them Mireille and Pierre Maugey. At first, the contrast between the man's anxious agitation and the resigned acceptance of the woman made me think he was the patient, and that he was younger than her. Tall and beautifully tanned, she was clad in a well-cut suit while he was casually dressed in corduroy trousers and a black roll-neck pullover, as you'd expect of an established painter. She complained of violent headaches, mainly in the temporal region, pains in the jaw, muscular tension in her back and extreme fatigue, which obliged her to lie down all day long. I examined her and asked a few supplementary questions. The diagnosis was immediately clear to me: it was a case of *Horton's Disease*, a rare but serious condition named after the colleague who first described it. I didn't want to say so before getting laboratory test results, but we needed to start treatment as soon as possible. I asked the patient if she was willing to be admitted straight away. Like most women in that situation she was slightly embarrassed; she hadn't brought a change of clothes with her nor any toiletries, her house was in a mess etc. I had to be firm with her, threatening to relinquish her care if she left the hospital. Her husband said he would go home and find the necessaries and she acquiesced. The tests confirmed my diagnosis. I administered a high dose of cortisone immediately, which she had to repeat every morning, without fail, for a long time. I kept her under observation for several more days, then agreed to discharge her home, on condition that she came for follow-up consultations at regular intervals.

It was a long and difficult battle, where my patient wasn't always compliant, as if she didn't really want to get better. One day, she telephoned me frantically from America, where she was accompanying her husband for an exhibition: she'd lost her box of pills! Two or three times, she forgot to take them properly and I had to consult my notes to remind her of the regime. But in the end, after five years, I was able to consider her cured. Down the road, as I said, I became a friend of the couple, since the worried husband consulted me himself, to keep me informed of his wife's progress, and he inevitably confided the most confidential information concerning their life together.

Don't be surprised: a long-lasting relationship with a doctor transforms him, if he's willing to allow it, into a confessor. We don't look after souls, we've neither the time nor the means, but souls sometimes come to us in desperation. Moreover, it's particularly relevant in the treatment of Horton's disease, where the exact causes are still unknown. After years of practice, I'm convinced that there are underlying psychological factors in the origin of the arterial inflammation characteristic of this condition. I'd be incapable of proving it scientifically, but I've almost always noted in patients who come to consult me with Horton's, unbearable mental torments alongside their clinical symptoms; furthermore it's the same for a number of cancers. Now as you can imagine, marital problems are among the most frequent disturbances.

Once again, I found myself confronted by a drama involving three characters, the sixty-three-year-old man, the sixty-year-old wife, and the mistress whose exact age I never knew, probably twenty or so, whom I never saw, but whose portrait I could make a reasonably accurate attempt at drawing. A classic story, you'd say, but stories like this are often most revealing of the human soul. Anna Karenina's suffering, which made her throw herself under the wheels of a train because she was rejected by her lover, is the same as that of Dido, the Carthaginian queen who, abandoned by Aeneas the Trojan, set herself on fire. Of course, not all marriages are tragedies, but nearly all, I'm convinced, are more or less dramatic.

The Maugey's formed an apparently happy menage, at least a tranquil one. He'd won a good position in the art market. A contract with a well-known gallery and several paying pupils in his studio on the Rue de La Grande-Chaumière, sufficed to provide a comfortable living for himself and his wife. He'd even bought an apartment in the neighbouring building, reserving the whole of the studio for his professional activities. Mireille Maugey was at last able to give up her job as an executive secretary, which had permitted the family to subsist during the difficult years of the painter's career. Now she spent her time agreeably in the company of friends, sang in a local choir and benefitted from guided tours of museums. She'd even resumed some piano lessons, abandoned since her marriage. The children, having left home long ago to lead their own lives, often came back to see their parents and demonstrated constant affection. Just like most happy people, the Maugey couple seemed to live uncomplicated lives until the day when one of the partners, in this case the man, which is the most frequent scenario, found it unsustainable, and as a result made his wife's life a misery. To put it succinctly, if Maugey was enough for his wife, he discovered that his wife and what she represented, no longer fulfilled him.

They could have continued living together, apparently it was chance that decided otherwise. (You're guessing that I don't really believe in chance in these matters.) Even if, as a true artist, Maugey started off painting for his own pleasure, and despite his relative success, he was still somehow waiting for something which never happened; perhaps one could call it glory, that is to say absolute success: not just to be considered an excellent painter by dealers, art lovers and colleagues, but to obtain worldwide recognition in the manner of a Leonardo de Vinci or Picasso. No matter the near-totality of people understand nothing of painting and never buy one, only that kind of fame, which transcends time and space, assures immortality.

That eternity, to which all artists aspire more or less consciously, suddenly took the form of a young woman. Marie-Odile, a journalist and admirer of Maugey, came to interview him and was sufficiently seductive to give off the right signals to the painter, who had, unknowingly, been waiting for them. After a drink at La Palette then several meals at La Couple, she became his mistress. It wasn't the first time he'd had an affair, models aren't exactly off-putting, and Montparnasse is full of lonely women patiently waiting for a lover on the lookout for consummation. But it was too easy, nothing to boast about, and that made it inconsequential. This time, in view of the girl's age, her childlike pink cheeks, her mouth which resembled a half-open bud, her wide-open eyes, fixed on him while he talked excitedly, he thought fate had rendered him an exceptional favour. He lost his head to the point of letting his wife guess the source of his new happiness; perhaps he had obscurely wanted her to do so, which is equally common.

Until then Mireille Maugey had turned a blind eye to her husband's probable misdemeanours; she'd even found some advantage in them; for example sparing her meetings with other painters where she was bored with hearing them brag about their work, put down their colleagues, or expatiate on their pet theories. How many times was she tempted to say: "Just paint and shut up!"

"Painters' stories", she used to say indulgently, remaining politely sceptical. Above all it relieved her from having to entertain them at home. She never asked Maugey the cause of his lateness; the certainty that he'd be coming back sufficed. She read while waiting for him, and sometimes fell asleep. When he finally came home, he tried not to wake her; he contented himself with tenderly watching her sleep, before slipping into bed. For the first time in their long conjugal life she developed the agonising intuition that one day, he wouldn't come home.

It doesn't take much, it's true, for a spouse to discover the peccadilloes of her husband... if she has a mind to. One day, after a period of persistent illness, he suspected he'd caught trichomonas, a contagious but minor sexual infection; it turned out to be a false alarm, but he'd had to take some precautions impossible to hide. Mireille didn't react, although she couldn't feign ignorance. Since Marie-Odile's intrusion into the menage, his colleagues and pupils openly teased the painter over his new aftershave, his unusual silk scarves, the scent in which he liberally doused himself. In order not to have to think about clothes, out of convention and artists' privilege, until then he'd limited himself to black corduroy trousers and a black roll-neck sweater at all times of the year, which he only took off in the evenings before getting into the conjugal bed. During very cold days, rare in Paris, he added a cap and a black Breton sailor's jacket, as if displaying that exoticism confirmed his identity as an artist and painter. Voilà! Now he was introducing light-coloured shirts and sometimes a suit jacket. His transformation, visible to all eyes, she thought, aggravated the humiliation of his wife. We know humiliation plays an important role in the pains of love. She thought she'd become a laughing stock, or worse an object of pity in the eyes of their friends and acquaintances, let alone their children. This time she couldn't refrain from action:

'He takes me for an idiot,' my patient repeated angrily. 'When he has to dine with "her",' "her", that was his mistress, Marie-Odile, whose loathed name she never pronounced, 'he makes up so many explanations and alibis that I feel ashamed for him; when he wants to spend the night with her, he invents a business trip; he who's incapable of negotiating the slightest thing. I'd almost prefer it if he told me the truth. If I question his childish fabrications, he gets angry like an adolescent accused of wrongdoing, or takes refuge in offended silence, which is all too convenient.'

Maugey wasn't taking his wife for an idiot, he even respected her. Setting aside age, he knew that she was more reliable than his young mistress; he could count on her: for example she'd always been in charge of the household economy, a task which had never suited him, above all during the period when his upper-class family hadn't forgiven him for his marriage to a "gold-digger", and refused to help. She advised him on the management and sale of his paintings. But love isn't simply the meeting of two intelligences, even on a background of tenderness and esteem. Now, she'd reached the age when love-play no longer seemed worth the effort. She wasn't yet like some of her friends who labelled it inappropriate, "in view of our age". That kind championed the virtue of separate bedrooms and bathrooms, only to be emerged from when already washed, purified and adorned. How can desire be maintained in the everyday comings and goings of shared beds and WCs? Mireille Maugey told me with amusement that one of her friends, an ex-psychologist by profession, had decided to reject all her husband's future advances:

'We know each other too well,' I explained to him, 'it'd be almost like incest!'

Others, a bit more understanding, confided indulgently that they were willing to "relieve" their gentleman, as if he'd been stricken by a skin disease; not asking anything in return for themselves, even stopping all attempts to go further.

Although she'd preserved a certain austerity, par for the course with executive secretaries, Mireille Maugey was normally very flirtatious, but for a long time this flirtatiousness had not been aimed in the direction of her husband; she was simply following the advice of magazines and competing with other women in titivating herself. On mornings devoted to housework, she wore old dresses; she only got dressed properly at the beginning of the afternoon, and immediately went out to meet her friends, so that Maugey lived permanently backstage of a performance at which he was never present. But equally, for a long time he hadn't paid attention to his wife's comings and goings or her efforts, and when, sensing the danger, she had her hair done more often and took more care to doll herself up in the mornings, he remained unimpressed.

At first she multiplied the allusions, the reproaches, jokingly calling him a bigamist and an old roué – which in an unexpected way, flattered him. Then, when she understood the affair was more serious, she lost it. She went from tears to supplications, which irritated the painter, but made him feel ashamed for her. To see this grown woman, usually so self-possessed, reduced to little-girlish blackmail, seemed to him a kind of disloyalty. Not knowing how to respond, he abandoned the terrain and fled the apartment. Then she gave herself over to insults and threats, accusing him of egoism, of mental cruelty, of sadism.

'I look after your meals, your clothes, you when you're sick, and this is how you repay me! Now that you're making money and you're a success, you chuck me away like an old sock.' How to reply without being cruel, that he was no longer happy with a mother, that at last he had a real lover? And now that he no longer had anything to hide, since Mireille knew it all, he no longer resorted to ruses and openly spent the best part of his time with Marie-Odile. One evening, Mireille didn't come home. He said to himself that to take revenge, she'd spent the night with one of her friends; all the same he couldn't stop himself insistently questioning her when she returned, and feeling troubled when she refused to give him an explanation.

Finally Mireille seriously envisaged leaving her husband, but since she was incapable of doing so, she ended up falling ill. He was upset and paid faultless attention to her in a quite unexpected way. He took down his easel, accompanied his wife to my consultations, kept her company through long hospital waits, insisted that she attend laboratory appointments without fail, watched over the regularity of her cortisone administration and the exact dosage; something that, bizarrely, patients sometimes forget, even though their life depends on it, or perhaps because their life depends on it. He shared her salt-free food, which was a gustatory abomination.

'Did you ever think of leaving your wife to live with your young mistress?' I asked him.

'Yes… sometimes… in a dream… I've never thought about it in reality, I knew it would be impossible… I'm more than sixty years old, one day she'd have cheated on me with a younger man, she'd have left me, and I'd have lost everything, my wife and my mistress… I know myself, I don't know how to live alone. Anyhow, I'd never have inflicted that on Mireille; I could see very well all around me what dramas separations are, frequent enough in our painters' milieu, even if they're sometimes desirable… so you want to know if I love my wife? I've never asked myself the question in that way… of course I love her! I don't think I could live without her… but perhaps I don't exactly know what it means to love…'

'You aren't the only one,' I consoled him… I've cared for many lovesick patients, I still don't know exactly myself… I'm not always sure I understand what a couple consists of, what keeps them together at a particular point… but if you love your wife, why did you do what you did?'

'I haven't done anything! Or nothing much, I just accepted what happened to me, it's true, the appearance of Marie-Odile…'

'Permit me to insist all the same, your friend didn't rape you! Why did you accept?'

'Why wouldn't I have accepted? Look, Doctor, I'm astonished that you ask the question… how would I have been able, at my age, to refuse that taste of paradise which fortune suddenly bestowed on me? Other women that I had… I no longer even remember their names. How could I ever forget Marie-Odile. A beautiful young woman. I who'd be incapable of swallowing soup if I found a hair in it, licked that extraordinary light down on her neck with delight. Moreover, I had the impression, quite frightening, that this was my last chance. If I'd let it go, it'd have been too late, I'd be finished... I almost didn't have the right to do that to *myself*... are you surprised (or I suspect pretending to be) that I could accept the love of such a young woman: isn't it all the more astonishing that she went along with it? That she agreed to rub her satin skin against my old boar's leather! I'm going to tell you a secret, if it is a secret for you: it's just as important to be desired as to desire. Women know it by instinct from puberty... oh, it's not as if at the same time, I don't reproach myself. Indeed, how could I do that to Mireille, my long-time companion in both good and bad days? The mother of my children. But again, how do you explain it? In relation to her I behaved badly, it's true; from my point of view, it was marvellous. I don't know whether paradise exists, later, after death, but a beautiful young woman, is a taste of paradise here and now... young and beautiful, no, not necessarily that, she doesn't have to be very beautiful (Marie-Odile is pretty, she needn't have been; Marie-Odile is blonde, she could have been a brunette), it's enough that she was a woman and young. With her I rediscovered my virility which was getting further away from me every day; I was her age, for example I began to play around, foolishly, like an adolescent, I made stupid jokes for the pleasure of seeing her laugh, I imitated people's accents (I'm quite talented at that), I climbed on a chair at risk of breaking my neck, and made a speech to an imaginary crowd, just to see her clap her hands... dinner with her was a ceremony which I prepared for, I dressed up; with her, two days in Florence outweighed a trip to Tibet without her; a walk in the park with her made it an enchanted forest...

'Was it the same with Mireille when we were young? Perhaps, yes, certainly, but it was in a past already so distant that it seemed to me imaginary. In any case, I couldn't do it with her now, she wouldn't be interested, she's too intelligent, too adult, I couldn't say the silly things that lovers say to each other, I'd feel ridiculous...

think about your own wife, Doctor… no, you're not married, you're lucky… with a wife, you can read the paper in bed, listen to the radio while eating a meal… with a mistress that's unthinkable! It's that with a wife you want to forget your life, with a mistress you want to be present in your life, you want to savour it like some rare food. Or better: one is reborn into Life, as if the creative process continued, extended itself through us… really, even more so than with children… more than with painting!'

Maugey hesitated, stupefied by what he'd just said… like many painters, he wasn't in the habit of thinking deeply, he wasn't an intellectual; he had the impression of having discovered an important truth, despite himself:

'Yes, love, is greater than painting… after all, the arts, religions, are attempts to extend life in the imagination, for fear of annihilation… yes, that's exactly it: I was living a new life, a young woman puts you back into the cycle of eternal life. Did I want to leave my wife because of that? No, how can I explain it better? I never truly dreamed of leaving Mireille because I saw no contradiction between what I was living with her and what I was living with Marie-Odile. Why would there be an exclusive contradiction between the trunk and the periodic flowering of a tree? I saw so little contradiction that I continued to see Marie-Odile while at the same time caring for Mireille with devotion, you're a witness to it… I could telephone one then the other, straight afterwards, with the same pleasure, scarcely surprised by my duplicity… but perhaps I'm a monster!'

I reassured him:

'You aren't a monster, you're a man.'

I reminded him of that passage in the Bible where the writer, obviously a pious and virtuous man, recounts without censure how King David warmed up his old bones through contact with young virgins. So the holy books are also peopled with men. If older women allowed themselves to warm up with young men, they'd be more indulgent.

Mireille Maugey could no longer be indulgent; she was suffering from what she saw as a betrayal. Naturally, I listened to the wife as to the husband, with the same benevolent neutrality required by my profession. I must confess, however, that deep down, I wasn't able to completely condemn the husband. To truly love a woman, is it necessary to only love her? Is it necessary to renounce all others? As Maugey put it, in his graphic language and naive cruelty:

'To really love artichokes, do you have to be disgusted by all the other vegetables in the world? Do you have to restrict yourself to shrivelled apples, left in the corner of a barn, even if you like their smell, when the new harvest brings a profusion of smooth-skinned fruit every year, puffed up and coloured like a baby's cheek? So good to eat!'

I couldn't stop myself from feeling a kind of masculine solidarity with Maugey, but I'm a doctor, I had to care for the arteries and perhaps the psyche of my patient. Luckily, the treatment of the Horton's and that of the heartache coincided. You have to gradually bring the patient back to health, crossing bumps and setbacks along the way. My best ally in that long battle was, perhaps, its duration; I had to wait until things moved of their own accord. They ended up by moving.

Pierre Maugey told me more and more frequently of his irritation with the behaviour of his young mistress, with things he had found delicious before, or simply maladroit; without seeming to be aware of the change happening in himself. Increasingly she made absurd, unexpected demands; for example, at the last minute, she'd refuse to go to a restaurant where he'd booked a table, obliging him to make an excuse and look for another one, which more often than not turned out to be disappointing. She'd stop at the entrance, turn up her little nose and decide: "It's not very cool," without Maugey ever understanding what that adjective, common in younger generations, signified. He was very fond of bistros, out of the romanticism of an old Parisian, and equally the memory of times when he could only afford such establishments. Marie-Odile, probably fearing that the establishment was beneath her, lacking confidence, suspected him of wanting to save money, refused to set foot in the place, "too much smoke", "too much noise", and decided: "It's seedy." He got embarrassed now when people took them for father and daughter, with a nuance of reprobation, while at the same time it amused and flattered him. In brief, he seemed to be slowly waking up from his dream and finding himself in a painful reality. Sometimes I'd see him beforehand in the waiting room, agitated, obviously upset that he had to take his turn like one of my patients, suffering in some way from a disease of guilt.

'I don't know where I am anymore,' he confided in me, 'while I'm with Marie-Odile, I often look at my watch… in spite of myself I cut short our date and leave earlier to get back to Mireille. And when I find her and she looks at me with her distraught eyes, like those of a faithful animal, attached to you since its birth, incapable of living without you, I want to leave again, and be elsewhere. Why must paradise be paid for with the hell of others?'

In fact, his liaison with Marie-Odile was coming to an end. They had been together for nearly three years. I've learned from experience that this kind of affair rarely lasts three years, to the point where I'd like to infer a kind of law for the attention of my colleagues: the first year is that of discovery, of astonishment; the second, that of exhaustion; the third sees erosion due to daily wear and tear leading to the rupture. So aren't there any liaisons which last longer? Which transform into definitive long-lasting relationships? Certainly, but it's precisely those that have changed their nature; they've become marriages: the enchantment has metamorphosed into habit; anyway it's the end of the illusion.

One day, Marie-Odile pronounced the fateful sentence:
'You'll never leave your wife!'

She meant: "Me, I'll never be your wife!" When your mistress, young or not so young, pronounces that sentence, she simultaneously reveals her secret hope and her spite; she takes note of her failure and proffers a threat: "I will never be your wife!" Yet, they all hope for it; they all want to transform a provisional liaison into a definitive installation. Even if, loyally, you've never promised anything, it makes no difference to the business. It's that men and women don't expect the same thing from a love affair. We're constructed differently biologically; why wouldn't we be psychologically? 'Forgive the unvarnished language of a doctor: the role of the male stops after copulation, as soon as he's deposited his semen, he can and he wants to leave; on the contrary that of the female begins then: in addition to the gestation, it's necessary to prepare for the arrival of the young, a nest. Today things seem to be changing, so it's said, that's not what I see in my consulting room. Women continue to behave in regard to men as if they expect fecundation and protection; it's understood that the man has to provide for their needs, even if he earns less money than they do. Symbolically at least, he has to cede the best place, put them first, protect them; we call that gallantry allowing us to believe that it's something given freely, whereas in fact it's not disinterested, neither for the one nor the other, and that's why it's perpetuated. On the part of the woman, marriage is always an attempt to capture the man. The fateful sentence announces that failure has occurred, it signifies: "You haven't fulfilled your duty as a male, I'm soon going to be looking for another." The young woman doesn't clearly know it yet herself, but she's preparing, she's making the liaison increasingly unviable.'

Maugey and Marie-Odile argued more and more often, and rather than telephoning each other an hour afterwards to make up, sometimes with tears in their eyes, each of them claiming to be in the wrong, they only telephoned the next day, then the day after. Soon they only saw each other on odd occasions;

Maugey discovering with astonishment that he could do without Marie-Odile:

'After all,' he told me, 'she hasn't always been in my life.'

He wanted to persuade himself that Marie-Odile had only ever been a pretty phantom born out of the imagination of an ageing man; that he hadn't so much been in love with that girl as with his own fading youth, which wasn't untrue. Or at least it wasn't a contradiction that matters in this domain. If he had, in fact, been passionately in love with her, passion being an illness, he would now gladly be cured of it. He promised himself from then on to remain faithful to his wife.

'I really owe it to her!'

'It's the least I can do,' he assured me, with unfeigned emotion; he had found a long-lost peace of mind, like a sailor who returning to port, is taken aback by its calm in contrast to the turbulence of the sea. He had married Mireille for her beauty, but also out of gratitude, because she'd taken charge of him: he was putting himself back into her hands with relief.

I only half believed him, not that I doubted the sincerity of his promise, but that he'd be capable of keeping it. He told me that after the period when his wife was truly in danger, when he forced himself to think of Marie-Odile as little as possible, he started wanting to see his mistress again; he telephoned her several times, but she was generally away on a story. Maugey having got her several interviews with his fellow artists; she'd acquired some cachet with her employers, who frequently sent her abroad to review exhibitions. He congratulated himself, with some regret. He could have persisted and ultimately found her, he didn't. Marie-Odile's youth had stopped time, even made it go in reverse, as if everything was once again possible. But he now knew that old age is an illness which is certain not to be cured, which gets worse every day.

On the other hand, I'm persuaded that he'll never leave his wife. Thinking of the future of his married life, he sighed.

'Ah, I so much wish that everything could be as it was before!'

Apparently everything had become as it was before, but nothing can truly become as it was before. Mireille Maugey resumed her meetings with friends, that she'd let go, took up the local choir again, and continued her shopping. She made real efforts at home; Maugey was a gourmet and hadn't always found his spouse understanding in this area; she applied herself to preparing better meals for him, exchanging recipes with friends. She stopped letting herself dress down in the mornings. She entertained friends useful to her husband's career more often, art critics, gallery owners, possible collectors. However, in spite of herself, she could no longer produce that vague atmosphere of tenderness in the home, always present in the life of couples, even during silences, which sustains them, as water vapour sustains the life of plants, without which they yellow and shrivel. She still hadn't reacquired the spontaneity of certain gestures, such as a squeeze of the hand without apparent motive, in bed while halfasleep, or in the obscurity of a cinema, which verify the presence of the other and reassure the other of yours; those stolen little attentions, which like all true gifts, have no need of recognition. When she met Maugey in the street, she did give that complicit smile by which partners indicate without speaking: "You're not a passer-by like others". But her smile was veiled in melancholy. Everything was apparently in order, but there were underlying troubles like hidden warts: they cause suffering even if nobody sees them.

Would she ever completely forgive her husband? What does "forgive" mean? If it was simply a question of making no further allusion to the betrayal, yes, she succeeded in keeping quiet; she was already practiced at that, persuaded that conjugal life always wins. But if, for things to truly be as they were before, it was necessary to retrieve their integrity, it wasn't yet the case with Mireille. Those last five years had partially whitened her hair, which she bleached and covered with a blue rinse. She told me one day how much she understood the expression "not being oneself"; until then in her life with Maugey she'd been altogether "herself", now she no longer knew where she was; she'd been totally, romantically, in love with him; had married him despite his relatives; she no longer knew what remained of that enthusiasm. After a period of restraint, Maugey plucked up courage to kiss her again on the neck, which usually pleased and moved her, but it had become difficult for her to let go, to not think that he'd perhaps done the same with the Other. She had to make an effort not to tense up. She refused to go on certain walks, particular outings, if she suspected that he'd done the same thing with her rival. At the same time, having received a very strict moral education, she felt guilty for not being able to give her husband what was due to him, particularly in bed, even if he'd been at the root of those impossibilities. She was punishing herself, and punishing him, I often told her, depriving both him and herself of most of life's pleasures.

Will she be cured of her wound? I fear it'll certainly take as long as the Horton's. To love, is it to be so attached to someone that without that person, one prefers to die? Recently, she tripped on the stairs of their building and broke her arm, which required plastering.

Julibellule
or the devil's darning needle

César Napoléon Gambini had been our Don Juan, a high school Don Juan, but all the same he'd taken our breath away during a shared adolescence, with his tales of glorious victories in that mysterious, frighteningly attractive field... women. A good pupil, excellent Latinist, he knew he was also handsome and well built; wide shoulders, blue eyes and a remarkable blondness, rare enough with us but even more exceptional in a Corsican, his muscles jutting from his chest perpetually covered in a white vest (one didn't say *T-shirt* in those days), a bit stocky, supported on solid gymnast's thighs. Our physical education teachers, who were putting on weight, asked him to demonstrate exercises on the trapeze or vaulting horse, that we then had to copy, which he gladly did with grace and pride, intending he affirmed, to dedicate himself to that noble sport when he left school.

However, those among us who met him later in Marseille, where he'd settled, and who invited him to join our annual dinner, reported with astonishment, near incredulity, that our Don Juan had ceased to be one. He'd been living with the same woman for years and seemed happy. Professionally, he'd become a respectable tax inspector, he negotiated the sale of properties compulsorily purchased by the city.

Thus, on that particular evening, he was with us for the first time. Without daring to ask the cause of his metamorphosis, we were very much hoping he'd explain it to us. When his turn to speak came, he wickedly said:

'I know what you're expecting me to talk about, I'm going to try to satisfy your curiosity… but it's a long story.

'I met Julie at a bus stop, yes, it's as simple as that. It happened two or three times, I mean in succession. Rare are the women who, when one addresses them in a queue for example, even respond with a smile. Alas, they aren't the prettiest; the pretty ones, when they reply, do it dryly, as if you'd offended them and then completely shut up, adopting a disdainful look which seems to say: "Do you really have the audacity to speak to me without having been introduced! I don't know you and don't want to know you", or at best: "My good man, you'll have to take a lot more trouble than that before I agree to even open my mouth". I didn't usually insist. Julie wasn't plain and she immediately entered into the exchange that I was proposing. Not that she was in any way duped by my pick-up strategy, she told me later, but she didn't find it offensive. Enveloped by a loden coat of non-specific hue, too big for a most probably slim body; hair disappearing under a large turban, I only really saw her face, whose fine features and tiny nose made her resemble a charming little bird.

'Standing in the shelter, our umbrellas closed, we chatted about the irregularity of bus appearances, the annoying waits, above all in bad weather, the obvious things that needed to be done if one really wanted to improve public transport, etc. All the banalities that one talks about because one can't talk about the essential, which is to say: I am a man, you are a woman, and we want to get to know each other better. However, she did let me know that she'd come from a local publishing house, where she was second in command of manufacturing services. And as the bus was decidedly not coming, I invited her to have a cup of coffee over the road. She didn't absolutely say no, but not today, she was in a hurry, she was going to take a taxi, maybe tomorrow… no, rather the day after.

'We were supposed to meet in the Place Saint-Michel, near the superb baroque fountain where the archangel, indifferent to the fury of the two dragons, permanently brandishes his sword over the devil lying at his feet.

'She didn't come. I waited three quarters of an hour, longer than usual on such occasions.

'I had no means of contacting her; I'd asked for her telephone number, she'd refused to give it, but she'd noted mine. "Me, I'll give you a call."

'A banal ruse for giving oneself the opportunity to stop short a possible affair, momentarily amusing, but which on reflection one doesn't want to continue. So I also wrote the episode off in the chapter titled "profit and loss" in the hunt for love.

'But the next day to my welcome surprise, she telephoned, made some vague excuse, and suggested another date, which I of course accepted. This time, she came, and even arrived early; I found her sitting at the back of the cafe on the other side of the square, Le Saint-Séverin. In the hubbub of the street that blinds and deafens you, I hadn't noticed her at the time of our previous meeting. Free of her awful loden and turban, she was a doll-like woman, pleasantly proportioned, with small breasts but undoubtedly present, a flat stomach, slender arms, rather like those of an adolescent; I was really surprised when she told me she was the mother of a thirteen-year-old boy. Married very young, she hastened to add, she was not long separated from her husband, for no other reason than a growing feeling of uselessness, stuck between a spouse absorbed by his profession as an engineer, and perhaps other things, and an adolescent son increasingly impatient to free himself from his mother's tutelage. The classic story of a petit bourgeois woman who, out of customary faithfulness to her background, to a marriage in front of mayor and priest, entirely taken up with her duties as a wife and mother – housework, education of the child, helping her husband's career – had for a long time renounced catching men's eyes and all forms of escape, until the moment when her husband's career established, her child grown up, the monotony of her existence, and the agonising feeling of time running out, had suddenly weighed upon her shoulders. Without even being aware of it, she was ready for an affair. But, having unlearned the flirtatiousness, which by dint of a few tricks makes women seem more attractive, she neglected her teeth, where two were starting to blacken, made herself up without conviction and wore cheap badly cut dresses in awful material. A crown of fine blonde hair surrounded and lit up her face but overwhelmed its delicacy so completely that I couldn't stop myself from comparing it to the fried doughnuts of my native country.

'However, like abandoned monuments which appear by chance on a journey in a deserted region, whose beauty one discovers with surprise under the dust of time; her lack of care hadn't been able to spoil the regularity of her features, the freshness of her complexion, preserved by a passionless existence, the velvet of her lips still just as tender as a young girl's. I said to myself that it would be easy to restore her radiance and that I should enjoy being the restorer.

'When the occasion is propitious, quiet ones like loners, speak abundantly and quickly, as if they want to make up for their mutism. I let Julie chat to her heart's content, until I felt able to say, without frightening her off, that I'd really like to see her again, elsewhere than in the hubbub surrounding us, and as soon as possible! (According to Napoléon, my illustrious compatriot and homonym, once the preparations for battle are in place, you have to charge your adversary, to prevent him from having time to regroup.) In addition, I rapidly explained to her, we needed to see each other again inside four walls… why not a hotel room… and as she seemed to hesitate: "We won't do anything more than you want, I promise… it's just to have a moment when we're truly, just us, together."

'That's what I say to apprehensive new partners to gently prepare them for more complete lovemaking, but she consented without further embarrassment, and the day after next, after a short stop in the same cafe, so she wouldn't feel too hurried, I took her to a small hotel on the Rue Quatre-Ponts. One where I usually went, and could sort everything out in advance by telephone, which had the added advantage of sparing my girlfriends the embarrassment of contact with the receptionist, in whom they thought they could detect, perhaps rightly, some ironic criticism.

'From the moment that the bedroom door closed, without first trying to undress her, I took her in my arms, clasped her to me, caressed her in every way, murmuring all the sweet nothings one says to a woman on such an occasion…

'I see you're smiling; some amongst you must think I'm a cynic. It's true I keep to the same line with virtually all of them, but the language of seduction scarcely varies. Goethe paying court to Christiane following Frédérique or Mme de Stein, Victor Hugo to Juliette following Adèle, must have repeated the same compliments. It's not cynicism, all women want to hear them, and we want to repeat them over and again to each one, because emotion is forever renewed.

'However, if Julie let herself be kissed and complimented, she was completely unresponsive, she remained stiff, arms flailing at the sides of her body, with a totally absent look. And when finally, deprived of an echo and fed up with her passivity, I undertook to relieve her of her dress and undo that curious get-up over her knickers whereby women keep their stockings up, intended above all to titillate us, which in Julie's case turned out to reveal solid cotton underwear; she was suddenly overtaken by panic, tore my hands from her body and pushed me away almost brutally; she was trembling.

'Evidently, I was her first lover, or her second if you count her husband, which I'm not sure about. People get angry with Don

Juans; aren't husbands even more guilty, who often deprive their spouses of complete satisfaction? Out of jealousy, or frightened by the possible ardour of their young wives, many husbands, young and inexperienced themselves, prefer to dampen the fire to the point where flames completely disappear. I tried to gently take her back in my arms, I caressed her head as one strokes a frightened horse; nothing worked. Cowering at the back of the bed, she arched her back against the wall letting out little cries of distress, as if she was running from some terrible unforeseen danger. I feared a nervous breakdown and got off the bed, all the time continuing to talk to her, assuring her that I wouldn't touch her anymore, since she didn't want it, that I was already grateful to her for having given me the favour of this intimacy. Mute, with clenched teeth and bright eyes, she hurriedly got dressed, looking at me as if, despite my promises, I was going to jump on her.

'She took flight. But, to my astonishment, perhaps only to console me, just after closing the door she whispered: "I'll call you."

'The next day, she telephoned: "Forgive me for yesterday… I behaved like an idiot. Of course I knew you wouldn't be happy with just a few kisses, I went with you all the same… but at the last moment, I don't know what came over me, I couldn't, forgive me."

'Of her own accord, she suggested another meeting. This time, she promised me, she'd be more… cooperative. She wanted it, she said; she was aware that she didn't really have a life, that soon it would be too late, etc. She chattered as in the cafe. I was, however, able to reassure her of my understanding, and of the great desire that I still had, me too, to see her again, and that I found her extremely attractive; a woman isn't old at thirty-two; on the contrary, it's her most beautiful age, that of her flowering, to which I'd be happy to contribute. This time I was sincere; the task was worthy of a true lover, especially a Don Juan.

'And when we met in the same room of the same little hotel, she undressed without waiting for my solicitations. I wasn't disappointed with my wait. To be honest, I rarely am; aside from the fact that nudity always surprises me, hoping one day to discover the ideal woman who'd be the sum of all the perfections, each one of them brings me closer in her own way. Set free, her hair, a rain of golden threads, enveloped her down to her chest, replaced on her stomach by a tawny fleece on yellow amber skin. To heighten her nudity, or to distract one's regard, she'd kept a choker on her neck and a belt around her waist made of the same metal. A delicate statuette, a Cérès, goddess of fertility, lovingly fashioned by the hands of the artist.

'This time, she accepted my caresses, even joined in, her hands still a bit clumsy, as always with spouses newly outside the conjugal nest. As for me, I did everything I possibly could, sparing neither my efforts nor my savoir faire.

'However, when judging the foreplay sufficient, I wanted to conclude and bring her to receive me, she lay on her back and stopped moving, as if her cooperation had to terminate there. I put her out of my mind, I confess, until my own head stopped spinning. Then I became aware that she'd behaved so weirdly that I wondered if she'd taken any pleasure at all. I thought it preferable not to put the question; a negative response would have been embarrassing for both of us. Better to give her time to dare to push herself to the limit, and to allow me to complete a semi-conquest, with which I couldn't be entirely satisfied.

'Before we parted, she suggested that we see each other again at her home, where we'd be more at ease, we'd avoid the inconvenience of the hotel, the expense. Her son increasingly preferred to spend time at his father's place, where he met up with his half-sister.

'For all that, her behaviour didn't change much. She lived together with her son in what had been the conjugal apartment, the top floor of a dilapidated building in the 13th *arrondissement*, too hot in summer due to the zinc roof, difficult to heat in winter. She asked if I minded her keeping her woollen Pyrenean dressing gown on, habitual companion of the curlers among lower-class housewives. Instead of sitting down near me, as I invited her to do, she kept moving about, coming and going across the room, busying herself preparing tea, showing me photographs of her son when he was a baby, chattering, to the point that I ended up becoming irritated, or worse, distracted: how can you pay court to a moving current of air?

'When, at last, she agreed to get undressed, she hurriedly slipped under the covers, where I joined her, after having switched off the light at her request. But however much I cajoled her, called upon all my experience, which, pardon my vanity, is very extensive, spoke sweet words to her (for example I called her libellule, dragonfly, then Julibellule, which stuck, and wasn't just an affectionate compliment, because it also expressed my inability to reach her), if she did nothing to prevent my caresses, she hardly responded to them either. If contact with her skin moved me, it was a damp fire, where I wasn't at risk of getting burnt, and which I despaired of being able to ignite.

'One day when she'd been particularly reserved, refusing to remove the heavy cover that hindered my hands, I impatiently asked her if, at least, she liked it, she replied limply: "Yes, yes, of course..."

'Then, I suppose to console me, she laughingly confided: "I had a cold the first time a boy kissed me, my nose was blocked; I let him do it because friends had told me that men liked it a lot, but I didn't feel a thing."

'Another day, when I was jokingly telling her about my far-off gymnastic exploits at school, I asked her if the sight of my body got to her, she replied in no uncertain terms: "We don't ask men to be beautiful, but we want them to be competent."

'It was certainly the first time, poor Don Juan, that anyone had suggested I was insufficient.

'Surprised, humiliated, I stupidly snapped: "You ought to try with someone else!"

'I wanted to hurt her with one of those things that lovers say, in the sure knowledge that they won't be believed and which they don't believe themselves. But she looked at me, not so astonished it seemed, as if she'd had the same thought herself, perhaps trying to ascertain whether I was speaking seriously, then quietly said: "Yes, that's an idea."

'Had she whispered, or did I just think I heard it: "You'd really like that…"

'In any case, soon all hell broke loose. We imagine hell is a dark valley where the damned suffer and burn; it can also be a luxurious meadow full of poisonous flowers, where those who breathe the scent become slowly intoxicated to the point of losing their senses, to the point of delirium and madness.

'Julie's metamorphosis began in the following days, as if in fact, she'd only had to wait for my permission. She had a wart on her shoulder that got in the way of my caresses; out of delicacy, I'd never dared mention it; the wart disappeared. The cotton bloomers which came down to her knees gave way to tiny silk knickers, the butt of our jokes because they turn us on so much. The single woollen Pyrenean dressing gown gave way to a collection of exotic robes, Spanish, Japanese, Arab, Hindu, which indicated as soon as you walked in the door, which dream we were going to live out together.

'Jean-Jacques Lambert talked about a festival just now, in candlelight with strains of music, kindly organised by a woman of the world, a bit flighty, who wanted to give him pleasure. With Julie, it was bright lights and brass bands, presaging fireworks.

'I said she lived on the top floor of her building; from the moment you entered, music and the smell of incense filled the staircase. She'd decorated the last steps leading to her landing with so many plants that you could have been in the middle of a garden; she put up coloured lamps, whose light, playing on the foliage, mimicked the front of a stage where some drama was about to unfold. And above all, the miracle! Julie finally became the mistress that I was despairing of, that I'd waited so long for and hadn't been able to create – active, inventive, playful. She gave me an all-singing all-dancing welcome: "I'm the bird of paradise, the queen, the goddess of the temple of love!"

'She was right – flowers, candles, music, incense, weren't they the ingredients of the cult that she'd given herself up to and whose servant I was? Already dressed as a geisha, she threw me a kimono and proclaimed: "*Soirée Japonaise!*" I had to rush and transform myself into the habitué of a teahouse; "Rogues Night", we both had to dress up, on the spot, in flat caps and velvet suits with turtlenecks. Everything suited her – the dresses, the kimonos, the skirts and trousers – due to the modesty of her bottom; everything contributed to her embellishment – ribbons, scarves, jewels, the inexhaustible work on her hairdo – my eyes weren't big enough to take it all in! How do chameleons do it, manage to surprise us time and again! Or on the contrary, divesting herself of her robe, she'd appear completely naked: "*Hamam Soirée.*" Get undressed! Hurry up!

'In her imperious impatience, she tore off my clothes and dragged me toward the bathroom. She played with the water as with love, patting it with her palms, splashing the walls, where she used to be so careful. She took hold of me in the water, to get me to make love in the bath. "Like whales!"

'I had to stop myself, for fear of messing up in that discomfort. I carried her to the bed where, still wet, I gave her what she wanted. I should have realised that she was overdoing it, that she wasn't quite so sure of herself, like people who never stop moving in order to prove their strength, whereas true strength is solidity, silence and immobility. But I was fascinated. I left her late at night, she who used to prefer to go to sleep early, and regained my domicile almost incredulous, surprised to find myself once again in the calm and solitude of my bedroom, wondering if I hadn't just woken from a dream, if I hadn't come back from a journey in a country where time didn't exist, because that's principally what love is, the only true paradise, outside of time, the only eternity. Julie really was the goddess of love, come down to earth, to give me a glimpse of bliss.

'So, would you say that everything in the end was for the best, in the best of worlds? I'd obtained what I was looking for, prior to setting out on new expeditions... no, altogether not! This time, it wasn't me that triumphed; it was Julie, who presented me with the triumph, having organised it in such a way that I played the character she assigned. Reversing roles, it was she who'd been in charge. "Don't move! I'm going to do it all."

'I didn't move, abandoning myself to her hands, until the pleasure became unbearable, I almost implored her to agree to finish off. "Ah, I'm happy! So happy!" she declared.

'She put on weight. "How awful! None of my skirts fit me anymore," she proclaimed, falsely alarmed.

'Have you noticed that happy women put on weight? A manifestation, I suppose, of their success in conquering a male. Perhaps I should simply have rejoiced in it; isn't the most beautiful present a woman can give to a man, to say to him that she's happy? But, apart from not being sure that I merited it, this excessive happiness, unrestrained like that of an adolescent discovering life, worried me: where had she found those forces which were making such a new Julie of her?

'Cursing my stupidity, I repeated to myself my imprudent provocation: "You ought to try with someone else!"

'Well, she had tried, and she'd done well! The miracle wasn't the result of my victory but that of an unknown rival, into whose arms I had pushed Julie, and who'd been more effective than myself. However, no matter how much I told myself that she'd stayed with me – proof positive that in some way she cared for me – it didn't suffice to show that she owed her liberation to me. I'd have liked to be sure that she did owe it to me. Suspecting the contrary, I feared, in addition, that I no longer satisfied her. Having at last thrown off her chains, why, in her freedom, would she content herself from now on with me alone? Why wouldn't she see the unknown stranger again? Perhaps strangers? Why couldn't there be feminine Don Juans?

'If love is paradise, jealousy is hell. The only serious drama between a man and a woman is that of suspicion. Jealousy is gut rot; one no longer lives, one agonises. As with a stomach ache or a toothache, one would like to make nothing of it, laugh it off, but it occupies everything, takes over everything, it excludes and paralyses all other thought. I was lying in wait, seeing the worst, interpreting possible signs of abandonment. One day, I no longer saw the wedding ring on her finger; braving her irony, I asked her the reason. "Oh," she replied distractedly, "it's because of the washing-up, I was scared I'd lose it in the sink."

'But she hadn't put it back on. The suppression of that conjugal symbol, which previously had annoyed me, made me feel bad, as if she'd liberated herself, not from her ex-husband but from me. Then, everything changes its meaning in jealousy; this woman who's a promise of bliss, becomes a source of permanent suffering. After that I telephoned Julie, no longer for the pleasure of hearing her voice, of confirming her existence, but to surprise her, to make sure she was alone, to detect any possible funny business. I went so far as to cancel a professional engagement in order to lie in wait outside her work. I positioned myself not far from the publishers and followed her to the bus. My torments began when I realised she wasn't returning directly to her home:

where was she going? Happily it was winter; she was wearing a Davy Crockett fur cap which made her stand out from a distance amongst passers-by. I leapt from one *porte cochère* to another. But how to survey all her comings and goings?

'I discovered with bitter amusement how difficult it is to control someone else's life. I could have had her followed by a professional, I didn't do it. On the contrary, I was quick to hang on to the slightest reassuring signs. Out of modesty, she'd never previously introduced me to her son; she brought us together for a tea, during which the boy, with that nice intuition for everything concerning his mother, behaved disagreeably. I took it as proof that she envisaged our relationship lasting. We went on holiday to Corsica, where I was happy because I had her all to myself, but my torments returned as soon as we got back.

'Out of discretion, so as not to make the ruptures more painful, I had in the past avoided publicising my liaisons as much as possible. She wanted to be introduced to my friends; I saw a happy omen there. I suggested she accompany me whenever I went out. But this proved an equally unexpected source of suffering. At the kind of party where women show off their naked shoulders and display their breasts and seem to compete, as if in a luxury brothel, I was more preoccupied with watching her than listening to my immediate neighbour. It was particularly galling to watch her dance. Dance, the great Tolstoy noted long ago, is a representation of adultery. At the sound of appropriate music, any old person has the right to hold your woman in his arms, chest against chest, belly to belly, where in other circumstances it would be unacceptable for him to touch her fingertips. Oh, it wasn't that I didn't laugh at myself. How, I asked myself, have I come to make such a scandal of what previously seemed pleasant and natural? If passion was the cause, then passion is stupid. To be in love is to feel good with someone; to be impassioned is to be made to suffer by someone. I came back from those dates irritated with her and furious with myself. "That imbecile Dunand never stopped making up to you."

"'All men flirt with me, be they as ugly as sin... including your closest friends my little darling, but be reassured,' she joked, 'it's you whom I prefer, my heartthrob little Corsican."

'That neither amused nor reassured me; it wasn't enough for me to be the favourite, I wanted to be the only one. During visits to my sister, I've been struck by the behaviour of her last little one aged eighteen months, who, sitting on the knees of his mother, wickedly pulls her hair while she's on the telephone. Was I going to tear out Julie's hair, to beat her, to prevent her from looking at other men? I wasn't lacking in desire. I was just discovering that one could hit a woman, even kill her, out of love. What to do, in fact, if a woman asleep by your side, begins to moan, dreaming, miming orgasm, encouraging a partner who isn't you: " Yes! Yes! Come on!" What to do other than strangle her in her sleep?

'Especially as, out of innocence or coquettishness, like Carmen with her lovers, Julie had no intention of sparing me. "All those looks don't seem to displease you," I said accusingly.

"'Why would they displease me? Between men and women, it's like an electric current; it's not always visible, but each one feels it in him or herself... it's a very agreeable sensation!"

'She was, of course, right; wasn't my attention immediately stimulated by the appearance of a woman in a drawing room for example? That's why no one has ever won the war against sex, neither churches nor political parties nor moralists. It's the great call of nature in each one of us; if convention and public order didn't oppose it, we would all eagerly respond. Especially as women encourage us in all sorts of ways, are always sending out signals; what are perfumes, make-up, jewellery? How could a dragonfly, bristling with all its multicoloured wing cases, fail to attract the attention of males, and how would they not want to grasp her, even if only a little coloured dust remained between their fingers?

'At the business where Julie worked, there were six women and four men, sitting side by side the whole day long; how could nothing happen? (I cursed this civilisation where women were free to go out in the morning, supposedly to work, and only return in the evening. Yes, I was still a little Corsican!) Hadn't she told me, approvingly, that some of her colleagues made love in the storerooms during the lunch break? "What do you expect, that's nature! The head to head between a man and a woman progresses irresistibly into body to body," she quipped laughingly; laughter that wrung my heart.

'The image of Julie, surrendering to nature, making loveless love with someone or other, in a storeroom, upset me; the image of her making love with a lover upset me even more.

'Ah, I'd rather she was frigid like before. She was no longer frigid with me, why would she be with others? Wanting to know, yet fearing the discovery of her infidelities, I searched through her things, yes, I shamelessly searched through them. I intercepted her mail, I opened everything I could without risk, I forced myself to recognise her correspondents' writing, I read and reread the letters that she left lying about; I listened in when she was on the telephone, suspecting her of giving me the runaround. One day, I came upon a work timetable carefully copied: it wasn't hers, hers I knew by heart. I asked her point blank the name of the colleague to whom it belonged, and why she had it in her possession. As she seemed to get agitated, I concluded she had a particular relationship with that colleague; I bitterly accused her of it. She played offended, then deigned to explain that their business was functioning according to a new system where everybody could choose the amount of time they put in; she'd taken a copy of her colleague's timetable to study a possible change of hours. It was plausible, but she refused to give me his name; she only affirmed it to avoid a row, and because my accusation was ridiculous. Then, because I was hassling her, she hit me with: "You don't have any proof!"

'I replied in pained triumph: "Well that's the spurious argument of the guilty. It doesn't mean *I'm not guilty* but just: *you can't prove it*, so it's an indirect admission."

'On another day while we were chatting, lying in bed after making love, out of carelessness or unconscious provocation, or was she making a childish boast, astonishing in view of her late awakening, she triumphantly declared: "I always start up on the first turn of the handle!"

'With me, she rarely came on the first turn; who did she come so quickly with? The vulgar comparison of a woman with a car was a man's expression, not that of a woman; she'd heard it, perhaps received it as a compliment from a grateful partner, flattered to have been so welcome, and to feel himself so skilful…

'But let's stop there on that awful feeling, you're all familiar with it; if you told me you'd never suffered from jealousy, I wouldn't believe you…

'Finally, I recognised my defeat; I decided to abandon the fight, to give Julie up; no longer the successful conqueror but following my Waterloo.

'However, I needed to cure myself of that burning wound. I knew from experience the best remedy for love, is another love. Not being in the mood to throw myself into a totally new quest, I decided to rekindle an old flame, which I had, as usual, prematurely put out; not worrying too much, I confess, about the suffering I sometimes caused. I just had an embarrassment of choice. I chose Raymonde (let's call her that). In general I avoided such reconciliations. Besides the fact that it's difficult to bring moribund embers back to life, and even on the assumption that one's successful, it's most often disappointing to find an old mistress now developing wrinkles or embonpoint. But it wasn't the first time I'd had recourse to Raymonde between two affairs. Good girl that she was, lacking excessive romanticism, remaining single by preference, she was always ready to get back together, free of any illusions or demands, a casual stopover. Under cover of making some purchase in the department store where she worked, I pretended to meet her by chance in the flow of staff coming out at closing time. She wasn't fooled, but simply showed her pleasure at seeing me again.

'We had a drink nearby, then I accompanied her home, where she offered me dinner. I told her everything, she made gentle fun of me and we made love quite naturally. As it was late, I spent the night with her. Ah, if only my relations with Julie could have been so simple!

'I saw Raymonde two or three more times, but it was only a calm between two storms. A few days later, having been informed by a friend aspiring to replace me, or by one of Raymonde's letters I happened to leave around, perhaps to take revenge, and show Julie she wasn't irreplaceable, she became aware of my betrayal.

'All at once the madness changed camp, or rather there were two mad people instead of one. Before even speaking to me about it, she telephoned Raymonde and, without giving her a chance to explain, called her a whore and a thief. "I'll tear out your eyes, you bitch! I'm going to kill you! I'll kill you!"

'She was shouting into the receiver, a terrorised Raymonde told me. I reassured poor Raymonde. "Julie's incapable of killing a fly; like some birds, she puffs out her feathers in order to seem more frightening."

'But I wasn't really so sure; hadn't I myself harboured murderous impulses?

'I used to telephone Julie every morning to say hello, chat for a few minutes, work out what we might do in the evening; sometimes, when I could, I called her again during the day. It was understood that she would contact me as little as possible when I was in the office. She began to call me several times a day, at random moments, under pointless pretexts, with no concern for the professional embarrassment she risked occasioning me. Sometimes, seized by panic, she demanded that I come and see her straight away. Luckily, I didn't depend on anyone at work and my office hours were flexible; I rushed out to meet her. She begged me not to leave her alone for long periods of time, to spend the night with her as often as possible, which I did more and more. But rather than calming her, my presence seemed to exacerbate her anxiety. She sobbed and called me names, suspecting me of all sorts of depravity (she even accused me of having "debauched her", since before knowing me, she'd led a quiet life; which wasn't untrue, but hadn't she been on the lookout for me?). Eventually, exhausted, she decided to retire to her son's bedroom to shelter from our tempest, but then I heard her sobbing again; I went in to console her. If I hadn't done so, she'd have come back and, standing at the foot of the bed like some haunted phantom, continued her insults and accusations: I was a monster, cruel and egotistical, who changed his women like his shirts! "Dirty little Corsican Don Juan."

'I'd never truly loved women, I took pleasure in seeing them suffer. Her friends had warned her enough about me, she hadn't wanted to listen. Sometimes, miraculously, the evening seemed to unfold peacefully, in a kind of reciprocal politeness, which I was careful not to disturb. We dined in silence, or exchanged a few banalities on the events of the day; only our looks, like rainclouds, betrayed our ongoing suffering. As a precaution, I pretended not to be sleepy; Julie wished me goodnight and retired. I didn't get into bed until I thought she was asleep, but scarcely had I become drowsy when the tornado broke out again, all the more impressive as it surged out of the calm. Julie beat the covers with her fists, and her feet, transforming herself into the kind of hysterical Furie which had impressed men so much in antiquity that they suspected it was a message from the gods. Hysteria, isn't that a feminine condition? It was as if she'd undergone a change of personality. She described in filthy language which she never usually employed, in obscene detail, very surprising coming from her mouth, what according to her must have happened between Raymonde and myself. She let out impotent cries of rage. "That's just how your whore makes love, isn't it? Answer me, damn it!"

'She started calling me *tu* rather than *vous* which we'd never agreed to use before, and then started begging, promising, "to do all the same things for me". "Tell me what you see in her? She's vulgar! She's fat!"

'How could I explain it was precisely that voluptuous female flesh that made me feel good, away from pointless troubles, that I forgot myself in her; that I liked a woman to be a woman, with a woman's breasts, with the backside and thighs of a woman. Could I cruelly retort:"Ask me rather what it is I find in you, Julie dragonfly, with your miniature breasts, non-existent bottom; actually you're an island bird, which makes a person wonder whether it consists of nothing but feathers, or the kind of rag doll which makes you wonder whether, if you took off all its layers of material one by one, its trimmings and its hair, there'd be anything left. Are you flesh and blood, Julibellule? Am I not crazy to love you?"

'When we were drained, she by her outbursts, me by the effort of holding myself back, we fell into each other's arms and made love frenetically, as if we were coming together to salvage the ruins of our love.

'Julie got thinner, she lost the kilos she'd put on; she paled, her nostrils became pinched, her little nose became pointed like a beak. I'm ashamed to confess: while her happiness had wounded me because I wasn't sure I was its source, her suffering wasn't disagreeable: she loved me so she was suffering because of me.

'She ended up falling ill, a stomach ulcer which burst one apocalyptic night, when she nearly died. "Don't leave me alone!" she repeated, as if I was about to abandon her!

'And because I saved her life, she's never been so dear to me. To better care for her I moved into her place, something I'd never agreed to do with other mistresses. I did the shopping, the cooking, the washing-up. I'd discovered that to love someone is above all to want to give, not just to receive.

'Then she became progressively calmer. We embarked on a long convalescence where we avoided speaking of past torments; like extensive burns we avoided touching them. And when I was appointed in Marseille, her son having decided to live with his father, Julie naturally followed me.

'There you have it, the whole story.'

Gambini remained silent.

However, he hadn't responded to a question which was burning our lips. After a silence, as if he'd guessed our curiosity wasn't completely satisfied, he said with a smile:

'You're wondering if I'm faithful to Julie, if Julie's faithful to me? I haven't responded to that question because there's no longer any point. I don't try to find out, I no longer search through her things, I no longer open her letters, I don't listen in to her telephone calls. As for the supposed unknown stranger, I've given up trying to verify his existence… perhaps it was nothing but a dream, Julie's dream, and each person, especially in a couple, must remain the owner of his or her dreams.

'Above all, I've ceased to be a love bulimic. If I've continued to play sport, I've given up playing competitive sport. I've renounced the role of Don Juan. Now I think all women are, in fact, one and the same dragonfly, which we unceasingly hunt in order to construct an ideal woman… who doesn't exist. So a single woman should suffice to assuage our anguish, because every woman contains the whole of femininity.

'And Julie? I suppose she thinks the same way. We never talk about that terrible time. In any case, if we happen to throw a party, she no longer asks me to dress up.'

The grit in the shoe
or the virtual child

Louise Gruson carefully cleaned her contact lenses before putting them back in their case, as she always did when she came home, then began to get undressed.

'Do you know who I ran into at Pahlares's opening?'

'I don't know.'

'Margarida… she's passing through Paris.'

Paul Gruson was immediately on guard, as if the history of his affair dated from the night before. One day, Margarida was bound to reappear… he succeeded in controlling himself.

'Ah, really…'

After a moment, which he prolonged as long as he could, he asked politely, he had to ask:

'What's become of her?'

'She's done very well! She's covered in jewels like a Monoprix display stand, only hers are real… she's staying at the Ritz! She married a big importer from Rio de Janeiro who used to be her boss.'

He wanted to say: "That doesn't surprise me, with her!", or something like that, but it would have revealed some emotion, better not to.

'So much the better for her.'

'Yes, she seems to be blooming… she even has a daughter, she was with her, she's called Amalia, prettier than her mother, obviously fresher, eighteen years old, and unlike her mother,' Louise added perfidiously, 'less flighty... she's studying seriously, she's doing... political science, as I understand it...'

Gruson's heart missed a beat; he held onto just one point: eighteen years! Fortunately his wife was engrossed talking about their former au pair girl. He enquired in a changed voice, this time scarcely able to master himself:

'Eighteen? How do you know?'

'I asked her, what do you think!'

He made a mental calculation, he repeated it once, twice, it wasn't possible! Amalia would have had to be twenty-one, he knew for certain, he'd made and remade that calculation so often. Hadn't he mentally celebrated her birthday...

'Has she got any other children?' he asked Louise.

'Er... no, certainly not, I asked her that question.'

Unless... he was reminded that Margarida had always refused to see him again, to introduce him to Amalia; she was capable of anything!

Margarida had come into his life exactly twenty-two years earlier: Margarida Rodrigues, with an "s", not a "z", she'd proudly proclaimed; she wasn't Spanish but Portuguese, Portuguese from Brazil. She'd been sent to his wife by an agency specialising in the placement of au pair girls. The two children were still small; Louise, an executive in an advertising agency, was hugely taken up with her profession, feeling guilty as career women often do, she was very demanding in all matters concerning her offspring. She imposed a work schedule on the young girls scarcely compatible with their time due in university, although for many, study and learning the French language were just an alibi to convince their parents to let them travel. The mirage of Parisian life, the hope for romances, easier to establish than in their native countries, were often the real reasons. One of them, very pretty, Gruson noted with regret in spite of himself, stayed for just twenty-four hours, time to introduce herself to the agency and send a telegram back home; she disappeared the next day without having opened her suitcase. It's true they sometimes awakened the concupiscence, more or less discretely, of the master of the house, aroused by their youthful femininity and being indifferent to the familiar charms of his wife and the mother of his children.

While, in order to make a good impression, most of the young girls claimed to have come from upper-class families to say the least, and were there above all, they emphasised, to please their parents, Margarida on the contrary let it be known that she'd run away from home because her father beat her, if not worse. She hadn't been any luckier with her first placement. She spontaneously informed the awestruck Gruson, that her previous employers, a couple of Brazilian compatriots, had taken her into their bed to mutually warm themselves up, in celebration of their common native country. She ended up returning to the agency to ask for a different placement, with the Grusons to be precise. These scandalous events in her life, light-heartedly depicted by the young girl, contrasted with her well-combed strictly pulled-back hair, straight tunic, as black as her hair, which, save for the white of her face, covered her from head to foot. Louise Gruson, a tall woman, model girl-scout leader, healthy in mind and body, incapable even of imagining such misbehaviour, especially towards very young girls entrusted to one's care, preferred to believe that Margarida was fantasising. She shrugged her shoulders.

'She's making it up, no? She's telling tall stories to gain our pity...'

The remark didn't favour the candidate, Paul Gruson knew his wife. On the contrary, being indulgent, since he was unconsciously seduced, he tried to joke about it. His experienced art critic's eye had perceived, beyond the modesty of her dress, the discrete beauty of the young girl, the regularity of her features, the continuous line of her forehead and nose; one of her doubles could have served as a model for Greek sculpture or the Black Virgins.

'All women fantasise,' he hazarded…

But, as soon as she thought the feminine condition was at stake, Louise's solidarity was immediate and total.

'Yes, because men are vile to women!'

'Not everybody, surely,' he pleaded limply.

'All! You included, my darling… moreover even between us, you always seem to be trying to get the upper hand… but especially with women… if Margarida fantasises, it's because she has to defend herself against men all the time.'

Thus, despite the first unfavourable reaction of the mistress of the house, Margarida was given a trial.

Louise explained what she was expecting of her. On getting up, to help the children sort themselves out, dress them, give them something to eat, then take them to school. Then she was free… until it was time to collect them and make their lunch at home; Louise didn't like them to eat in the canteen where they might pick up some kind of gastric fever. After having taken them back to school, Margarida was free again until four o'clock when she had to wait for them at the gate. Tea, supervision of homework, washing hands and getting ready for dinner and going to bed. Finally she was completely free until the following day.

Margarida raised no objection to this division of her time, which generally caused other girls to flee, since it clashed with the demands of their studies, with which Margarida scarcely seemed concerned. Often, she didn't even go out in the mornings, or only after lunch; then she went back up to her room on the sixth floor, or mooched around the apartment exchanging a few words with Rosa, the cleaner, also Portuguese.

Gruson, a columnist in the arts pages of a prestigious weekly magazine, usually did some work at home before going out to exhibition openings, which always took place at the end of the afternoon. When he sat down to eat, Margarida forbade Rosa to use the hoover; Gruson, who didn't understand a word of Portuguese, guessed what was going on from the furious look on the cleaner's face. When, after washing up and a final tidying, Rosa left the house, Margarida asked Gruson if he'd like some coffee, accompanied by a glass of iced water according to the custom in hot countries. Then she read or watched him write. Sitting on a cushion, or even on the carpet, she remained immobile like a big black cat, until the journalist having pushed his papers aside, indicated it was time for another break, during which they chatted amicably.

Coming, like his wife, from an old bourgeois family, austere if not puritan, Gruson had only ever cast a distant look on the various au pair girls they'd had. A long tradition had taught him it was necessary to respect women but at the same time be wary of femininity. However, it was difficult for a normally constituted male to remain altogether insensible to Margarida's charms and attentions.

Slim, but perfectly proportioned like an ebony statuette, quick-witted with an ironic intelligence, playful and a little sarcastic, she was too different from the Scandinavian or German girls (tall placid sporty blondes who resembled his wife), to fail, at least, to awaken his curiosity. And when she suggested teaching him a little Portuguese, "so as to understand Rosa and me better", she added with a smile, without taking it too seriously having always been a bad language student, he accepted with pleasure above all because it created a kind of mutual understanding between them.

Margarida was very clear in giving him three keys with which to get hold of her native tongue, otherwise it would indeed remain impenetrable to a French ear. Like the Portuguese, Brazilians swallow most of their vowels, thus *general* becomes *gnrl* and *admiral, mral*; they don't make use of melodic support in their sentences, so their speech, deprived of the internal music found in French or even more in Italian, resembles the regular firing of a machine gun; finally she stressed, they sprinkle everything they say with that famous *cheu cheu*, the only recognisable thing in a conversation between Portuguese, which makes it no less opaque.

But if Margarida wasn't jealous of her time during the day, once night fell, she seemed to suddenly emerge from her stasis. As soon as the children were asleep, she went up to her bedroom, and came back down an hour later, transformed, nearly unrecognisable in her make-up. It could scarcely be called make-up since the layer of foundation on her face was thick, violent. On an orange-coloured base, nearly yellow, she'd superimposed patches of red, acid blue around her eyelids, and so much carbonaceous matter on her eyelashes and eyebrows that they became stiff. The overly violent carmine turned her mouth into an exotic flower. It was as if there were two Margaridas: during the day an angel made of unvarnished wood, at night a bizarre multicoloured face, scary like primitive people's grimacing totems where the clumsiness of the painter has caused the colours to run. Possessed by an unusual degree of agitation, she rushed out of the house as if some urgent task was waiting to be done.

'You could say a cat going out on the tiles hunting toms,' Louise murmured, ill at ease and scandalised, 'one expects to hear her miaow...'

She wasn't seen again during the evening and on her return she went directly to her room. The next day she came down, still half-asleep. "The multicoloured angel is becoming a smeary angel," Gruson joked; her face was crinkled, almost stiff with the accumulated products on her skin, badly washed, with traces of red, orange, and kohl on the wings of her nose, her temples, her forehead, in the roots of her hair and around her ears, which disgusted and irritated Louise, who was always spruce on getting up as if she'd just got out of a bath. Gruson wondered why Margarida spoiled the purity of her complexion under all those layers of horrible paint, which aged rather than embellished her, and must surely, in the long run, be damaging to her skin. Perhaps she wanted to dissipate that bluish pallor of Mediterranean women, resulting from centuries of feminine confinement. Sometimes, having got in very late, exhausted, and having sunk into the heavy sleep characteristic of her age, she didn't come down in time in the morning, and Louise, in a hurry and furious, had to go up and fetch her.

One evening, they were woken by a commotion; violent knocks on the door to which Margarida responded with shouts. She'd been pursued by a suitor, most probably drunk, met in some dance, who not wanting to give up, had followed her home up to the floor of her building. Gruson had to intervene, together with the concierge, to threaten the intruder with the police. It made a fine scandal in the posh apartment block. But Margarida seemed so terrified, trembling like a bird buffeted in a tempest, that Gruson refrained from reproaching her at the time; he even had to reassure her, and to his embarrassment, she cuddled up to him like a frightened child.

All the same, the next day, he remonstrated with her about her extravagancies; one day she'd come across someone more brutal, even dangerous. He threatened, to be honest without conviction, to tell her parents; wasn't she somehow his responsibility? He told her about Louise's growing impatience. Margarida burst into sobs. Her father, jealous like all fathers in her country, would force her to return immediately; he'd beat her if he found out about her little antics, oh, so innocent, but you can't play around like that at home. She was happy with the Grusons, she loved the children, she was attached to them. She begged him to plead her cause with Mme Gruson, whom she was afraid of, not like him, Paul, who was so kind… embarrassed in the face of those torrents of tears and supplications, Gruson promised to intervene with his wife and, to calm her, he put his arm round her shoulders. She threw herself against him and, to thank him, kissed him effusively on both cheeks, several times, without him responding in kind.

It became a habit with them. As soon as Rosa was on her way, they sat side by side on the sofa and drank the exquisite coffee, prepared by Margarida and chosen by her from the best specialist shops.

'Portuguese coffee, the best in the world,' she averred with pride, 'even better than Italian coffee!'

Gruson wasn't very loquacious; Margarida told him amusing stories from her bohemian milieu, or recounted with emotion that brought tears to his eyes, the extraordinary opulence of a minority of her people in contrast to the extraordinary poverty of the majority. And when Gruson laughed or sincerely sympathised, Margarida kissed him in gratitude. Sometimes she lay on the sofa and, head on Gruson's knees, continued to talk. Spring, which was beginning, gave the journalist allergies, headaches and unstoppable sneezing attacks; while remaining seated at his desk for long periods of time, it froze his feet. He agreed to let Margarida rub his temples and feet with hot oil, as they did back home; he didn't really believe in the remedy, but he found it amusing and agreeable to be massaged in that way.

To be blunt, one doesn't place oakum next to a flame, above all one as ardent as Margarida, with impunity. Later on, he couldn't have said when they first made love, in so far as it happened insensibly, and without him really knowing how one thing led to another. He followed her upstairs to her little bedroom, for fear that their exertions would make a mess of the apartment. In any case, he'd never have agreed to use the conjugal bed, which would have seemed sacrilege and a betrayal of Louise. They made love on the young girl's narrow divan, from which Gruson, being used to the king-size double bed that Louise had ordered at the beginning of their marriage, was perpetually in fear of falling.

With the exception of some nascent heaviness, barely noticeable in her breasts, and the promise of a future expansion of the hips, Margarida's buxom nudity, that of a young woman, deceptively disguised under her clothes, surprised Gruson with a perfection worthy of her facial features. Above all, she astonished him with her mastery in bed, her passion, her inventiveness, unexpected in such a young woman. Sometimes, her young body being unavailable for complete conjunction, she took him in her mouth. Out of delicacy, fearing that he'd hurt her, when he felt himself carried away by the dizzy abandonment of orgasm, Gruson wanted to withdraw, but she held him in, explaining:

'It doesn't bother me! On the contrary, I like it! And I want you to reach the peak of your pleasure…'

He was grateful to her and at the same time experienced a kind of obscure apprehension, as if she was imposing her law, sucking out his life. Sometimes she arrived, hair unloosed in a glittering cascade ("I washed my hair this morning, for you!"; she called him *tu* familiarly from time to time; he never used that word, even in moments of the greatest intimacy). He was disturbed and fearful of the dark power of that hair. The ancient comparison between snakes and the Gorgon's hair was apposite. After coming downstairs, both of them relaxed, as if nothing had happened. She sat on the sofa opposite him and watched him work, her large eyes fixed on him like those of a dog, or murmured loving words so excessive that Gruson felt uncomfortable.

However, time being limited by Rosa's departure and the children's coming home, and because in spite of his fascination, Gruson was ill at ease with the affair, they didn't make love very often. His life with Louise suited him; she lacked the sultry beauty of Margarida but nothing in her troubled him. On the contrary she embodied, *la femme forte* of the classics, on whom one could rely. As for his dreamy side, he found it sufficiently satisfied in museums and galleries. No affair, even with Margarida, seemed worth the risk of destroying the edifice of his conjugal life with a companion beyond reproach, and affectionate well-balanced children. Wasn't Margarida going to bring back some infection from her nocturnal escapades, that he'd perhaps transmit to his wife, despite the moderation of their sexual urges and the growing intervals between their encounters in bed?

And then there was that old anxiety which obsesses the conscience of every responsible man: the possible pregnancy of his partner. It was he who regularly asked Margarida if she'd "taken precautions", to which, as if she was scarcely bothered by it, she responded evasively: "yes, yes", or even one day, in an unexpected manner, slyly: "you're worried!", which he believed signified, it'd be unfortunate for you! Her father, the men in her family, she explained to him one day, would react violently if she became pregnant outside marriage.

On another day, in one of those moments of abandon where nature is overwhelmed by desire, she told him with almost perverse jubilation, that she always looked for people's weak points, men especially:

'Then, that's where I press!'

He tried, slightly afraid, to persuade her that the moral thing to do was exactly the opposite: to avoid profiting from people's weakness, to look, on the contrary, for what would do them the most good. She sneered, abruptly vulgar.

'The moral thing, do you know a lot of moral people?'

Having imprudently confided to her, that coming from a large family he would have liked to have had more children, but Louise hadn't agreed:

'I could give you one, if you like,' retorted Margarida.

'You're crazy!'

'Yes, I'm crazy,' she agreed.

Briefly, like many settled men, if he professed indulgence for a lapse every now and again, on a trip for example, "a bit on the side", he carefully avoided lasting attachments, which couldn't fail to cause trouble in his life, which is to say especially the life of his loved ones. In any case, Louise would never have tolerated it; he didn't know how she'd react. He often discoursed to Margarida on loyalty, as if loyalty occupied a great place in his affairs; she listened, her beautiful black eyes fixed on him, without him ever knowing if she took it seriously or if she was laughing at his fears.

And when, weary of Margarida's renewed misbehaviour, fearing it would end up giving a bad example to the children, who were too influenced by her, Louise decided to let her go, he was almost relieved. He no longer knew where he stood, where he was going, and he'd never have had the strength to break off. Moreover it turned out well: the Easter holidays were coming soon, and the Grusons usually took the children to the mountains. The au pair girl, Margarida, was due to accompany them, so the parents could both enjoy skiing. Well we can give that a miss…

So Louise announced the end of the contract to Margarida, who began to cry, leaving Gruson unsure whether she was thinking of the end of their affair, her attachment to the children, or whether she was simply worried about finding herself unemployed once again. Louise harboured none of those perplexities.

'Latin theatre! Hysteria on order!' she decreed.

Gruson, although not unmoved by the theatre, did wonder if his wife had a point. Margarida looked to Gruson for help who, for fear of weakening and thus showing his complicity, left the room. The only indulgence he allowed himself, without telling Louise, was to give Margarida an excellent reference, although unsure whether the agency would take such a dithyrambic text seriously, above all when written by the master of the house. He tried to compensate her a little by offering, still in the absence of his wife, a drawing by Pahlares which was on his desk, a gift from the artist following a particularly complimentary review, which he knew Margarida was fond of.

Several weeks after returning from the mountains, when Gruson, still divided between nostalgia and a sense of deliverance, a danger avoided, regretted and reproached himself for not having taken Margarida's new address, in order, he thought, to give her some possible help, he found a letter in the mail from the young woman. It briefly announced that she was pregnant, by him, no possible error, and, as in crime films, didn't give an address.

'I'll call you on the telephone.'

She didn't call him, but shortly afterwards he received another letter, thanking heavens it hadn't fallen into his wife's hands. It was very well written, whereas Margarida wrote pretty bad French. This time, there was a deluge of reproaches, it accused Gruson of having seduced her; she no longer had a penny and was living in a squat.

Luckily she had friends!

In her condition, she obviously couldn't find a place in a family. Conclusion: she demanded a fixed sum every month, she hoped that he wouldn't leave the mother of "that little life which came from him" in destitution. (How many times following that was he unable to sleep at the thought of that little life…) She also had to prepare a layette, buy a cradle…

Several days later, he received a telephone call at his journal office, where she more or less reiterated the terms of the letter. Gruson tried to suggest that it would be better for the child and for herself, if she didn't keep it. Of course, he employed all the arguments, wise and unwise, that men give in those circumstances, dictated by good sense, guilt or bad faith. In vain.

'No; it's my child… moreover, my religion forbids it!'

He wasn't aware that Margarida's religion was so demanding; for example she'd never asked to go to Mass. He suggested that they meet to talk about it somewhere, not on the telephone…

'No, I'm too ugly! I've already got fat; you men, you aren't deformed, you sow your seed and then goodbye!'

He had to deliver the sum fixed by Margarida every month into the hands of Miguel, a waiter at Select, the "Café des Copains". In exchange, she promised to quit trying to see him. It wasn't exactly blackmail, but Gruson had no choice.

Then, in effect, there was silence for several months, during which he regularly supplied the allowance required, until the day when he received word at the office informing him that she'd had a girl and that she'd named her Amalia. At the same time she announced she'd decided to return to Brazil with her daughter, but in order to do so she needed the price of an aeroplane ticket. After that last bit of help, she promised he'd never hear a word from her again.

Gruson immediately supplied the requested sum.

Margarida kept her promise; he received no more news. He felt relieved, he'd escaped the cyclone.

But that was to forget that he was one of those people who fan the flames of their own hell. All the same, how had he been able to let himself behave that way! A young girl, and under his own roof! He wouldn't have admitted it to anybody. Sometimes he accused himself, burdened himself, sometimes pleaded, defended himself, going over the same arguments. Margarida wasn't a young girl like the others; she was a bomb placed in his life and the life of his family! Sooner or later, it would have exploded. He rebelled; he blamed Margarida, all women including his own; if Louise had been more affectionate, instead of only thinking about her career, he would have been less attracted to Margarida. He'd wanted more children.

'You can make them on your own!' Louise quipped.

Well, he'd made one without her! Now that women had control over their pregnancies, hadn't men's responsibility been largely diminished? Hadn't he regularly asked Margarida if she'd "taken precautions"? What could he have done, other than trust her? Perhaps she'd even consciously wanted that child, to make a rod for his back? But he also recognised that in those matters, both women and men lost their minds. Perhaps Amalia was the fruit of calculation or carelessness on Margarida's part, she wasn't any the less his daughter. She was the fruit of a folly but a shared folly, whose consequences ought to be shared. He sometimes dreamed that he was assailed by thickly moustached black men, or so he imagined Margarida's father and innumerable brothers and cousins to be. Other times he reminisced with nostalgia, reminding himself of their unrestrained embraces. He nursed an increasing desire to at least have some news.

To get hold of Margarida's address, he telephoned the agency ostensibly because the young girl had forgotten some effects that he'd like to return to her. He was gently laughed at. It happened frequently enough that the master of a house sought to re-establish contact with a young girl. Their addresses were never given out. He could bring her things to the agency, which would take responsibility for sending them on, if possible, since sometimes they'd been given false information.

He returned to the "Café des Copains"; the waiter, Miguel, confirmed that Margarida had left without warning. By going through Margarida's postage stamps, he was able to deduce the location where the squat she'd lived in must have been situated: there was nothing there; most of the old buildings had been demolished to make way for new developments. He had the impression that fate had permanently robbed him of a part of himself. Perhaps that was punishment for his bad behaviour and cowardice.

Then, little by little, time did its work. Once or twice, suffocating under the weight of that secret which he hadn't confided to anyone, he came within an inch of opening himself up to Louise. But his wound was causing him less and less pain. His daughter, Amalia, simply belonged to another world, a kind of virtual world; she lived within him, in an imaginary Brazil. He noted the dates of her birthdays in his diary, her first communion, her confirmation, in a code known only to himself, and sometimes he even celebrated them mentally, on his own. When he was asked how many children he had, he hesitated, two, no three, Jacques, Jaqueline... and Amalia. When they moved home, he took account of Amalia; one day perhaps... he would have gladly decorated one of those little shrines that Asians build in their homes, in memory of their ancestors, a coloured lamp permanently alight, some dried flowers, some fruit: his virtual daughter's altar.

Louise finished getting undressed, all the time continuing to say mean things about Margarida; she must have put on weight round the hips, like her countrywomen, her face must have begun to dry out, her nose was pointed…

To stop this demolition job, which annoyed him, he asked his wife if Margarida was still angry with them (he meant with him).

'No, she didn't seem to be, why would she be?'

'I don't know… because of the children… after all we threw her out…'

Louise shrugged her shoulders.

He waited till she got to the last of her underwear before leaving the room; he knew she didn't like him seeing her that way.

He ensconced himself in his study and called the Ritz. He was told that they hadn't any clients named Rodrigues. How stupid he'd been! She must have changed her name on getting married… Margarida, he insisted, wasn't there at least someone called Margarida? A Brazilian lady with her daughter? Yes… a Margarida Pinto.

He was put through to her room. He immediately recognised her voice, she didn't seem in any way surprised that he'd called; she was expecting it after having run into Louise. They exchanged the usual banalities concerning their mutual health, the time that had passed… she'd found Louise a little more portly… she became a bit more animated when asking for news of the children…

So he was able, with beating heart, to put the only question that mattered to him: Amalia? No, she wasn't his daughter; she was her husband's.

He hesitated.

'Were you really pregnant?'

'Yes… but I didn't keep it… you were right, it was best for everyone…'

'But then why…'

She laughed farcically.

'It was a friend from the squat who suggested it to me, he wrote the letters, I wouldn't have known… we were broke, you understand…'

She went on talking; Gruson was no longer listening to her.

He no longer knew whether he regretted it or not: that child, who'd been present in his thoughts and behaviour, that he'd carried with him for twenty years like a piece of grit in his shoe, had never existed!

'But why did you call your daughter Amalia… like…'

There was a silence, then it seemed to him her voice changed, Margarida replied:

'In memory of our history.'

The Sonotone

Standing in the bath, Vera Lumbroso finished washing herself. It was an ineluctable rite, especially for women, who should never forget it; she felt her granddaughters weren't always clean enough; their jeans for example, which allowed them to sit down on the ground any old where, result: they had filthy, shabby backsides, like shepherds. She preferred the shower to the bath, where one soaked in dirty water. It's true she also had some difficulty in getting in and out, despite the handles that Maurizio, her husband, had installed.

'The bath's a trap for old people,' he'd declared.

He'd even thought of getting rid of it and just keeping a simple shower, but there was no point; anyhow, baths are absurd receptacles, too narrow and slippery; one of her friends, Lucia, a lot younger, had broken her shoulder in a fall. Vera had discovered a little wart on her temple; she'd have had it removed if the doctor hadn't advised against, and she was able to hide it under a lock of hair. She could no longer see her toes clearly, with or without glasses; she'd nearly cut her little toe, the most difficult to get at, it's true, hard and knotty like olive tree wood; she had to make extraordinary efforts to cut her nails, which she couldn't sustain for very long and which made her hand tremble. Even the children today have difficulty with their vision; it's all to do with glasses; perhaps she should change hers. She'd noted with satisfaction that in past centuries, if wealthy people were read to, it wasn't out of laziness or ostentation, but because they were quite simply, long-sighted. Eyes age more quickly than the rest of the body; she'd transmitted that information to her ophthalmologist, who'd smiled without responding. She'd resolved to periodically entrust her toenails to a chiropodist and the practitioner had clumsily consoled her:

'You know, madame, everything wears out at our age…'

At our age! At our age! His hair was all white! She regretted having called him, perhaps his hand wasn't so sure. She refused to allow herself to be counted among the "old people". Furthermore, there were no old people, there were only people who believed themselves to be old, age doesn't matter, it's in their heads. Truly old people are repugnant and messy; their flesh is transformed into meat, with blueish varicose veins on their legs; she was proud of her legs just as firm as those of her daughters; she enjoyed her food, a little less perhaps, slept well and did some exercises every morning, before going out for her local shopping. She'd have responded to her husband's advances more gladly, if she wasn't afflicted with that horrible half-denture and if, like cats, she hadn't needed to sleep separately, in the little bedroom, more and more often. Without doubt there were brown spots on the back of her hands, but they were scarcely more bothersome than freckles; Julia Sitbon, for example, had them all over her face. She looked at herself in the mirror; some wrinkles were definitely coming on her temples and cheeks, but Maurizio claimed that they disappeared when she smiled, making her look just as she did when they were courting. They'd married very young; Maurizio was twenty-one years old and she was twenty-three; it would have been better the other way round, but she felt more vigorous than him.

She was in a hurry to finish her grooming; it was going to be a long day. Once a year she entertained friends to celebrate her birthday. It was her big private moment, the only one. Even Maurizio wasn't invited; he wasn't keen on it anyway. Those present would be exclusively female; the majority of the guests, with whom Vera played bridge three or four times a week, had been to the same educational establishment, the School of the Sisters of the Rue de Hollande. Their chatter seemed like that of a strange tribe to him, even Vera seemed a bit alien.

After having vaguely helped his wife with her preparations, Maurizio, a retired civil servant for several years, usually went to the cinema, then hung around in a cafe waiting for the apartment to regain its calm. That particular year, Vera's birthday fell on a Sunday, the usual day for grandchildren to visit. They were always welcome without prior notice, but Sunday was the day. On that occasion Maurizio had very much wanted to offer his wife a short cruise around the Greek Islands, which he was also keen on doing; she'd refused, supposedly because a birthday ought to be celebrated at home; in actual fact she didn't like travelling. He suggested that she cancel the children which she was, of course, opposed to. It was another unfailing rite. Their own children, all married and occupied with their large families, came to see them intermittently and in no particular order; on the other hand the grandchildren, six boys and four girls, loved meeting up regularly with their grandmother, and consuming a sumptuous couscous that Vera, although of Lebanese origin, made marvellously, and which required thirty-six hours' work. They chatted, especially among themselves, cleaned their plates with alacrity, then left the table one after the other, like little birds who, after waiting for a moment, take flight.

Vera busied herself making innumerable cakes for the birthday, exceptionally there was no couscous, but the refrigerator and the cupboards contained enough food for an army. The young people, all there to wish their grandmother happy birthday, ate, with plates on their knees, which they refilled as and when required. Excited and all speaking at once, shouting in order to be understood, they exchanged gossip and told each other the latest funny stories. They highlighted the exiguity of the living room, which barely contained them.

After their last daughter's marriage and departure, Maurizio, now more comfortably off, had frequently suggested to his wife that they change apartments. They had, of course, recovered use of the children's bedrooms, but it was narrow all the way through, not light enough for his developing cataracts, in any case too small to accommodate all the books, whose number ceaselessly increased now that he was spending a good part of his day reading, and which were overflowing into the corridors and even into the loos. He was repossessed by a dream abandoned since the birth of his first baby, a huge room, reigned over by waxed wood, as he'd seen in the cinema, lined with books from floor to ceiling, even though his eyesight had deteriorated and he couldn't make out the titles above head height, and the effort of bending down had become uncomfortable. But, although apparently in favour of the project, one room for each of them, a nicer bathroom, a more spacious kitchen, and above all, a lift, which they increasingly missed, he ended up realising that Vera always somehow managed to find fault. He'd taken her to visit several dozen apartments.

'Too big! I'll get exhausted cleaning it...'

'Badly designed! You have to run between the kitchen and the dining room.'

'Lack of storage space!'

Etc., to the point where he became discouraged.

'You're playing pigeon-shooting with me,' he said, 'I put up the apartments and you knock them down, one after the other!'

She acknowledged it with embarrassment:

'You understand, I'm used to it here, I know everything...'

He sensed an anxious quaver in her voice at the idea of leaving those places where she'd nested for so long, where she'd given birth four times, brought up her children, entertained her grandchildren. Over the course of the years, the apartment had become an extension of her own body, like her children and grandchildren. So he gave up the idea. Age, that's also it, one no longer undertakes anything new, one's resigned to seeing tapestries yellow and paintings crack, as if things irremediably grow old with you. Maurizio even sometimes wondered if during all those years of life together, the promiscuity, the inevitable upsets, hadn't blunted those subtler emotions which inform the life of a couple at the beginning. He assured his wife that he would always desire her, that she was still desirable, but he saw clearly that she didn't quite believe him; that she knew "always" meant "hardly", and that tenderness played the greatest part. When he kissed her on the neck, which she used to particularly like, he was well aware that he wasn't placing his lips on the skin of a young girl. As if she didn't want to put both him and herself to the test, she multiplied obstacles to physical contact, more and more rare, increasingly furtive. Allegedly to spare him because of his insomnia, or because he snored. So women don't snore? Less forcefully than men, it's true; men simply don't draw attention to it out of courtesy, and because at first, desire more or less overcomes everything. She slept more and more frequently in the children's ex-bedroom, now her husband's study. In addition, Maurizio fulfilled his duty as a male with less and less appetite, but habituated for so long to a living presence, to the warmth of a body at his side, he wasn't resigned to sleeping in separate rooms, and so had difficulty getting to sleep. Possibly out of modesty, rather late, or to hide the wear and tear of time, she retired into the little bedroom when she needed to get undressed. She asked him to knock before coming in.

'You understand, a woman always has to take care,' without him knowing exactly what care she was talking about, nor why she only needed it now.

However for Vera, as for most women, a bottle which once contained an expensive perfume, is never completely lacking in scent. On the way back from those trying visits across the streets of the capital, which ended up putting Maurizio into a bad mood, due to the absence of results, and the meticulous attention she'd paid to unpityingly exposing the tiniest flaws in the apartment being looked at, to the point where she attracted a hostile irritation from the owners, she walked briskly along, as if she was more than happy to have finished with that chore, too fast for her husband in spite of his objections, caused by an old pain in his ankle that nagged at him. Unable to keep up with her, as in those shopping expeditions in large stores which never seem to bother women and leave men exhausted, he wondered if she was still really concerned about him. But when the distance between them became too great, she'd stop and patiently wait. He noted with relief that they were still attached one to the other by invisible threads. One day he had decisive proof, if there is such a thing in the domain of feelings. At the time of his heart attack, when he was taken to hospital urgently, the doctor hadn't at first hidden from Vera the fact that he was worried. She burst into tears and for one of the rare times in her life, began to pray.

'My God, don't let me lose him!'

It was the doctor who told Maurizio, who was very moved by it. He was reassured by his wife's upset; so he was still important to her. As usual, she'd simply responded and calmly organised everything. In that respect the two spouses were similar, either by temperament or because they'd ended up resembling each other as old spouses often do. When he came back from a medical consultation, she rarely asked him about it straight away, as he'd have liked her to do, but he knew that she wasn't particularly worried about health matters, even her own, and probably it was her way of downplaying the importance of illness. When children are sick, the captain has to remain impassive, emotion only being permitted on return to port. Moreover, wasn't he astonished by the tenacity of his own attachment? Even today, if she was late coming home, beyond her usual time, he felt a familiar anxiety reborn in himself.

Certainly the time was far off when, with that exquisite naivety of first love, Vera had declared, her eyes shining, and perhaps secretly delighted:

'If I cheat on you, you're going to kill me, aren't you?'
He'd replied, mocking her a little to hide his own emotion:
'And you, if you leave me, I'll kill you!'

He would have been completely incapable of killing anyone, and above all his precious wife and lover. He wondered now – if by misfortune she disappeared before him – if he'd be able to survive for very long. Such was the entanglement of their lives that they had become like plants whose roots, having developed side by side, are so utterly intermingled, that if one is pulled up so is the other, and vice versa.

In essence, Vera was the captain, the rock and the nourishing tissue of the whole family, Maurizio understood that. The family museum was situated on the windowsill and in a chest of drawers in the living room, both entirely given over for this use. The display was regularly enriched with specimens from different cultures from all over the globe, which the children and grandchildren brought back from their travels for Vivi's benefit (Vera had become Vivi; "Nanna", "Granny" being banished at her own express request, because it's nicer that way): a bull's head in "ebony wood", "real ivory" tusks, spiked with tiny multicoloured banderillas, brought back from Spain by Marco; a gri-gri which could cure the pains of love, bought by Jean-Jean from Black Africa, where he'd been a development worker; a Tunisian tambourine, a *darbouka*, which vaguely resembled an amphora; a knitted green-yellow-red-black beret, rallying sign of the South-African resistance; a Statue of Liberty, souvenir from Madeleine's honeymoon; and, of course, enough photographs of all of them to make an illustrated monograph of the family.

The young people, ultimately satiated, did not, however, leave. Only Alberto, nicknamed Al-denté, an old joke, continued to feed his obesity. Their grandfather, tired out by the exuberance of those young lives, had discreetly withdrawn. They'd vainly tried to get Vera out of her kitchen, on the unusual grounds of celebrating her birthday together; she never ate a real lunch; she just nibbled whilst standing in the kitchen.

'We poor women, nature leaves us little choice, wrinkles or bums; when the time comes I'll choose wrinkles.'

She placed that moment far off, but nature hadn't waited for Vera to choose, who was beginning to put on weight; her proud waistline was already fading, her fallen arches had made her almost flat-footed, she walked a bit like a bear.

But this time her presence seemed indispensable to the young people; they'd hatched a project concerning her. They were whispering:

'Go on!'

'No, you!'

'Jean-Jean! You're her favourite; she'll listen to you…'

Jean-Jean, the favourite, was occupied with unsticking, bit by bit, the label on a bottle of muscat; he was forced to interrupt that interesting task under the unanimous pressure of the assembled company.

They'd noticed for some time that their grandmother had difficulty in hearing, particularly in the left ear. She blasted out her little radio (television didn't exist at the time, and not many families had succeeded in obtaining a phone); she often repeated what was said to her, replied at cross-purposes, and claimed that the younger generations articulated badly ("What do they teach you at school!"); she didn't set foot in the theatre since apparently modern companies of actors muttered ("Ah, only the Comédie-Francaise… the professionals, they're the only ones!). She obviously arranged things so that she presented her right ear as much as possible, but she got irritated when people were surprised by it. How could she hear distinctly when they were all talking at once?

All the same, the young people had decided to overcome her resistance, persuaded that in the end she'd be grateful. On the occasion of her birthday, they'd all contributed to offering her one of those recent gadgets called Sonotones, the trade name, which were supposed to help the hard of hearing.

At the decisive moment, however, they weren't quite sure how to go about giving the present to their grandmother, without provoking one of her sudden outbursts, like April showers. Jean-Jean went to look for Vera in her den and apparently succeeded in his mission; she appeared in the doorframe of the living room, her spectacles on her nose, drops of sweat on the hair of her upper lip. Thrilled by this first success, the young people intoned "Happy Birthday...", with some extra couplets written by Alexandra, where she had rhymed all the words ending in *a*, and where the refrain affirmed that:

Qui longtemps vivra
Verra vivre Vera
Vivat vivat Vera!

Finally, they clapped hands.

Their grandmother softened, listened to them with affection, and got ready to go back to her stove, when Alexandra indicated that the session wasn't over. She pulled out a bit of paper from her bag and began to read. She wished many happy returns to Vivi, so she could continue making them the best couscous in the world, and even make use of her left ear, every Sunday, to hear their extremely intelligent and witty words, etc. Then, suddenly, lowering her voice almost to a murmur, she announced to Vera the nature of their birthday present, and asked her to try it out there and then.

Vera desperately tilted her right ear, without altogether understanding what her granddaughter was proposing. But when Jean-Jean presented her with the little packet, wrapped in pink ribbons, she understood the ruse and exploded:

'You insolent creatures! Snotty-nosed kids, who think they can insult their grandmother while they've still got milk on their lips!'

Then, she furiously went back into the kitchen, without even taking the little packet from the hands of her grandson.

A profound silence fell in the living room; the young people, stunned, realised they'd hurt their grandmother. Alexandra rushed into the kitchen on the heels of Vera, without quite knowing how to excuse herself. Seeing a full plate of semolina cakes on the sideboard, *farkas*, she asked Vera for the recipe, pretending that nothing had happened.

'Ah, I see, *farkas*! Tell me how you make them… Mum doesn't know how, doesn't want to know, because of her bloody work… you really brought her up badly… tell me what you put inside…'

Vera, already softening, touched by her granddaughter's question, not wanting to make a thing of the incident, when she was, perhaps, not altogether in the right, joined in the game.

'What you put in the *farka*! Ask me rather what you don't put in it! As well as semolina, of course, almonds ground and unground, soaked dates, then mashed with a fork, raisins, cinnamon, a lot of sugar, some—'

'Hang on! Slowly! Please… give me time to note it down.'

She picked up her notepad, turned over a page and prepared to write.

'How much semolina? How many almonds?'

Vera made a gesture with her hand half-closed in a fist, like a Bedouin eating couscous with a spoon.

'This much, you see? If not you add.'

'But no, I don't see! How much do you add? When?'

'You add when there isn't enough! Now leave me alone, my oil's going to get too hot.'

After having rolled up pasta ribbons, she threw them into the frying pan where, under the effect of the hot oil, they were transformed into large yellow flowers.

Alexandra didn't insist; it was enough that the diversion had more or less succeeded; she rejoined her acolytes. The young people, sheepishly, went into the kitchen one by one, where Vera allowed herself to be kissed. Soon afterwards, they left, discretely taking with them the object at issue.

After their departure, Vera melancholically recounted the incident to her husband. He'd heard her outburst, he agreed with her; moreover he also didn't like it when people made an issue of their age; an elderly spouse reminds you that you too are growing old. As for himself? His prostate was enlarging, or so it seemed, obliging him to run to the toilet more often; he could scarcely read with his right eye, that cataract would soon need doing; his ankle which brought back memories of windy days; to say nothing of forgetting people's names more and more often, even sometimes friends… he had to note that he too was undertaking that curious reverse apprenticeship that old age is, but he also preferred not to think about it too much. He embarrassed the well-intentioned young girls who offered him their seat on the *métro*, by refusing, and joking that he wasn't yet old enough for that. One day, after having renounced the search for a new apartment, he'd succeeded in convincing Vera to visit a kind of institution for retirees, which a friend had spoken of very highly. They were taken by the excellent running of the establishment; unfortunately it was full. The director, a young enough woman, apparently not yet familiar with the fear of death, advised them to put down their names on a waiting list.

'Be assured,' she added unthinkingly, 'you won't have to wait very long, people often die here.'

They didn't sign up and spoke no more of it.

Before leaving his wife, Maurizio spread an embroidered cloth on the dining room table, put some pre-prepared cakes on it, candlesticks, bottles of wine and orgeat, replaced the bottle of muscat defaced by Jean-Jean, knowing that Vera would change the arrangement.

He too went to kiss his wife, who seemed weary.

'When everything's ready you should lie down for a bit.'

She murmured something that he didn't understand; like most people who are hard of hearing, she was speaking too softly.

He'd decided to go and see *Ben Hur*, a film which had received excellent reviews, especially because it lasted a long time; that way he'd get back after the departure of Vera's guests. The number 70 bus which served the Beaugrenelle area, where the film was being shown, was also taking its time.

He wasn't disappointed; he loved those grand historic epics where, immersed in images of the past, he could forget the present.

When he left the cinema, it was still light; he sat on the terrace of a cafe, ordered a milky coffee and read while dipping into *Le Canard Enchaîné*, which amused him less and less. When he was a student, he wouldn't have missed buying the Wednesday paper for anything in the world; had *Le Canard* gone stale or was it he who'd lost interest?

Rather than waiting for the number 70 bus, since he still had time to kill, he crossed the Mirabeau Bridge to catch the number 72, and took a marvellous walk along the Seine.

On the bus, he found himself opposite an old lady whose face was nothing but a field of wrinkles. The nose, which emerged from it, was still small and fine; the lips, crinkled, preserved an agreeable shape. A man, he thought, perhaps several, had kissed that mouth passionately; doubtless, if one took off the mask woven by age, one would find a pretty woman. She noticed that he was staring at her; she looked at herself in the window and adjusted a curl of hair. He looked away, but she smiled and addressed a word to him, complaining about the rarity of the number 72 and the length of its route. As he couldn't hear what she was saying very well, he asked permission to sit next to her, which was graciously accorded.

She was going to visit her daughter, but she lived in Saint-Cloud, at the "Club"; she enumerated its advantages; above all relieving residents of all domestic chores and entertaining them; it had a restaurant, an infirmary, cleaners, a leisure room where one played bridge, listened to lectures, and had parties. One thing she didn't like: the dancing evenings. It was painful to see old people waddling about, breathless, gross or skeletal. Once, the director had organised a kind of ballet: it was grotesque, pitiable. The women were most ridiculous, made up outrageously, dressed like gamines, short skirts and décolleté. It was all the more painful that they looked like men, moustaches included. If it weren't for their hair and their backsides, you wouldn't know who were the men and who were the women... she'd thought about it all a lot, she'd lived alone for such a long time, since the disappearance of her husband... it's true that it's not easy for women...

'Oh, nor for men either,' Maurizio assured her.

'Perhaps, but for women it's awful, they've lived in relation to men, obsessed by the body image they wanted to project, by their face, they wanted to continue to please. Aging requires permanent refurbishment, but there's no point in having any illusions: youth is just a dream, there are dreams that will never come true. Dignity, wisdom, is to accept the facts.'

The old lady continued speaking for a long time in front of a thoughtful Maurizio.

'Old age is the antechamber of death, and fear of old age is the fear of death, however age has to be accepted since we all have to die one day...'

The bus was now nearly empty. A young woman had spread out a whole array of cosmetics next to her and beautified herself with the insouciance of a cat.

The old lady got off at Châtelet, after having bid farewell to her travelling companion.

Was Maurizio frightened of dying? No, he didn't think so; he'd had some turns; his head sometimes spun when he made an effort and he had the impression that he was going to lose consciousness. One day, he'd have a more serious episode, a deeper absence which, instead of dissipating after a few seconds, would invade his head until he was dazed, unconscious, and then there would be a void. Or maybe a second heart attack, this time decisive? He feared decrepitude above all; progressive degeneration. Or again it could be a sudden accident, unpredictable; several days earlier he'd knocked the end of his shoe on an uneven paving stone in the Place de l'Hotel-de-Ville, he lost his balance and fell down; apart from a few bruises he wasn't really hurt, but he noted on that occasion the growing difficulty he had in getting back up from the ground; luckily he was helped by a charming young girl, and he had to lean against a tree for several minutes afterwards. He promised himself to walk more slowly, to pay more attention to where he put his feet, why not a stick, there was no shame in it, his father had a collection. The physiotherapist who'd treated his sciatica, had joked one day that if she had power over people's behaviour, she'd prohibit rugs for the over sixties: she spent her time looking after old people who'd fallen because they'd tripped. One day, perhaps, after a fall, he'd be stuck in a wheelchair, how awful! He wouldn't like to impose that on his family for anything in the world, especially not on Vera; he'd rather go into some quasi-medical institution; he had to stay in his right mind! Sometimes he forgot names, even of his oldest relations…

When he got home, the apartment was silent, Vera must have been asleep; he was glad; all those preparations, as well as the always overexcited presence of the children, had visibly tired her. In order not to wake her, he took off his shoes and put on slippers. He was hungry, he hadn't eaten since midday; there must surely be some leftovers from the party. Before eating, he went to check that the gas tap was closed, as he did every night, ever since Vera once forgot to do it. Then, making as little noise as possible, he went into the living room; to his surprise, like a forgotten bride, the party table was still pristine. The candles hadn't been lit, the birthday cake was intact, the bottles hadn't been opened, the bowls of olives, cheese cubes, roasted almonds and pistachios were full to the brim. And then he noticed the light under the door of the small bedroom-study. He knocked and entered. Still clad in her red velvet dress with the lace collar, Vera wasn't asleep; she was lying on the bed, a book in her hand, which she wasn't reading.

'What's happened?' he asked.

'Nothing… they didn't come.'

Clearly she'd been crying; the tears had left traces on her face powder.

'All of them?'

'Yes, all.'

'That's very strange…'

Then, suddenly, he guessed what must have happened; he put on his shoes and went down to the mail boxes. Theirs was so full of overflowing letters that he could scarcely open it. He pulled out a random scribbled note: the two Cartoso sisters, both widows who lived together, surprised, almost annoyed: they'd knocked on Vera's door for a long time, they'd gone away with their cakes… all the same, one doesn't forget to inform people when a reception is cancelled! The message in the second letter, carefully calligraphed from the "still beautiful" Élisa Fiorentino, conveyed more or less the same message.

He emptied the box and went back upstairs, placed the whole bundle next to Vera, who picked up one note, then another…

'I think I must have been asleep, you were right, I was too tired, I mustn't have heard the doorbell.'

Maurizio tried to console her:

'A missed reception, it's no big thing!'

'No, it's no big deal… but I think I'm a bit hard of hearing… tell me, what is a Sonotone?'

The ogress

Agatha Miraviglia was fourteen, Charlotte my sister six, and I was nine. We called her the ogress because she was always hungry and devoured our snacks. She came rushing over from the big children's playground to hassle us; she demanded half our sandwiches, which we handed over without objection; she stole our sweets and cigarette cards; she made me listen to obscene stories, preferably in front of Charlotte, which humiliated me even more; then she boasted about being a woman and described herself in detail which repelled me; sometimes she made me accompany her home and carry her school bag. If I made the slightest sign of resistance, she got hold of me by my shirt collar, which on one occasion she tore, until I begged for pardon; even today, I'm terrified someone will pull on my tie!

Anyway, if I'd been able to, I think I'd have joyfully strangled her, but I'd have been quite incapable, she was so much bigger and stronger than me; I wouldn't even have dared to touch her. Even more than her strength, her bone structure and her angular frame which made her look like some kind of dinosaur, the sounds which emanated from her, terrified us. It was rumoured that she lived in darkness with her blind father, who insisted that the shutters should always be closed; she was said to feed him, nobody knew how. She said she was going to become a doctor when she grew up, in order to care for him, which seemed absurd to us, for a woman, but it made her appear all the more redoubtable.

Once however, I thought I'd discovered a way out; she had a very full head of hair, tied in a single large braid which bumped against her back when she pounced on us. So while she was berating me about, I no longer know what – our sandwiches that day were too small for her liking, or maybe I was too slow in giving her a marble – I suddenly grabbed hold of her hairy appendage and pulled with all my might. She cried out in pain and anger, which gave me great satisfaction. Unfortunately, as luck would have it, Charlotte came up and thought it'd be a good idea to join in our enemy's torture. This proved to be the salvation of the giant who, in her turn, reacting with the rapidity of a snake, seized hold of my sister's two minuscule plaits, and pulled with all her might, screaming:

'If you pull, I pull! If you pull, I pull!'

Charlotte screamed back in her turn; what else could I have done, other than once again, submit and abandon the struggle? She was stronger than the two of us put together. So in bed that night, I was reduced to imagining fights where I was always the winner. I put my fist into her left eye, which swelled up and bruised; then into the right one, which swelled up and bruised, that way she'd be obliged to wear horrible black spectacles in the school playground; then I gave her a big punch on the nose as well, which resulted in its becoming as large as a potato... ah! She'd make a good clown with those enormous glasses on that enormous nose! Then I'd get her into a neck hold and bring her to the ground, where she'd be crushed by an appropriately oncoming vehicle, or better, without fear of contradiction, by the local train, accidents quite frequent in summer, or again, she'd be inanimate, lying on the beach, drowned, only just washed up, a hideous Gorgon's head, dangerous Medusa even in death, with sticky algae all over her hair and salt water disgorged from her mouth and nostrils... those daydreams were neither effective nor very edifying, but they expressed what I was feeling and they helped me get through the hell of my schooldays, while waiting to become an adult when I could take vengeance, for good, as I swore to myself; I kept repeating that I'd take my revenge later on, and that also helped considerably.

Happily, life separated us; first thanks to the *lycée*, where I had the unhoped-for luck with my background, to gain entrance, and where as a girl she was unable to get in; then my studies, quickly interrupted by the unleashing of hostilities, the duration of the war; then travelling, meeting my future wife at the Cité University, getting married.

I never saw her again. Just once, I heard my sister Charlotte speak of her, on the occasion of a quick holiday I spent with my parents to give them pleasure. To general astonishment, the ogress was married, and even to a boy from an upper-class family. But one day we received the explanation for that unexpected happening: the unfortunate husband was prey to severe nervous attacks. She devotedly cared for him, dividing her attention between her father and her spouse, until the day when the latter cracked open his head in a fall, Charlotte concluded, in a tone which made me feel ashamed.

Much later, on returning to the country for good, I thought, I set up home with my young wife in a neighbouring area, several kilometres from the capital, in a kind of village for government officials. We'd obtained the necessary loans for the purchase of a small piece of land and the construction of a "villa", as we pompously called it. I was utterly happy with that arrangement, which though neither one of us had much money, allowed us to immediately enjoy a comfortable house and garden, whose plans had been drawn up by my wife. It was situated on a hillside which due to the climate, was practically always covered with perennial plants and flowers.

However, the terms of the loan weren't as advantageous as they seemed. We were committed to large repayments over a long period of time, which didn't leave us much to comfortably live on. And, above all, we were held to a strictly punctual mortgage system, we risked losing everything if we failed to pay twice in a row. However, in anticipation of the forthcoming arrival of our first child, I'd just requested a second deferment from the village's Management Committee.

On that particular morning, little clouds which had no bills to pay, were enjoying chasing each other in a perfect sky. For my part, I was thinking about dealing with the snails on the geraniums, when I heard the front doorbell chime. I glimpsed a woman at the gate, a poor soul dressed in an awful faded lacy skirt, pretty filthy it seemed to me, and a worn-out camisole. She was dragging an old leather suitcase which had seen better days, tied up with string. No doubt some humble pedlar lacking a shop, going from door to door, trying to sell useless objects. A well-known type represented by innumerable little ill-defined occupations at the limit of swindlery, small in numbers, it's true: vendors of lighter flints or individual cigarettes, special sunglasses for viewing eclipses. Poverty excuses many things, but all the same I couldn't buy what I didn't need, often damaged or stolen goods, especially at that difficult time. I was going to shout to the untimely visitor not to persist when, suddenly, I recognised in her... our tormentor! The manner in which she smiled and her sweeping hand gesture proved that she, on the other hand, knew very well on which door she was ringing.

'Hi! Hi! You OK?' she said to me, speaking familiarly as if nothing had changed in such a long time. I felt a pang in my heart, to my surprise, a rush of anxiety, irritation and, resurging intact from the depths of my childhood, the desire to at last take revenge. Of course, I judged myself ridiculous: I wasn't going to settle an old score now, at my age and at hers! Confronted by that poor woman, so visibly maltreated by life, I remembered the story one of my uncles often told: he too had been persecuted by a bigger pupil and had sworn to take vengeance later on. When he finally found his torturer, he was spitting blood; how do you punish an ill person? Vengeance had slipped through his fingers.

Dragging my feet, I went to open the gate.

'Hi Mordidou!'

I hated being called that, it was the diminutive of a first name I didn't even like, and which moreover in dialect, took me back to a past I wanted to forget. But I tried to be objective, she'd always called me that, and perhaps she'd never known my true first name.

'They told me you had a house here, I came expressly to say hello!'

Then, quickly, inveiglingly:

'Well, since I'm here, I'm going to give you the benefit of my superb shirts and pyjamas! But I'll give you a good price, a friend's price of course...'

I couldn't remember having found her so charming in the past; the monster had become monstrous: excessively bony, her head too big, too heavy, on the end of a neck that was too long, dragging her downwards toward the ground and making her move forward in a swinging way like some prehistoric animal. Her features had hardened losing all feminine grace, if she ever had it; in addition, hair all over the place and un-made-up, she had visibly renounced all those preparations which contribute to the permanent artfulness of the human female. Perhaps she'd never been so tall after all, and was it just me who felt tiny in comparison, in any case I'd preserved the memory of a giant. Now I was a good head taller and would at last have been able to smash her *couperose* nose in (she must have been a drinker), with a single punch. Life had more or less already avenged me; our tormentor stood before me, begging pitiably, dressed like a tramp; I on the other hand, in my own house, with a respectable profession, almost a notable, if it hadn't been for those money worries, which I hoped one day to bring to an end... I felt ashamed of that vengeful feeling, even if it was involuntary. I had to be all the more careful with Agatha, as I was sure she'd make the same comparison to her detriment, with her shabby clothes, ragged skirt and crumpled blouse. No, not at any price I decided, would I even make allusion to her erstwhile nastiness… when to my amazement, it was she who evoked our common past.

'Do you remember,' she said to me with a knowing smile, 'when I used to put the screws on you?'

She used the words "put the screws on", whilst smiling as if it was a big joke. I grimaced a vague smile, as if I'd recovered some old school camaraderie.

'Is your father OK?' I asked, in order to say something.

'Yes,' she replied dryly.

She obviously didn't want to pursue the subject.

Of course I abstained from speaking of her unfortunate marriage.

She'd opened her old suitcase, which was full of awful pyjamas in garish colours, covered in strange birds with outspread wings, flimsy shirts, probably retrieved from unsold stock, and undertook once again to convince me of the quality of the material, the elegance of the cut "à la mode", and especially of the relative modesty of the price, which was true: what could such garments be worth! I tried to explain to her that my wife usually took charge of buying that kind of thing; that anyhow, I didn't really need anything at the moment, without, of course, giving her the only true reason, which would have hurt her: I wouldn't have been seen dead in those ridiculous clothes, not even in the intimacy of the marital bed. Brushing aside my arguments with her hand and head, she kept on talking without stopping for breath, with the self-confidence and stubborn tactics of canvassers, who don't themselves believe what they're saying, who know that they aren't really believed, but who hope against all odds that a moment of inattention or weakness in their target, will allow them to unload a superfluous object. She was, in fact, trying to bamboozle me, but I didn't give the hoped-for response. No, really, I wasn't going to put on those shirts with poor collars and too-short sleeves, those strangely low-cut pyjamas. However, I committed the mistake of lightly fingering a pair of pyjamas, made of the worst quality artificial silk.

'Good,' she concluded, 'I see, these are the pyjamas that interest you! Take a couple, I'll give you a reduced price…'

'Ah no! I don't want any!'

'Well then, a shirt.'

'No!' I stammered. 'No, I don't want, I couldn't wear…'

In my haste, I'd been almost brutal; in spite of my promise, I had perhaps wounded her.

'Good,' I capitulated, 'I'll take a shirt… just one.'

'Are you sure you don't want two?'

'No, no, I assure you, it's fine like this!'

I thought it wise to quickly change the subject; I asked her how she was getting on…

She cut me off forcefully, not willing to dwell on the subject; yes, she was fine. I couldn't find out anything else.

She looked around, slowly pivoting her large head. Bitterness, envy, hostility? She said:

'But you, you've done all right for yourself, eh!'

Despite the lack of means, my wife had worked hard: waxed furniture, pastel-coloured curtains, reproductions of masterpieces bought in museums during our holidays, a few knick-knacks, heirlooms from our respective families.

While putting her substandard merchandise back in her shabby suitcase, the ogress had resumed vaunting the "guaranteed" quality of the fabric, print resistant to all washing, and above all, above all, the unbeatable modesty of her prices! She sourced her products directly from a wholesaler, Le Comptoir de Denise, you see; that way she benefitted from the same prices as the retail shops, but she didn't have the "overheads", the rent, the staff, not even a "patent", nobody asked any questions, and she wasn't going to stupidly declare it to the taxman! So she could offer the best prices in town… she was happy to give her friends the benefit, especially a friend like me, that she'd miraculously recontacted, after all those years and with so many shared memories...

I thought I'd misheard, was she making fun of me?

'Although,' she went on as if she suddenly remembered something...'I must be stupid, a week ago, Valensi you remember? He was talking to me about you, and he bought some nice pyjamas, he said that you'd come back, that you were teaching in a *lycée*, and that you lived here, so I came to the village, specially to see you... and of course for my business... can you believe, just now, I sold a shirt to the head of the Village Management Committee, Mr Temam isn't it? He was talking about you with someone I didn't know, but perhaps it means something to you, a fat man, bald, with an enormous red bow tie... when I heard your name, I pricked up my ears, you're thinking... from what I was able to understand, you've asked for an extension to your loan...'

I made an immense effort to roll with the punch, and waited for what followed, which didn't come. Apparently there was nothing more to learn from her; in the end I couldn't stop myself from saying:

'And so?'

'So what? Nothing; I don't know anything else, they continued speaking, but I didn't pay attention to the rest.'

An old murderous desire resurged in me.

She pointedly did up her case then, lifting her head and looking me in the eye, she added with a detached air:

'Oh, they didn't seem very positive, no, it didn't seem to be going very well for you... good, are you going to pay me now?'

In fact, what else could I do? Strangle her perhaps as I'd so often wanted to do!

I opened my purse, then my wallet; I didn't have the necessary sum. To be honest, I didn't have any money at all, except a single one thousand franc note. It was the beginning of the month, I'd just received my trainee teacher's salary the previous evening. I asked the ogress if she had, herself, any change.

She made as if to look for it: no, she didn't have any either.

It was a godsend: I gave her back the shirt.

'Never mind,' I said quickly, 'I'll take one another time... perhaps two... when you're next passing by.'

'No,' she replied firmly, 'I won't be coming back; I made this whole journey specially to see you. No, I'm going to go to look for change in the village grocery.'

She pulled the note out of my hand and turned her back on me.

I saw her retrace her steps, unhurriedly, along the little stone garden path, with her strange swinging gait, head in advance. Arriving at the gate, she turned round, and with her sly, little crook's, poor street pedlar's smile, called out:

'Do you remember you once wanted to fight with me? You started pulling my hair? So I got hold of your sister's hair and I also pulled. You pulled, I pulled! You pulled, I pulled, so you really had to let go!'

And, laughing all the way, she waved my mint thousand franc note at the end of her fingers, which I anxiously watched disappear.

The whore goddess

Our generation, we all know, wasn't favoured by fate; after the anguish of the war and the horrors of the German occupation, we underwent the austerity of the peace. Scarcely had the guns become silent and France being still devastated, we, the survivors, rushed back to the University of Algiers to continue our long-interrupted studies. We were still living through hunger and cold. We weren't the only ones; Algiers – immeasurably overpopulated with refugees, the families of politicians and administrators evacuated under Vichy, waiting to return to the motherland – were all living parsimoniously. Still I was lucky, if you could call it that, to share a disused warehouse with Barrucand, a fellow student originally from the same town as me, who secreted tins of corned beef under his jacket, and to occasionally receive a few coffee beans from my parents, which served as precious currency. We had a washbasin in which we urinated, but strangely no water, the supply pipe having for some unknown reason been bashed in. We didn't have a WC either. The only WC in the building was situated on the ground floor, and being often blocked, on busy days we had to run to the public toilets in the Place du Jama-el Aoua… which were themselves often blocked. As for the cold, we had to resign ourselves to sleeping with our pullovers on; it's well known that in winter, it's colder in southern countries than northern ones, which are prepared for bad weather.

However, at our age, the most painful deprivation was that of the flesh and the heart. During those apocalyptic years, we'd hardly had time to think of love, which was reduced to quickies in the Rue Abdallah-Guèche, Tunis's red-light district, which smelt permanently of sweat, sperm and oil burnt in the prostitutes' stalls, which opened onto the road. It was worse in Algiers where our new-found freedom highlighted our privation even more. Muslim women were untouchable, for fear of being lynched, it was said; one scarcely saw others in the streets and those whom one did encounter, most often accompanied, covered from head to foot, only revealed their sparkling eyes through the kohl; the Jewish and European women around, minus the lynch mob, were scarcely more accessible; before the first favour, they demanded a promise of marriage, that we couldn't possibly give without brainwashing ourselves. Anyway, undernourished, clothed as we were in ill-fitting old jerkins and military fatigues made of coarse, yellowing canvas material, purchased in army-surplus stores, which kept us warm but transformed us into shapeless bundles, we wouldn't have even dared pay court to an honest woman. The Americans, of course, sent crates of clothes, but probably had us mixed up with pygmies, other Africans it's true; if the jackets weren't too bad a fit, the trousers scarcely reached our calves.

There were, as in Tunis, the hot alleys of the Casbah, where easy women made up like marionettes, eyebrows shaved and repainted in black, blood-red mouths and cheeks, resembled those in the Rue Abdallah-Guèche. But, through a suspect inconsistency, they seemed more dangerous than the women of our adolescence, who were somehow more familiar. Besides, as future doctors we knew, and had sometimes verified to our cost, what could happen to those who had recourse to their services. From time to time, one of us who had succumbed to the pressure of his glands, found himself afflicted with gonorrhoea, which made him hobble comically for weeks. Thus have the sins of the flesh been punished ever since the sanctions inflicted by the Eternal on Adam and Eve.

A welcome came from Mme Gaby, a war widow who'd fallen on hard times since the death of her husband, a chief warrant officer in the Zouaves. She was a good-natured, chatty, motherly lady, generous in body and spirit, who'd transformed her villa on the heights of Algiers into a modest *maison de rendez-vous*. Replacing the rattan furniture, seen in most small colonial homes, with high-quality stuff bought at bargain price from friends who were leaving the country, judiciously locating lace or knitted lampshades in every corner, hanging a few local tapestries on the walls, together with reproductions of famous paintings alternating with the work of young Algerian artists, she'd succeeded in creating a petit bourgeois interior which reminded us of our parents' houses and was a nostalgic consolation for our loneliness. Moreover, clients were only admitted after careful questioning, the place was imbued with an atmosphere of good company. It was a small enterprise which only employed five personnel, but all young, friendly and discrete: Paula, Stella, Rosa, Fortunata and Cécilia, obviously assumed names; it was even rumoured that they weren't professionals but married women who were there to augment their meagre household budget or, perhaps, still more troubling, out of a taste for adventure.

Among those ladies there was Cécilia, not much older than us it was unanimously agreed. She gave priority to students, on her always full waiting list.

'At least they wash!' Mme Gaby explained laconically.

And, tenderly:

'And they're little darlings.'

Except for Barrucand, who didn't fancy women, all my friends were infatuated with her; not, however, to the extent that I was soon to become. With the crudity of guard-room language, they went into ecstasies over the softness of her thighs, especially their insides – "satin!" – the firmness of her bottom – "marble!" – to the point where they'd nicknamed her "The Goddess", or again "The Venus de Milo". I'm going to tell you why. Right from the start I was looking for something more in her than bodily perfection, something other than the transparency of her skin, the porcelain blue of her eyes, or the featherlight down on her neck, as in a Dutch portrait. Even her accent, which I couldn't at first make out, a kind of basic American, which seemed to have Scandinavian harmonics, Swedish or Norwegian, made me all the more fascinated. I tried, unsuccessfully, to explain to Barrucand how she got to me.

'What more do you see in her than other women?' he ironised.'What do you find in them anyway? Without their half-pear-shaped breasts, most often flabby and saggy, their long hair and their ridiculous high-heeled shoes, so high that they always seem about to lose their balance, we'd take them for fat, whiny, little gentlemen! Puddings with big bums!'

How could I convince him that Cécilia's breasts in the form of apples not pears, he hadn't seen them, were the most beautiful and mysterious fruits in the world? That her feet, minuscule by comparison with her height, in sophisticated shoes rather like theatrical cothurns, were ravishing? That her exotic accent, with the deep inflections of an accomplished woman, suddenly interspersed with childlike high-pitched giggles, oboe and flute, carried me away, moved me to the core? Because, yes, one can fall in love with a voice! A voice can capture all of femininity! As for comparing the superb Cécilia to a pudding with a big bum, you must have to be blind, or in possession of the bad faith of a homosexual!

'And you, I retorted almost angrily, what do you see in boys? Explain that to me?'

In a word, I'd fallen in love, without yet understanding what it meant; have I ever understood, even later? At the time, I needed to see Cécilia more and more, even without touching her; I wished her all the good in the world without wanting anything back and after all, isn't that the real essence of love? To the extent that my resources permitted, a derisory grant and some mathematics lessons, I visited the villa on the hill as often as possible. I who'd gladly and proudly embraced the common medical student adage: "Medicine is a demanding and exclusive mistress!". I'd have moved in to Mme Gaby's, if she'd let me. The beloved woman is a goddess whose courtship rites are immutable, always and everywhere, on whose altar offerings must be continually placed. Denying myself, I'd offer Cécilia my coffee beans, which were in cruelly short supply in Algeria, having been replaced with horrible ersatz stuff; dates which my parents had also sent me, to their own cost; one day I brought her a precious tin of corned beef that Barrucand had derisively traded; she scolded me, knowing my circumstances, and made me take it back. A date with a beloved woman is a ceremony which demands that you purify yourself beforehand and put on your best clothes; I, who'd taken so little care of my appearance during those terrible years, smartened up. Barrucand taught me how to look after my skin and do my hair; I shaved as closely as possible with those blunt razors available at the time, grazing the skin on my cheeks in order to spare Cécilia's. On days when I saw her, I put on my American jacket and the only civilian trousers I had which reached my ankles.

Cécilia often arrived late; one waited while chatting to the other girls and Mme Gaby, who looked delighted, quite excited herself by her lovely students. Sometimes Cécilia cancelled, leaving us to our hunger for her. Then, Mme Gaby explained in whispered innuendoes, that something impossible to avoid had got in the way of the poor dear, with her life, you understand. I didn't understand what life she was talking about, but I respected the mystery which disturbed me all the more. When I was sure of her forthcoming appearance, I preferred to wait in the street to meet her, to spot her in the distance under her umbrella, her perfect Scandinavian blondness, wearing a simple white skirt, due to the heat, which moulded her exquisite femininity, and a silk blouse in pastel colours, yellow or pink to match her hair, difficult to distinguish at first in the flickering light. I played at being afraid, delicious anxiety, that she was only a creature of my imagination, but soon her contours fell into place, a concentrated paragon of beauty, to me finer, even today I swear it, than any work of art; since no sculpture, no painting could rival her, because no artist however talented or conscientious, could infuse their work with what shone out of Cécilia: life. Through what fascinating mystery was this embodied miracle, slowly coming towards me, swinging her hips rhythmically with the supernatural grace of a living goddess?

However, when finally present, she didn't address a word to me in the street; just a look, a batting of the eyelids, to indicate that she'd seen me and accepted my homage, and she returned my wave. I rushed ahead of her to Mme Gaby's steep steps, which led up Algiers' hill (but isn't an ascension necessary to arrive at the altar of love?), and triumphantly announced her arrival. Mme Gaby, having dispensed with the ritual of "the display" used in most *maisons de rendez-vous*, humiliating for the women and embarrassing for sensitive clients, who have to choose as in a cattle market, I was able to go directly to Cécilia's room. Nor did she receive me in a dressing gown, like most girls, who out of laziness can't be bothered to get dressed between tricks, sometimes keeping a fag end between their lips, which makes them seem indifferent, sloppy, and destroys all romanticism: one knows that one has succeeded someone and that one will be followed by someone else. With Cécilia, I had the impression of being a particularly favoured guest; she spoke respectfully and politely enquired after my news. While I was undressing, with beating heart and hands almost trembling, and before getting undressed herself, like a hostess putting the finishing touches to a reception, she lit a candle and a stick of incense in the shadows, blinds and curtains being drawn against the heat, transforming the room into a temple of love where she was about to officiate in her radiant nudity. Then, after having carefully placed my clothes and her own in the cupboard, she lay on her back and gently opened her thighs; she didn't speak or move, abandoning herself to my bashful ardour, her arms inert alongside her body, as if I was making love to a statue, indeed the Venus de Milo.

I gathered from the outrageously proclaimed confidences of my comrades that it was exactly the same for them. Despite everything, I hoped we weren't altogether interchangeable. Hadn't she given me, exclusively it seemed, nobody else having alluded to it, some light caresses on my head and neck, while, paralysed by emotion, my virility was slow in manifesting itself? At first, she allowed me to do everything without ever protesting, but she did ask me to avoid her mouth.

'You have all my body, except my mouth, please...'

I respected that, until the day when she gave me a quick kiss, which I returned with gratitude, and soon I made wide use of that privilege, which she herself seemed to appreciate. I tried to find out more from my comrades, as discretely as possible, in order not to provoke the inevitable jokes. I had the joy of learning that none of them had the right to the candle or the incense, nor, above all, to kisses on the mouth. Soon, she let me stay on a little longer after making love, lit a cigarette and put a record on the gramophone. We chatted, more exactly I talked and she listened; I reported the local gossip which I thought, in her situation, she probably missed out on. I told her the funny stories with which Barrucand in particular, tirelessly provided me. She didn't always get the drift, due to the language barrier, or misinterpreted what I was saying; one day confounding the words Ricains (yanks) with Africains, she took offence at some objectionable traits she thought I was attributing to Americans, when in fact I was talking about Moroccan tabors. I patiently began all over again until she finally smiled, making little comment, simply changing colour like translucent statues lit from the inside. I learnt to avoid certain subjects which were painful to her; for example our often envious irritation with allied soldiers who, disposing of their chocolate, cigarettes and dollars that opened the hearts of even the most virtuous, conducted themselves as if they were an occupying force in a conquered country, assaulting lone women in the street when they were drunk, making obscene propositions. Holding religion a taboo subject, as prostitutes and Anglo-Saxons often do, my statue objected when I allowed myself to ironise in a Voltairian manner against the faithful and the superstitious; I was obliged to apologise and soften my comments. But those rare jousts ultimately enabled her to be more objective and heightened our togetherness.

Anyway, the teeming, dirty and malodorous town, where I was cold and hungry, where I was homesick for familiar Tunisian streets whatever their similarities with those of Algiers; an overage student in a ruined world which hadn't even buried all its dead, turned out to be magnetised by Mme Gaby's *maison de rendez-vous* on the flowery hill. And within that villa, by the secret perfumed room, deliciously fresh in summer, comfortably heated in winter, where the most precious jewel sparkled, the smile and the glowing body of my friend. I knew then that paradise existed and that it was located in a woman, even if that woman was one of Mme Gaby's personnel. Just once, I shyly asked if we could see each other elsewhere, for example go swimming together since the summer had set in. No, that wasn't possible, she said emphatically, almost severely. I didn't insist, my happiness was unhoped for, it was already more than complete and didn't really need augmenting. Wasn't paradise a tiny garden in the immensity of the universe? I only prayed heaven that nothing would happen to put it in peril, as with Adam and Eve.

But heaven had decided otherwise.

Our studies were going to finish earlier than expected. In order to give some recompense for all those lost years, and get us active more quickly, especially since there was a dearth of doctors, the faculty decided to spare us some placements in the more recondite reaches of current medicine, and granted us passes in the relevant examinations. Soon there would be no further reason for me to be in Algiers. But, a paradox of passion, I was less joyful at the prospect of shortening my difficult daily life, than alarmed at the risk of being separated from Cécilia. That idea seemed unbearable.

With the passage of time, it happens that one surprises oneself, one scarcely recognises oneself: was I really thinking that? Whatever got into me? The obvious solution impressed itself on my mind: since I couldn't, it seemed, bear to live without Cécilia, nothing remained but for me to take her with me; I wouldn't be thrown out of paradise, I'd carry her in my bags. There's method even in madness; I feverishly constructed a plan which seemed resistant to all challenge: armed with my diplomas we could set ourselves up anywhere, in one of those war-ravaged countries where they lacked practitioners, always except in the light of good sense, my homeland, to spare us the inevitable scandal among relatives and the stupid jokes of their friends. Then, as soon as I saw Cécilia, I revealed my plan in the most natural way, as if she could only adopt it with enthusiasm. By the time I found out what jobs were available, she would have several weeks in which to make preparations, say her last goodbyes to the absurd life she'd been living up till then. As for me, burning my boats, and to avoid painful confrontations, I decided not to go home, and to announce my decision to my parents by letter.

I knew I was being a bit impulsive and didn't expect her to throw herself into my arms spluttering with emotion, nonetheless I was surprised by the manner in which she reacted.

'*Crazy...* you're mad,' she murmured unexpectedly, as if overwhelmed, a far-off look in her eye as if she was looking right through me. I couldn't make out whether it was me she judged mad or my project.

I wanted to believe it was simply surprise in the face of my sudden announcement, but a happy surprise, altogether unhoped for by her; she'd no longer need to earn her living at Mme Gaby's. I needed to give her time to get used to the idea of her new existence as the wife of a doctor.

On getting back home, I joyfully poured my heart out to Barrucand, sure that he'd approve.

'But she's a whore!' he exploded.

I wasn't expecting such a negative reaction from such a non-conformist.

That she was a prostitute, not only didn't bother me but constituted a lucky chance. I patiently undertook to convince him of it, thanks to an argument that I heard myself construct as I went along. Being a prostitute made her all the more within my reach, she offered herself to me unconditionally, without all the traps, the invisible but so effective circle that surrounded most women from our community, always wives, sisters, daughters of other men, who fiercely defended their chattel. Precisely because she was a prostitute, Cécilia alone represented all the women that I wasn't able to have, of whom our unfortunate generation had been deprived. Cécilia wasn't just Cécilia but all women and the essence of femininity. What is a prostitute other than a goddess of love? 'Some tribes,' I explained dogmatically to Barrucand, 'even sanctify their prostitutes and consecrate them to the gods. Prostitutes are good luck for both men and gods, etc. And anyway, she loves me, isn't that the most important thing for a man? Don't prostitutes have the right to love?'

'Perhaps she loves you, but all the same, she sleeps with anyone—'

I interrupted him with irritation, desperately searching for favourable arguments:

'And so-called honest women only sleep with their husbands, do they? Only they do it secretly, is that better? And why should women who have several men be scorned when we men, boast to each other about our various affairs?'

'And your parents?' he said at the end of the argument.

'I've decided not to go back home!' I cried, 'Since they wouldn't want Cécilia, I don't want anymore of them… I refuse to transform myself into a bigwig in a tiny community of a small town! I don't want to spend my life in that tepid water! Cécilia is my Statue of Liberty, my America, my Indies.'

'She's right. You are mad,' he murmured, 'she's more sane than you are.'

So be it, I was mad, mad on Cécilia, madly in love, in the same way as some are mad on God, I was mad on the goddess Cécilia! Barrucand wasn't entirely wrong, it wasn't a comfortable love, but it filled me with pride: it seemed to me that I was engaging in a heroic act against all the cowardice of the existence we'd been given.

But it was then that fate told me, even more clearly, that its decision was irrevocable.

The American cultural attaché had organised a series of receptions for the elite of the country; it was part of a more general plan aimed at winning the hearts and minds of the newly liberated population, to the great displeasure of the old colonists. Students were considered a particularly worthwhile investment.

I didn't have the luck to be part of the first contingent, which I at first deeply regretted, given the idea of the victuals that the Americans would be liberally distributing. I was glad I wasn't there though, when Barrucand who'd been among the first guests, came back with the stupifying news, as much for him as for me: Cécilia, whose name wasn't Cécilia but Catherine, Cathy, was the wife of the cultural attaché! She'd played her role as hostess with natural grace throughout the whole evening, supporting her husband's career. Being aware of my friendship with Barrucand, of whom I'd often spoken, she had a few more kind words for him. Her accent was very American, with a touch of Swedish, because her father, also a career diplomat, had been posted in Sweden for a long time, where she'd spent her adolescence. As for her husband, Barrucand who was expecting to meet a superb cowboy, informed me disappointedly, he was a fat gentleman from the Midwest, with a protruding stomach, a thunderous voice, and clearly older than she was.

The news, one can imagine, spread like wildfire. I was supposed to rejoice like my comrades, flattered at the idea of having made love to the wife of a high-ranking official, American to boot. I was devastated. I understood why she thought I was mad. Ah! She'd fooled us all, me infinitely more than the others. The goddess didn't exist, the earth was only populated with lovesick housewives. I swore to myself never again to set foot in that villa on the hill.

Naturally, a drunken oath, I ran back several days later with rage in my heart. Mme Gaby received me with a pitying air, visibly aware of what had happened. When I placed the usual payment for service on her desk, she refused my money on Cécilia's orders, who was waiting for me.

I didn't give her time to light the candle, I shouted:

'Why did you do that? Why!'

I meant: "You, why are you a prostitute?", forgetting that if she hadn't done that, I'd never have made love with her, perhaps never have even known her. But such are the consequences of passion: I really wanted to love Cécilia as she'd originally appeared to be, to share my life with a prostitute who made me happy. I couldn't bear the idea that Catherine, Cathy, lawful wife of Howard MacLarren, a career diplomat, could have so ignominiously cheated on her husband, with whom I now felt an obscure kind of fellowship. I really wanted my whore to be a goddess, I couldn't admit that my goddess was a whore, as if I'd discovered that my own mother, or one of my sisters were prostituting themselves. Now, to imagine her receiving my comrades in her belly, one after the other, who laughingly exchanged their impressions afterwards, was making me suffer as if she was already my wife. Beside myself, I mixed insults with retrospective questions. Why? Why? And in the face of her silence, I suggested to myself possible answers: to make money? Mme Gaby's other girls, lower-class women or wives of impoverished people, OK, but not the wife of an American cultural attaché whose earnings were higher by far than those of his European colleagues, to say nothing of the bargain domestic service, the perks, the car. Perhaps for the satisfaction that her husband wasn't giving her? So she could take a lover, but because of that to collect coitus in series! Apparently, she didn't get much more satisfaction from her clients, since apart from a few superficial caresses, she wasn't very responsive. Out of tenderness? My comrades assuredly didn't dream of giving her any and moreover she didn't seem to be looking for it. And above all, the most painful: so I wasn't enough for her! It only remained for me to suspect her of some hidden vice, in that shadowy part of most women, which frightened me and at the same time, made me all the more attracted. But which?

'You're frigid? A nymphomaniac? You need the whole Faculty of Medicine!'

As with gladiators who each possess their own particular weapon, the trident for one, the fork for another, Cécilia's was silence, she remained impassive under the avalanche.

Then, suddenly, as in fairy tales, two tears pearled in the eyes of the statue and a wistful smile appeared; she held out her arms to me.

'Come,' she said.

That invitation, issued in familiar language, instead of calming me, just reminded me of prostitutes' normal vulgarity.

'Whore! You're nothing but a whore!'

I fled, running down the steps then the hill, and happily found Barrucand in the house. Instead of telling the truth and reporting the scene of my rupture with Cécilia, I told him straight out that I was going to carry her away, whether she agreed or not, and other stupidities. I was delirious. Seeing the violence of my grief, he spared me his habitual sarcasm concerning "females"; he cautiously suggested that I console myself with another of Mme Gaby's girls; why not Rosa, who was just as blonde as Cécilia and who looked like her, or Stella, perhaps with finer features... I nearly hit him. Passionate love is, decidedly, incommunicable.

A week later, I revisited Cécilia, I made no reproaches, I asked no questions. I threw myself into her open arms; our tears mingled which had the same taste. We remained immobile, enlaced, not even thinking of getting undressed.

When I left her on the doorstep, as if to avoid a new discussion and more tears, she shyly announced that her husband had been posted to Ankara. She'd known it for some time; she hadn't dared tell me for fear of spoiling our final weeks.

I burst into sobs, sobs born deep in my chest like a howl. I repeated:

'And me, what's to become of me?'

She gently consoled me:

'You're going to become a great doctor... you'll help thousands of people who'll be grateful to you, who'll love you... you'll no longer need the love of a single woman, above all one...'

I closed her mouth with a kiss.

'You'll see,' she said melancholically, 'you'll even end up forgetting me.'

As you can see, I haven't forgotten her.

Why did she go to Mme Gaby's? I never had an answer to my question. I only hoped that she had no further need of a madam in Ankara. During our remaining time, I rushed to Mme Gaby's almost every day, who tenderly looked after us. I don't think Cécilia saw anyone else, I could tell from my comrades' disappointment. Sometimes we went swimming, as far away as possible from the town, leaving the popular beaches for the rocky creeks in the surrounding area.

It was the middle of the dazzling Algerian summer. Lectures had been over for a long time; my parents were waiting impatiently. To economise and because of the exhausting long journey, twenty-four hours in nasty wooden coaches, I'd spent long months without returning home.

The day after Cécilia's departure, I returned home to join my people, the sneaky beach boys with girls of my own age and background, already short and fat in their heels, future puddings. Barrucand was right, a young doctor about to become a local bigwig, I was going to have to choose a wife who would be neither a goddess nor a whore.

The Buddha's smile
or love's good fortune

At Châtelet station, close to where I lived, on returning in the evenings, I often saw a middle-aged woman standing at the junction of two corridors with two plastic bags at her feet, covered in large red and white stripes and overflowing with bits of material and paper. Surveying the intermittent flow of hurrying travellers, she seemed to be waiting for someone. As I'd never seen her speak to anyone, and because she was always there whatever the time, I ended up supposing that the person in question, husband, lover, child, hadn't ever come. Perhaps that person didn't even exist, and the poor woman was mad. One encounters such people in Paris, as in all big cities, talking to themselves, gesturing with their arms to threaten an interlocutor or convince an imaginary crowd. This unfortunate woman simply waited silently.

There was nothing special about her, and I wouldn't have noticed her if I hadn't seen her almost every evening. She'd reached the age where men only vaguely look at women, if they aren't brought to their attention by some physical peculiarity or some eccentricity in their dress. Châtelet's stranger, I learnt her name later, simply possessed one of those interchangeable faces of the Parisian street, which she made no effort to embellish, save for some light traces of red on her cheeks and lips. Her hair was clean and properly combed – so someone must have been looking after her – but without any special prettifying. Her clothes were modest but not neglected, and indicated the thriftiness of her lower-middle-class background. She had nothing of that haggard, abandoned air, belonging to most of the *métro*'s mad.

Perhaps I'd have ended up ignoring her if I hadn't been struck by her astonishing permanent half-smile, which strongly reminded me of Uncle Ho's, a little rubber Buddha I'd bought in New York, which had been adopted by the whole family due to its calming smile, and whom my daughter took with her every time she had to sit a university examination. What was the Châtelet stranger's secret? What was the meaning of her smile, full of serenity and happy confidence, which seemed to come from deep within herself, as if she found some reassuring presence there? So that when you looked at it, instead of pitying her, out of a kind of spontaneous sympathy, you wanted to smile along with her.

One evening I didn't see her, nor the next day, nor in the following ones. Every time I hurriedly passed by the windy junction that she habitually occupied like a statue, I couldn't stop myself casting a glance in that direction. Then I went away on a business trip for a few weeks.

On returning and resuming the routine commute between the Ministry of Public Works where I had my office and my home, I saw no more of the strange Châtelet woman. I felt a kind of regret and was vaguely worried, as if she'd been a distant relative. Before renewing my season ticket, I took the opportunity to question staff at the ticket office, which wasn't far away.

Oh, yes! They knew her well; Parisians love their *métro* but not to the point of lingering in it; that immobile passenger hadn't failed to capture their attention; they'd even nicknamed her, at first jokingly, the Phantom of Châtelet. Feeling pity, they sometimes offered her a hot drink and when she stayed too long, they persuaded her to return to her domicile. Occasionally one or other of them offered to accompany her to her brother's place where she lived. Unfortunately, at the moment, she was bedridden with bronchitis, which wasn't surprising given the amount of time she spent in that windy area. By chatting to those young ladies, I was able to piece together the poor woman's story.

Claudine Bartillat used to lead a quiet life with a husband she loved, who was a *métro* employee, which explains why she was waiting there, and a son whom she adored, all the more so, since according to doctors she couldn't have any more children. One day Providence or the devil, jealous of her happiness, decided to strike at the heart of her wellbeing: in his fourteenth year her boy developed a serious illness. Struck down by leukaemia, there was nothing anybody could do to save him; neither regular doctors nor quacks whom she consulted one after the other, nor pilgrimages, nor the blood transfusions which she gave to the limit of her strength. Then, after his death, she continued to celebrate his birthdays; she forbade anyone to touch his bedroom, even to clean it; she persisted in regularly setting three places on the dining room table, and despite the concerned remonstrances of her husband, preparing enough food for three people.

However, luckily, some means were available to help in her misfortune. She lived in one of those workers' districts in the suburbs of Paris where her husband, a militant trade unionist, had obtained a three-roomed council flat in social housing, where an admirable solidarity made the local population into a large family. They shared her grief, tried to take her mind off it, invited her out, visited her as often as possible. As she was also a member of various associations, including a club, "The Ramblers and Friends of Nature", which organised frequent excursions, her leisure time was also taken care of. After a period when she refused to leave her home, she even ended up, although as she said, "with a hole in her heart", letting herself be convinced to resume some activities. So, surrounded by her husband and affectionate and devoted friends, she gently picked up the strands of her life.

But Providence, or the devil, hadn't finished with her. She was struck severely a second time. During one of their backpacking outings at Fontainebleau, her husband who was in front, rock climbing with a friend, was seen to stop short, open his mouth wide like a fish out of water, and lift up his head, as if lacking air he was trying to suck in as much as possible. Then, he folded, collapsed like a puppet whose strings had been cut, "like a man who'd been shot", his group said, who'd known the horrors of the war and the Resistance. His closest companion and the other hikers – there was even a doctor and nurse among them – rushed to help him up. But he remained inert; his heart, which had stopped beating, didn't want to restart, despite their prodigious efforts. Claudine Bartillat, who was at the tail end of the group, also wanted to rush toward her husband; she was stopped from doing so by a sign from the helpers, and taken aside. She fainted.

The whole thing was too much for her already overburdened head; when she regained consciousness, she went to fetch her husband and even her son, in order to return home together, as if nothing had happened. Her friends tried to gently bring her back to reality; in vain. Leaving the doctor and nurse to take care of the dead man, they accompanied her home. They suggested staying with her at least for that first night of grieving, but she politely showed them to the door because, she explained, she had to prepare an evening meal for her two men.

Her reason never came back. But, as the only apparent oddity in her behaviour was her daily stationing in the *métro* corridors in expectation of her husband's and son's return, and in every other respect she led the same life as before, she was left in peace, to be visited in turn by friends and watched over by her next-door neighbours. One day when the smell of rotting food which had accumulated in her kitchen began to bother them, and when, in addition, it was discovered that she was forgetting to switch off the gas more and more often, her brother was alerted and managed to affectionately put pressure on her to come and live with him in Paris. As she resisted, he brought to bear a decisive argument to which she could only accede: it'd be more convenient for her to wait for her two loved ones in the corridors of the nearby *métro*, with her two large bags full of warm clothes and food, one for the child, the other for the husband.

It was on returning from another trip that I learnt from the *métro* receptionists, that Claudine Bartillat had died of pneumonia complicating her bronchitis. On telling me the sad news, the young women were sincerely sorry, as if they'd lost a friend; the brother had to console them by saying she hadn't suffered and that she'd died in the same serene manner with which they were familiar.

I, in my turn, tried to console both them and myself; I told them, all things considered, at least in the last part of her life she hadn't been unhappy. Hadn't they themselves declared with astonishment that the Phantom of Châtelet was a happy phantom? I told them about one of my discoveries concerning death, made during the course of my travels. According to quite widespread beliefs, if a person was loved during their lifetime, and if one continued to carry out the duties due to the dead, he or she didn't torment you. What is it that gives rise to those strange ceremonies and offerings, or closer to home, Catholic Masses? In Madagascar, the dead are taken out of their tombs once a year, they're richly dressed and paraded around the town in the middle of a joyful crowd; at the end of the day they're brought back to their graves, where they rest in peace until the following year. Similarly, Claudine Bartillat probably had a peaceful soul, because she'd never ceased to care for her lost loved ones, waiting for them every evening with a good dinner and warm clothes. Having never stopped loving them, her love was certain to be returned. Wasn't that the secret of Claudine Bartillat's happiness? Of the Buddah's smile?

The Seine's castaway
or love's misfortune

We were on our way back from a dinner with friends who lived on Ile Saint-Louis. Huddled together we were rushing to our cars; whipped by a cold wind, the heavy rain, mixed with the humidity rising from the river, was threatening to penetrate our coats. At the exit of the Pont Louis-Philippe, we thought we could hear some shouts for help, little cries of anguish which seemed to be coming from the water. We leaned over the parapet and discovered through the haze, like a beast stemmed by the flood, a woman standing on the narrow edge of an enormous pillar to which she was desperately clinging. Soon we were able to make out her abundant hair falling all over her face, and its youthful style, emphasised by a very short dress adhering to her body.

Who was she? Why had she climbed onto that perilous perch at that late hour? How had she managed to do it, despite the tempest and the slippery quays? Everyone offered their own hypothesis (later, we'd have more details concerning her history) – overwhelmed by a family drama, upset by some sentimental setback, exasperated by an obnoxious husband or betrayed by an inconstant lover – in any case the hapless woman had decided to renounce what was for her, an unbearable life. As Parisian suicide candidates often did, she'd chosen to drown in the Seine. But the river, usually so placid, had transformed itself into a monstrous beast, exhaling sinister vapours, moved by a howl coming from its entrails, swirling like so many mouths seeking to engulf her. Just as she was about to sink into a death that seemed more terrible than she'd imagined, in a panic, she'd managed in a last-gasp attempt, to climb onto the life-saving pillar.

Now she was repeating a litany of:

"I don't want to die! I don't want to die! I don't want to die!"

But how long could she hold on to that unstable equilibrium before her arms became ankylosed in contact with the icy stone? We were seized by the horror, common to most humans, when confronted with the inevitable death of one of their own. We shouted the usual derisory encouragements: "hold on!", "stay strong!", "we're going to get you out of there…", with no idea how we were going to do it. We were no longer young and fit, and even if we'd been able to get down onto the quay without breaking our necks, we wouldn't have been able to reach her on the pillar.

It was then that I happily remembered the existence nearby, on the Boulevard Henri-IV, of a Republican Guard barracks. To my friends, who immediately suggested we rush over there together, I objected that it'd be better if I went alone; we'd get in each other's way, hampered as we were by our large overcoats and slowed down by the high-heeled shoes of our companions. Then I ran to look for help.

Having reached the enormous building, constructed in the form of a blockhouse to protect the Republic from possible rioters, and after passing through the tall, open, unguarded doors, I had to cross a couple of courtyards, both equally deserted, before finding myself in the presence of a young soldier who was huddled by a stove, reading a newspaper. I explained to him as rapidly as possible why I was there. He carefully folded his paper, and without saying a word, went back to one of the desks, behind which he sat, opened a large black register, and finally said:

'Your papers, your surname, first names, address, occupation, relationship with the victim.'

I felt anger take hold of me.

'I'm telling you,' I nearly shouted, 'that a woman's in danger of her life! I don't know her! I refuse to give you all that information about myself beforehand! I'm going to get back to her to see what I can do on my own! Assuming she hasn't already been swept away by the current!'

He lifted up his head, looked at me as if he'd just made a discovery, and at last seemed to understand the urgency of the situation; he closed his register and got up.

'Wait here,' he said.

After a time which seemed unending, he came back accompanied by two comrades, one of whom was carrying a rope ladder and the other a large blanket. From that moment on they were wonderful. They ran so fast, I couldn't keep up with them; when I got to the bridge, they'd already fixed and unrolled the ladder, on which one of the two was getting ready to descend to the voluntary castaway, who was now silent.

We assisted, equally silently, with the rescue. The guard straddled the parapet and lowered himself down the length of the pillar as quickly as possible. As soon as he reached her, the desperate young woman relinquished her immobility and threw herself onto him, encircling him with her arms. We couldn't hear what she was murmuring. He gently released himself, then as she refused to let go, he had to struggle to get her to agree to mount the ladder on her own, in front of him. But having got to the top, she seemed to quickly recover all her energy and jumped lightly onto the bridge. She really was very young, scarcely out of adolescence, very pretty, with fine doll-like features, large eyes as black as her opulent hair. She was shivering in her soaked little dress, which was too thin for the season. One of the soldiers put the blanket over her shoulders and added his own cape.

We'd have liked to know more about our rescuee, but it was late and we too were very cold; our coats were also soaking. We were reassured as to her fate, and it sufficed us to entertain the pleasant feeling of having helped to save a life. We left them walking to the barracks together, and we headed back to our cars.

In the following weeks we often spoke of that memorable night, we kept asking ourselves how such an attractive young person could have wanted to put an end to her existence. Persuaded that it must have been a broken heart, we blamed the imbecile who'd rejected her. Then time passed, which blots out everything; we only mentioned it on rare occasions. Until the day when, having to consult a book in the Arsenal library, which is also situated near the Pont Louis-Philippe, I got it into my head to drop into the Republican Guards' barracks to get some news of the escapee.

After having gone through the two tall doors and the two courtyards, which this time I crossed like a habitué, I had the luck to run into my Cerberus from the original night, who would, I thought, facilitate my request. Indeed he did recognise me, and didn't go to open the big black register; he didn't ask me my surname, first names, address and occupation. He'd guessed why I'd come back to the barracks. Moreover the whole affair had made an equally strong impression on him, he said, he'd frequently discussed it with his comrades. He'd no need to consult the archives; he remembered the information given to him by the family of our heroine very well. She was called Lucie Martineau, a management secretary, living with her parents in this very quarter of the Bastille, to whom her body had been returned.

'Her body!' I yelled...

'Yes, she died, she tried again just a few weeks after her first suicide attempt... it's often the case you know, when they truly intend to die, they end up doing so... this time, she reached the end. It wasn't raining, the water wasn't particularly cold... nobody was on the bridge, nobody heard her shout for help... if she did shout, which wasn't even certain... we found her not far from here, trapped between a barge and the quayside... they never get very far.'

'So it was a broken heart, no?'

'Yes, that's what the family told us... a pathetic story, as always in these cases. She was madly in love with her boss, a married man; he'd promised to get divorced and live with her, then he went back to his wife... she broke off with him, but couldn't bear the separation.'

Yes, I thought, a pathetic story, but that's the way it is: excessive attachment kills; even dogs lie down and die on their masters' tombs. The poor girl probably didn't know that there is no love without suffering, that the book of love without pain hasn't yet been written... if it ever will be.

As if he'd guessed my thoughts, the young soldier said gravely:

'Yes, sometimes it's a misfortune to love.'

Then, dreamily, he added:

'It's almost always women, poor things...'

The double secret

Several months ago I received a phone call from a colleague who'd come back from a trip to the Middle East. He wanted to share some news which he knew would interest me: he'd met Aurélia Feijtö!

Aurélia had been part of the distant, troubled world of my adolescence; caught up in the torment of the war, she and her whole family had disappeared. Now, according to my friend, not only had she survived, but after having emigrated to Israel, she'd become the wife of a high-up civil servant in the Ministry of Public Works. So she'd fulfilled our youthful commitment and I hadn't, it's one of my regrets, accompanied by a feeling of failure. Perhaps I'd have followed her if she'd asked me to and if history hadn't decided otherwise.

It was while dining at her home that my colleague learnt we'd been close in the past.

'We talked a lot about you and those times,' he told me. 'Aurélia Feijtö, alias Mme Davidson, even confided a secret concerning you.'

'Tell me!'

'No, you first... she made me promise not to reveal it before you'd brought up your own memories, you'll understand why...'

'Oh, it's a sad story, and quite banal I suppose: in short, I was hopelessly in love with her, as one loves or thinks one loves for the first time... I was seventeen years old, Aurélia was sixteen...

Like Romeo and Juliet, but we, we never dared to declare it, we didn't live through a tragic love story…

'This might sound stupid today, attitudes have changed so much… perhaps if we'd had a few more years? No, even then not; we belonged to the same young people's political movement; to pay court to a "comrade" would have been an unpardonable weakness, almost a betrayal of our common ideals. Moreover, the Movement preached chastity before marriage; we had to devote our energies to the triumph of the Cause. The miniskirt hadn't yet been invented by a naughty English woman, Aurélia used to wear embroidered central European blouses, buttoned to the neck with military-style collars, very long skirts or trouser-skirts that reached to her calves. Nothing to attract attention. Her hair was gathered in a strict crown around her head, I don't remember ever having seen it let down, even on the beach. Just once, a memory which has stayed with me because of its rarity, on the occasion of a party, she allowed herself a décolletage sufficiently open to reveal the cleavage which separated and reunited her breasts. Alcohol being equally contrary to our principles, we drank lemonade together. When a button on her blouse came undone, she tried to make it good, but her fingers got stuck in the lace on her front, revealing yet more flesh; she became so confused that she blushed, and me too even more, as if she'd undressed in front of me. Without being aware of it, I would have indignantly denied it, I was in the process of discovering through Aurélia, beyond Aurélia, what today still seems a mystery to me: the attraction between a man and a woman, however naive they may be.

'We saw each other at meetings and numerous demonstrations organised by the Movement, where I admired her seriousness and the rightness of her opinions. My zeal was increased tenfold by her presence. She attended the young girls' *lycée*, not far from the boys' school, so I was able to wait for her at the gate under the pretext of gallantry. My heart raced as soon as I saw her, always spotlighted in the gang of pupils, where I only focused on her. In good weather, luckily it often was in my native country, stripped of our militant armour, we became simple sun and sea-worshippers, together with all the young people of the town, politicised or not. The main thing was to be seen in everybody's eyes, both girls and boys, as the most well built, the most skilful at throwing and catching a ball, the person who swam fastest and furthest from the shoreline.

'I joined in with the same ardour, but solely to capture her attention. In her swimming costume she seemed the most fascinating creature in the universe, more moving than any sculptural masterpiece; since, apart from the firmness of her bust and loins, she was miraculously high-spirited; she talked, moved, threw herself forward daringly to parry the attacks of her opponents, unafraid of falling flat on her face on the sand, shouted with exasperation or joy, burst into peals of laughter, quickly overtaken by her usual mask of seriousness. Not very tall, but so well proportioned, with a skin so evenly tanned under the streaks of salt, that it seemed to me our sun, usually so cruel to blonde girls from the north whom it burned, frizzled and pealed without mercy, must also have been in love with her, since it had transformed her without bruising, into a marvellous exotic fruit. I found the freedom of movement in sport which permitted some bodily contact between the sexes, almost disagreeable, in so far as it got me flustered. Happily, with the exception of folk dancing, which we made respectful use of in our outdoor activities, smooching was prohibited by the Movement. How would I have been able to control my hands, my eyes; would I have been able to cover up the rising flames of my body against hers! To overcome my embarrassment, I adopted the darkly romantic air of the eternal adolescent. "You're weird!" she gently reproached me.

'Or, going to the other extreme, I became excessively agitated, as if I'd taken some kind of drug, cracking silly jokes, making stupid puns I thought were clever, and which to my shame, she treated with disdain, or with a mocking smile that transformed her eyes into narrow slots over her high cheekbones, reminiscent of her Hungarian fatherland. Had I been more sure of myself, I'd have thought that her brusqueness was, on the contrary, a mark of esteem; which I could have won by simply being natural. I could have sworn that just seeing her ravished me, that I'd have pranced in front of her like a dancing bear, just to please her. But I'd have needed to be more capable, that's to say less in love and more sure of her. In ignorance of her true feelings, terrorised by the idea of being found out and perhaps rebuffed, I preferred to live in doubt and cultivate hope, rather than risk the suffering of an out-and-out rejection.

'For the first time in my life, for someone so given to action, I started writing an intimate diary. I wrote poems; me poetry! I haven't done that with any other woman. What I couldn't say to her, I was able to confide to paper. I compared her ridiculously to a candle, to a crystal stopper, due to "their light which illuminated my days", a wax doll, due to its blondness, and for the same reason a canary; to a cork goddess in memory of the statuettes I used to sculpt with my knife to relieve my childhood misery during horrible summer camps in the forest of Aïn Draham… luckily I never dared to show her all that nonsense!

'To be honest, I couldn't have been more distant. It wasn't only shyness that paralysed me but the feeling of being incomparably far away. I'd never known a girl like her. Up till the apocalyptic intrusion of the Germans into our small community, we lived ignored by and ignorant of the wider world. We needed the arrival of the allied troops to convince us that Australia wasn't uniquely populated with kangaroos and that Hindu soldiers, with their long black oiled hair, like snakes under voluminous turbans, came from the same planet as we did. Did Aurélia also come from another world, was she light from a distant star, a meteorite fallen from heaven? One doesn't pay court to a meteorite, one puts it on a pedestal and addresses it with silent prayers.

'Daughter of a well-known militant in her own country, Hungary, who'd fled the advance of the Nazis in successive stages, finally reaching North Africa, she belonged to her father's prestigious struggle, of which we were only a pale replica. Professor Feijtö was also said to be a distinguished doctor. At the time, for me, son of a shopkeeper, he was a respected notable. Among the products of that terrible war, Aurélia had miraculously appeared in my life, I who'd never left our shores, at the same time as those fabled emigrants who alone knew how to resist the Nazis, whom they resembled, all slim and blond with steely eyes; an emanation from that imperial Europe, Vienna, Berlin, Prague, Budapest, where our great men lived, venerated models, Marx, Freud, Einstein, and before them Kant, Goethe, Beethoven and Mozart. How could I even dare to think that I was worthy of the daughter of such a father? How could she not have seemed inaccessible, forbidden? Had she, extraordinarily, given me some sign, I'm sure I wouldn't have understood it. To hope to reach her, I imagined, some upset in our lives would have been required, for example some brilliant feat, which would have covered us both in glory, where I would have lost an arm or an eye in order to save her; or in the aftermath of it she'd remained injured, and as a result needed my permanent help, and consented to let me look after her forever... how adolescents fantasise!

'Of course, I wondered, if being more mature than me as girls often are, while I was hesitating on the brink of virility she would become an irresistible woman. If, despite the injunctions of the Movement, she wasn't going to end up letting herself be wooed by one of those slick-haired cravat-wearing winners (at the time we greased our hair like Rudolf Valentino, except of course for the militants). We never wore cravats in the Movement, but white shirts with collars open over our jackets, like butterflies, symbols of our purity. They were close-shaved, scented (how awful!), and not being paralysed by our virtuous inhibitions, permanently lurked around all the girls, sometimes even obtaining favours from the prettiest. And God only knows how tempting a prey Aurélia was! But the idea of Aurélia being brushed against, being touched by one of those brilliantined dandies, seemed monstrous sacrilege, just as a child can't bear to conceive of its parents' lovemaking. And worse still, even more inconceivable, the idea of Aurélia as a consenting prey! Until the day when she came to ask me, with unusual humility for her, which hurt more than her disdain, to lend my so carefully maintained exercise book, to one of those boys, stylish and handsome – I have to confess – but a notorious dunce, who frequented the racecourse more often than the philosophy class. That, of course, filled my heart with rage. Probably taking me for a redoubtable rival, he thanked me for it, handing it back, still through the intermediary of Aurélia, shamelessly crumpled, covered in coffee stains, studded with a single inscription repeated on page after page: "I'm pissing in your ass! I'm pissing in your ass! I'm pissing in your ass!". How could I fail to understand the meaning of his fury? Why didn't it occur to me that Aurélia must have said something positive about me?

'Then, in our turn, the real war came, after the misleading palinodes of the armistice commissions. The Nazis got hold of her father once again, whose life was temporarily saved because he was a doctor and therefore useful. For my comrades and myself, militants and layabouts alike, whose only use was to break rocks on the southern roads, there were the round-ups, the forced labour camps, the executions and the deportations; for the girls, the rapes and the disappearances. By a stroke of luck, unlike Europe, the occupation didn't last long enough for the Nazis to impose their usual progressive extermination. The Africa Korps, Rommel's famous army, lacking air cover, harassed by American bombers – whose passage overhead we welcomed with restrained joy, even if they pounded us as well – retreated, chased by the Allies, until it locked itself in the mousetrap of Cape Bon, where it was caught and soon completely taken prisoner.

'On returning from the camps, in a hurry to resume normal life, I renounced, so I said, our youthful utopia, for the dream of making a living; peace, almost as uncomfortable as the war, made any other plan derisory. As a delayed student, like many of my comrades, I was able to get to Algiers to finally finish some rapid studies. Engineers, among others, were needed to reconstruct what the folly of men had destroyed; I became an engineer of Public Works and was quickly sent to Europe for my first posting.

'I'd lost all trace of Aurélia and her family long ago. Had she continued the sacred fight, gloriously realising our adolescent dreams, or had she been taken, pistol in hand, and like so many of ours, sunk into some hell invented by our enemies? Or, what I preferred to believe, had she perished in a last stand, and taken her place among the heroes of the Panthéon? Not being able to imagine what had become her, I tried to erase her from my thoughts, if not from my heart, and believed I had just about succeeded, as with dormant cysts that lie encapsulated in oneself, sometimes throughout one's life. In any event, the meteorite metamorphosed into a shooting star and disappeared into the immense universe.

'But she never ceased to occupy my dreams; the various women whom I fell in love with later on always resembled her; rather petite, firm and self-possessed like our apricots, a serious manner, with occasional ironic smiles, sudden peals of laughter and above all angelic blonde heads surrounded by a halo of light... but I ask myself if I ever truly loved another woman; certainly not in that way.

'Well, that's all. I told you it'd be a sad, banal affair...'

'Not altogether,' my colleague continued warmly after a silence, touched I think. 'On the contrary it's a beautiful story;

sad yes, banal, no... now I understand why Mme Davidson... Aurélia, made me promise to hear yours first: she wanted to be sure if, according to you, you'd truly loved her. In case of the negative, as she'd ordained, and as I promised her, I'd have kept quiet; I wouldn't have revealed Aurélia's secret.

But, after what you've just told me, with her permission, I can confide it, here it is: she was in love with you, she too never dared tell you; she was always hoping for a sign from you.'

I thanked my colleague. I took a note of the address and Aurélia's new name as a married woman. But, up till now, I haven't sought to see her again; I'm not sure whether I ever will. I haven't even written to her.

How would I find her after so many years? Has that crease which used to appear in her forehead when she laughed and disappear in repose, permanently settled there? Has her amber brown skin resisted the harsh sun of her new homeland? Has it wrinkled and withered like that of the imprudent women in her country of origin? What remains of my Aurélia?

'She must have been very beautiful,' said my colleague, with that nostalgic regret that men have when faced with the ruins of beauty.

'And she? Would she recognise under the grey hair of an ageing man the adolescent down? We'd say to each other hypocritically, as civilised people must: "you haven't changed", or even talk to each other more formally with embarrassment, politely addressing her as Mme Davidson: "how do you do?".

'Isn't it better to preserve our images of the past intact? Isn't our double secret itself now the most precious thing for us? We never touched each other, never even exchanged a kiss. If we'd lived together, would we have necessarily got on? We can't go against body chemistry. Perhaps, like so many couples, we'd have ended up looking miserably elsewhere. An electric lamp, however powerful it might be, ends up exhausting itself; isn't the fate of meteorites, originally balls of fire, to be transformed into cold cinders? Perhaps a dream of love is more constant than a love that's lived…

'At least, that's what I keep repeating to console myself. On the other hand, what I regret almost painfully, is that Aurélia didn't know how much I loved her, and still more, not to have myself known for all those years, that I was loved by Aurélia.'

A true friend

If like me you happen to walk along the banks of the Seine, Fernando Ingrassia said, and you stop behind the back of a motionless fisherman, his gaze fixed on the end of his line, you've probably witnessed an astonishing event: on the stroke of midday the man gets up, sorts out his equipment, then empties his bucket full of fish, wounded by the hook, mouths bleeding but still alive, into the river. If you'd asked him why he behaved in that strange manner, he'd have replied that the widely polluted Seine's fish are inedible; even his cat wouldn't touch them. So why bother to fish at all you wonder? Perhaps he wouldn't know how to explain it, if he could, he'd say that in fishing as in the quest for love, the most important thing is the pleasure of conquest and the wait which precedes it, which magnifies the quarry in one's imagination.

Things were going badly for me, continued our comrade, and I'd broken with my girlfriend of the time.

After having worked for years in an accountant's office, I'd decided to set up on my own. Working together with younger recently employed colleagues, more enterprising because they wanted to show their metal, was becoming increasingly excruciating. If I don't take my independence now, I said to myself, I'll never dare to do it. But the months went by without my succeeding in building up sufficient clientele to make a decent living; I remained alone for many days, in my spanking new office in which I'd invested all my savings and a bank loan, without even having a secretary.

I no longer remember why I broke off with my girlfriend, or why she left me. Perhaps it was my business worries and the feeling of a setback that ended up invading everything, and lacking energy for anything else, I'd let our relationship die out, as a candle consumes itself. In any case it seemed to me more judicious to devote myself entirely to the office, and I did eventually succeed. But I wasn't yet of an age where one can put the yearnings of the heart and above all, the body, aside for long. I began to need a woman again, when fate, which had been so opposed to me during that period, deigned, for once, to smile on me.

What do you think the percentage chance of running into an old girlfriend is, or a friend you haven't seen for twenty years? I calculated it: supposing that one made the same return journey on a bus and local train, going and coming twice a day, about one in twenty-five thousand, five hundred and fifty! You'd need a kind of miracle; well, that miracle, Providence provided for me.

I was hurrying to get out of the *métro* at the Concorde station, when I nearly bumped into a woman who, apparently equally keen to get into the coach that I was leaving, got in my way. In the huge rush that nearly all of us in this town are in, due to the distance travelled, the congestion caused by sheer numbers, the collective agitation, we scarcely take time to look at faces. Even when we're at ease, sitting in a cafe or at the theatre, we know that others are only furtive shadows which, in a few minutes, or the time it takes for a show to reach its conclusion, will irremediably disappear, sink into the crowd... save for a miracle, one in twenty-five thousand, five hundred and fifty!

However I had the impression that I'd found myself in front of a familiar face; I had immediate proof of it because its proprietor let out a cry of joyful surprise:

'Ah, could it be! It's you, Fernando!'

At first I was overtaken by a feeling of unreality, confronted by that tall woman with overpainted cheeks, blueish eyebrows, opulent platinum blonde hair tied in an impressive bun on her head, dressed in an ample sack dress as if she were pregnant, who hailed me so familiarly. And just as she realised who I was, I remembered her name:

'Michèle!'

We hastily exchanged the usual pleasantries between old friends, strange after all that time, and because the train was just about to leave:

'How are things with you?'

'And you? What are you up to?'

In that limited flash of time, becoming almost painfully aware that I was going to lose her again for years, perhaps forever, I let out a kind of anguished shout:

'What's your address?'

She replied, already inside the coach, in an equally absurd manner:

'It hasn't changed!'

'I no longer have it,' I yelled, 'remind me!'

Without worrying about the other passengers, probably amused by that little drama, but like *métro* users all over the world not letting it show, no doubt part of the everyday street theatre between a man and a woman, she shouted her address just before the doors closed and the train juddered as it picked up speed. She waved to me through the window and disappeared into the railway tunnel.

Only then did it occur to me that I could have got back into the coach, and we could have found out more about each other, before alighting several stations further on, but that's the way it is with ideas that come afterwards, and anyway I was already late.

I got to know Michèle Parinaud as a result of our respective professional activities. She was a tax advisor in a large textile business, that's to say, she laughingly explained, she taught her bosses how not to pay what they owed. Her department had asked for some extra advice from the office to which I was then attached; we had to work out our analyses and suggestions. An agreeable liaison resulted from our collaboration, for both of us I think. Her body a little too weighty for my habitual taste, her face a bit plump, her mouth a bit large, which in addition when she was thinking, she kept comically half-open like a large fish; nonetheless she had an appealing face, light coloured agreeably full lips, skin covered with excessive layers of make-up, eyes small but flecked green. I can't resist a pretty face; I rarely fall in love at first sight with a body; for me, one sexual organ is the same as another, it's the look that's important, the rest follows. Moreover Michèle turned out to be a charming companion and a cooperative lover, attentive without being overbearing. Talkative but jovial like so many garrulous people, she loved to tell stories and she told them well, with spirit and vivacity, funny stories which made her burst out laughing with a contagious chuckle, even before one had grasped the sense of the story. She told me the office gossip with amused indulgence, she unveiled the ruses of her profession without resentment or any particular objection.

So we spent some months together outside time; it was a luminous, gentle summer, surprising, like a welcome gift. We called each other nearly every morning before going to work, and even sometimes when we found ourselves alone in the office, just to confirm our luck at having met, which lightened our day until we reunited at dusk. Then we used to go and listen to the street singers in Montmartre or the boulevards, whose jokes made her laugh heartily, and then we supped in a bistro. We went rowing in the Bois de Vincenne or the Bois de Boulogne, then, between times, ate fries and drank cold wine, which she was fond of, on the banks of the Marne, the whole lot copiously seasoned with untiring kisses, like newly engaged couples; most often returning to her place, we still had the strength to make love; we were, as I said, in the summer of our days, a time of carefree nonchalance.

However, our affair didn't last long; autumn came, and would soon extinguish the lanterns of the beautiful season. Our shared project having come to an end, she had to go and sort out the finances of one of their subsidiaries, she was very frequently away and our timetables didn't coincide. At that point I was still worrying about getting a promotion in the staff hierarchy, and it's in the nature of romanticism to give birth to loss; not having formed solid enough links to resist distance and time, our separation was mutual without bitterness or resentment. To start with, my love life used to resemble one of those machines for automatically changing records where one disc is quickly replaced by another. I ended up thinking I was in love with another girl in the agency, and left Michèle without excessive regret; I only remembered our best moments, without really asking myself, I have to say, how she'd experienced the end of our affair.

During our very brief encounter she hadn't been able to give me her phone number. As soon as I got to the office I looked for it, and using her address easily found it in the telephone directory. Besides, I'd phoned her so often in the past it seemed as familiar to me, as if we'd split up the night before. She hadn't got home yet and I had to wait until evening to hear her voice.

I suggested we see each other again very soon, perhaps for dinner; she gladly accepted my invitation but only for a dozen days later; she had to travel to the provinces. I didn't press her; I was used to that kind of delay, which each new partner thinks they have to impose on us. Perhaps women aren't as impatient as us or don't need us as much as we need them, or, more probably, teasing is their natural means of arousing desire; in any event, when I phoned her again, she delayed our meeting for another week. But far from discouraging me, that slow waltz only increased my impatience. Already, in a single flash, the whole world, its colour, its density, had changed; the moroseness into which I'd plunged as a result of my professional worries was almost gone.

The simple appearance of a woman in my life, especially after a period of continence, has always had that effect, as if I become an adolescent again about to conquer the whole world, not just a single being. It was as if I was going to experience an absolutely new affair, bringing with it a new triumph. That's why, let it be said in passing, infidelity, morally questionable, also seems to me the sign of a healthy love life, of renewed youth.

Anyway, twenty years on, it was once again summer, I wanted to believe it. And when, after having imposed the second delay, and following several messages, she finally called and invited me round, I was persuaded that we were going to relive an enchanted episode; that we would be making love with the same ardour that I remembered, and I confess that as much as tenderness and emotion, it was that which I needed.

She was living in the same little apartment, fourth floor without a lift, in the Rue de Babylone, where I arrived, heart pounding in my chest as a result of climbing too fast, just as in the old days, but in those days I didn't get out of breath (time really has gone by, I said to myself sadly). I was reminded with pleasure that it gave onto the park of a neighbouring property that she'd explained, belonged to a nunnery; her flat seemed to be an extension of it in so far as it was untroubled and above all, now, full of all sorts and sizes of pot plants. In the middle of that miniature forest, was a collection of ravishing dolls, whose expressions and gestures were astonishingly lifelike; big babies clutching their bottles, smiling or sleeping soundly, little girls and boys perfectly miniaturised, clothed like helmeted bandits, like peasants, or waiters in a cafe, filled all possible spaces in the living room, occupied the tops of all the furniture, chairs and shelves, including the top of the wardrobe.

'I'd like you to meet my children,' she declared proudly.

How could she, especially with her corpulence, even move about in that crowd? There wasn't any visible space for a second inhabitant: I concluded with satisfaction that she probably didn't have a regular companion.

She was wearing a pair of shiny black silk indoor trousers and a bra in the same colour and material. I hadn't realised during our rapid meeting in the *métro* to what extent she'd put on weight, her stomach in particular, protruded like a pumpkin being carried in front of her, almost like a false one, like an actress with a pillow simulating pregnancy; her breasts, compressed by the stretchy material, foretold an avalanche. I understood the purpose of the sack dress: its floating amplitude effaces forms, absorbs nature's excesses. Whatever the inconveniences of the skirt, most women are wrong to abandon that efficient instrument of camouflage in favour of trousers, which reveal the size of hips and big bottoms... or the lack of them.

She noticed my glance.

'No, I'm not pregnant,' she said with forced gaiety.

Then, as if to excuse herself:

'It's true, I'm fat... but I'll tell you why: it's either that or being perpetually deprived, not eating when I'm hungry, not drinking, missing meals, being obsessed with bathroom scales... I've tried draconian diets over the years, no dairy, no ice creams, no cakes, no sugar in my coffee, no bread; one day I got fed up, I said to myself: "Enough of all this, I'm going to eat!" Since then I've eaten and drunk normally, good wine and Coca-Cola, which I love, I enjoy all the delicious things that the good God puts at our disposal... if men don't like it, too bad!'

I assured her, with as much conviction as possible, what we always say to them in such circumstances, that for my part I preferred women to be real women and not "ironing boards"; that a woman's embonpoint was a relative affair, varying with different conventions and civilisations and at different historical periods; I reminded her of Rembrandt's, Rubens' and Raphael's superbly plump creatures; in the East one fattens up girls for marriage; in Greece even today, a beautiful woman is a well-covered lady, living proof of her husband's prosperity, etc. I was so prolix that I wasn't entirely speaking in good faith and I could see that she wasn't duped.

And to prove I desired her, I tried to take hold of her waist; she barely had one, she was as round as a tree trunk, a barrel from armpits to thighs. I wanted to kiss her, but, she turned her head away playfully and leapt off the sofa with the surprising lightness that fat people have.

'No, not so fast, if you please! I've only just come home,' she explained, 'I rushed in order not to keep you waiting, I'm all in a sweat, I'm too hot! First I'm going to put myself at ease! Look, while you're waiting, I've prepared a surprise...'

She took a large plate of scented and very sweet, yellow Spanish melons out of the fridge, that I happen to be very fond of – she'd remembered, which touched me. She placed it on the table then ran off to the bathroom.

Leaving the door open, she continued to chat telling me, as in the past, the latest gossip from her office, where she'd grown in stature and which now completely occupied her, so much so that she scarcely had a private life, other than with her doll-children, but she wasn't complaining, etc. I could follow her ablutions equally well.

'I don't even have time to pee!'

I heard the sound of a stream in the toilet bowl, then that of water being flushed.

How disappointed I was, even angry, when I had to admit in my adolescence that my mother and sisters also had bowel movements, as if they'd betrayed me: how could they allow themselves to engage in activities so contrary to their nature! Dirtiness and smells had to be, just like brutality and obscene talk, the sad preserve of males. Women shouldn't have to defecate, urinate, have periods, give birth, they shouldn't even have to eat, except in secret. Angels! Multiple examples of Virgin Saints. I think I'd never been completely resigned to not considering women a particular species of angel, non-corporeal... lacking that body which on the other hand fascinated me. Make whatever you like of that contradiction; well, even today, I'm not sure I've sorted it out.

She came back at last, naked torso under a white Judo dressing gown, with red silk knickers edged in black lace, so minuscule that they scarcely reached the edge of her pubic hair, and over which spilled a double roll of flesh. Her breasts, liberated from the straightjacket of her bra, the avalanche having been produced, abundant and formless, joined the fatty cascade of her abdomen. She'd made use of the time to make herself up, but too quickly; in order not to keep me waiting, she'd neglected the traces of red and blue in the creases on her forehead, on the side of her nostrils, around her ears. She'd have done better to have left her make-up as it was, since she just seemed more of a mess.

'Would you have guessed I take belly dancing lessons, they're fun and they do me good, better than physical exercise, which bores me! Here, look!'

Singing and beating time on an imaginary tom-tom, whose boom-boom she imitated, she made a few pelvic movements, which to her mind were gracefully oriental, making her enormous bust wobble about. Having not yet acquired the suppleness of an experienced dancer, she rather evoked the antics of a dancing bear. Her liberated breasts, too heavy, swung from one side to the other like badly packed parcels. Despite myself, I couldn't help visualising the mass of viscera, intestines, liver, spleen, that she must have been shuffling about. You've perhaps read a short story by Colette that struck me forcibly, where an officer suddenly loses interest in his mistress because, being completely naked, she looks ridiculous wearing his *képi*...

I put an end to the exhibition by retiring to the bathroom to get undressed; I had a long shower at the same time.

When I came back, it was time to decide.

I tried once more to kiss her. She was abundantly sprayed with a perfume I recognised I'd given her in the past, which hadn't completely succeeded in dissipating the smell of her sweat, which was acidic as is often the case with people who eat too much. I was finding out just how much, in the absence of desire, sexual congress becomes an unbearable chore, almost repugnant. Through what malevolent transmutation, does a mouth, that red floral receptacle for kisses, return to being an orifice for taking in food, a harbourer of microbes, exhaling dubious breath and fetid stenches coming from the stomach or bad teeth? The kiss, the most delicious thing in the world, no more than an exchange of saliva; too full lips become mouthfuls of raw Japanese fish, impossible to swallow. Or perhaps, quite simply, the spur which had driven me forward in the past and made everything acceptable – because all food seems delicious when you're hungry – had become less imperious with age. It was no longer summer, but for me as for her, the beginning of autumn.

However, despite everything, out of human respect and because of her expectation, I wanted to do it. But my body didn't want to. Who among us has never found himself in that ridiculous situation, where we have the impression of a serious defeat, where we feel humiliated, diminished in front of a sarcastic or furious female? But I also know the suffering of a disdained woman equals that of an impotent man; I persisted, without result.

'We have our little pride,' she gently mocked me, 'come on, it's not serious…'

However, good girl that she was, to console me, she wanted to take me in her mouth; I pushed her away.

I felt irritation come over me, not so much because she teased me – all's fair – I wanted to take vengeance – but for what? I think more than the need to overcome my disgust, I was furious with her for not fulfilling her role as female-angel, and stopping me from fulfilling my role as a man. Ah, you no longer want to make any effort to please, well indeed you don't please me! You'd rather eat? Go ahead, eat! I wanted to say nasty things to her, to throw all those unfair insults in her face – who can be fair in those circumstances? I'd lied, she was indeed too fat, her skin was too pink, too stretched like a pig's, she was… I didn't know what to say… bland, yes bland, like the uniform cream in which one drowns in her native Normandy, all the food smells… when she burst into tears, her large mouth open wide, distorted by a little girl's suffering.

'Anyway I haven't become that ugly!'

My anger suddenly abated, transformed into pity, I tried clumsily to reassure her; I told her she'd "preserved" – I bit my tongue – a pretty face, with almost no lines. I couldn't think of anything else. She sniffed, blew her nose, dried her tears which were still running in the traces of make-up on her cheeks.

When she'd calmed down, she smiled at me sadly; in my turn I suggested relieving her by other means; she refused.

I got dressed in silence and went off, after having kissed her on the cheek.

During the weeks that followed, I didn't call and neither did she. I'd finished fishing, I'd thrown back the fish; she too probably; perhaps she'd never thought from the start that the catch could be eaten.

Then I telephoned her, we saw each other again, in a cafe. When she isn't travelling, she comes to see me in my office and we discuss my management problems together, on which she gives me good advice. We dine in some bistro or on the banks of the Marne, we sometimes even dance there, but we don't make love. We've become good friends again, perhaps deeper and better than before, as the most faithful friends are those with whom we don't sleep. I'm just taking care not to lose her again and not to risk having to wait for one chance in twenty-five thousand five hundred and fifty to find her. So that's how I discovered it's the day when we cease to see in them, above all, their sex, that we can finally see women as human beings.

The two spoons

We know the devil's the cause of all our misfortunes, but we have to add our own stupidity, this story proves it.

An Evil Spirit boasted of being able to break up even the most united household. According to him, it would be enough to sow a few suspicions, and even in the case of the most virtuous wife and the most trusting husband, the couple wouldn't be able to resist.

One day when he was bragging about his awesome power over humans, another Evil Jinn threw down a challenge: he knew of a couple so perfectly matched, so perfectly happy, that it would be impossible, even for a devil, to destroy it.

The devil accepted the bet and, filled with excitement over the difficulty of the task, launched his campaign from the very next day. He began by gathering information; in point of fact, there was a rich merchant, well liked for his urbanity and esteemed for his loyalty, which contributed to his success. He offered his wife, who was young, gentle and beautiful, all the gifts that a woman could wish for and that his fortune permitted.

Very much taken up with his business, he used to leave her alone for long periods of time, but, trusting her completely, he had no worries about going away.

The devil judged those conditions to be very favourable for his enterprise. And soon, not a morning went by without the merchant's wife receiving a visit from some supplier, come to make a particularly appealing offer, of fish, of which her husband was fond, of meat for succulent grills, of fresh vegetables or sweet fruits. And it happened by chance (of course it wasn't chance: it was the devil who'd sent them) that all those men were stunningly built, each one more handsome than the other.

But no matter how hard they tried, come hither looks, deep sighs, thinly veiled propositions, even letting their merchandise go for derisory prices, nothing worked. In the evenings she told her husband of her platonic encounters and they laughed together over those stupid men, and savoured the good food that all that nonsense delivered them.

The devil was despairing and for the first time in his life, began to think of admitting defeat, when he was accosted by a neighbour of the couple, as jealous of the beauty of the young wife as she was envious of the husband's prosperity.

'I understand your problems,' she said, 'give me a hundred pieces of gold and I'll see to it that you win your bet.'

'How could you do it, you crazy fool? I've tried everything, me the devil, in vain!'

'That's my business,' she declared, 'give me what I ask and you'll see.'

A hundred pieces of gold, that's a sum, but not for the devil, and then his honour was at stake: the bargain was quickly concluded.

The next morning, the wicked neighbour, after having disguised herself as an old beggar woman, went to sit under the faithful wife's window and began to moan lamentably. After a moment, the merchant's wife, full of compassion, opened her window and asked her what was the matter.

'Hunger,' replied the old lady, 'I haven't eaten for two days, already my legs will no longer carry me, I feel death prowling around me...'

Overcome with pity, the young woman invited the bogus moribund hag into her home and offered to share her meal. The beggar woman accepted with eager and prodigious thanks and a blessing for her benefactress.

'But,' she added, 'first I need to ask you something: I should like to have two spoons.'

'What for?' exclaimed her generous hostess. 'Surely one is enough? Do you have two mouths?'

'Don't mock me,' the guest implored, 'I know it might seem strange but it's a family tradition, according to the wishes of my great-grandfather: we'd abstain from eating rather than use a single spoon.'

'So be it,' conceded the hostess, 'in the state you're in, I wouldn't want to have your death on my conscience.'

Indeed, the old woman set to eating with her two spoons, as if she'd never eaten in any other way.

She was finishing off her plate, when the door opened; it was the merchant coming home.

'This is my husband,' said the wife to the old woman.

'How come?' exclaimed the beggar woman. '*The other one*, the one who was using the second spoon, wasn't he your husband?'

'What other one?' asked the wife. 'Was there any man here? Are you crazy, you wicked witch?' cried the terrified wife. 'There was no-one other than the two of us!'

The old lady feigned huge embarrassment, as if without intending to, she'd committed an indiscretion.

'It must be my poor eyes,' she quickly said, 'I thought I saw someone... no doubt it was just a shadow...'

'And the other spoon,' the merchant cried furiously, 'no doubt that's also a shadow? The shadow of a spoon!'

No matter how his wife protested her good faith, her jealous husband wouldn't be persuaded.

'You're not just fickle,' he shouted at his wife, 'you're also a barefaced liar!'

And he immediately threw the unfortunate woman out.

And that's how the devil won his bet.

And since the merchant needed a wife to manage his household, he married the wicked neighbour – which he soon came to regret.

This only goes to show that the wisest of men loses his head as soon as his wife's virtue is in question.

This proves still more that even the wisest man can behave like a fool.

And this ultimately proves, that an ugly, envious woman, can be more dangerous than the devil.

My neighbour's dog

'Stories about couples, I've got hundreds to tell you,' Laurent Bastide assured us, the portly and rubicund director of the Matrimonia Agency. 'I've sometimes thought about publishing them, apart from the fact that I've no talent as a writer and it would contravene our ethical standards. As we do have them, and they're quite strict. We're often lumped together with flesh pedlars, kind of pimps, when we're only practising the ancient, respectable and very useful function of matchmakers. We share something in common with priests, psychologists and lawyers. Thus, in the course of an already long career, I've been persuaded that most of my clients are not so much seeking to find a passing affair, as to put an end to an isolation that's become intolerable. So much so that I've introduced the question into our information sheets. Here, out of many others, are some stories about solitude.

'Jean Garnier, an engineer by training, retired after thirty-seven years in the same establishment, a factory manufacturing household appliances where over the course of the years he'd become technical director, a promotion well deserved for his competence and devotion to duty. As he was getting older, he'd made the decision, as he put it, "to shut up shop", that's to say, he explained, to put a bit of distance between himself, people, events and obligations. Not that he was less occupied, but from then on, he devoted all the time which he used to devote to work, to leisure activities.

'Living in the Rue de Tournon, two hundred meters from the Jardin du Luxembourg, he was able to register with the ASJL, a logo which had always intrigued him, though he'd never had time to work out what it stood for, a club for boule players which had its own special pitch, where he could play or watch others play whenever he felt like it; he assiduously followed Professor Martineau's lectures, the eminent specialist on Sumerian civilisation, which had always fascinated him, though he'd never had time to take a real interest in it. They were given at the Collège de France, situated not much further away on the Rue Saint-Jacques. He benefitted from guided tours of the Musée du Louvre, principally those which covered the people of the Middle East. But all of his activities were carried out at a leisurely pace without undue passion, with wisdom; the words "wise", "wisdom", "wisely" recurred several times during our first interview.

'And regarding women, assuredly together with professional worries, one of the prime causes of men's troubles. "Ugh! I've finished with them! What a relief!"

'He'd boasted about it with his friends; he'd even thought, renouncing all attempts at smartening himself up, of letting his beard grow. To be honest, had he not made that decision, his natural appetite, now less demanding, would have forced it upon him. But men always need to rationalise their behaviour, it made sense to recognise it and make a philosophy out of it; he believed he'd succeeded.

'So why, after all those good resolutions, did he have need of my services? "Because of the evenings," he declared. "During the day one's distracted, one doesn't have time to think about oneself."

'Throughout those past years, he used to get up at 5am in order to be first in the factory, from which he returned in the evenings at indeterminate times. On reaching home he'd find his wife, whom he'd unthinkingly separated from, now a source of regret as he hadn't taken account of the extent to which her presence had become indispensable to him. "The evenings, they're a void; one's just faced with oneself."

'He sometimes dines with a friend, or lady friend, but it's not the same thing, and then, of course, you have to go home; neither television nor radio can replace the presence of a living being; there's reading, but apart from the fact that he'd never been a big reader, it's also a solitary activity. Every so often the children come to see him, but they have their own lives, and share their time between himself and their mother, whom they probably prefer because she feeds them. Taken up in the whirlwind of the days ever since his entry into active life, he'd never felt anything like it; one only discovers the weight of solitude when one experiences it, and he'd always lived surrounded by people, both at work and at home. Why couldn't he peacefully enjoy his well-earned leisure! He was almost angry, perplexed at what had happened to him.

'Furthermore he wasn't the only one to suffer like that, he confided to me; most of the people he knows who've become single, widowed or separated from their partners, complain: "It's hard…"

'Finding it unbearable to live in their deserted apartments, they rush from one event to another, exhibitions, lectures, group outings. Women especially, some of whom swear they're "dying of solitude". "I don't live anymore, I just survive…", "since my husband's death, I'm like a worm cut in half, as if a part of myself has been amputated", "luckily the telephone exists!".

'Many of them confide their anguish there, making permanent use of it, especially in the mornings. According to management, they're the cause of chronic blockage of the network. Even Pierre Delaroche, a childhood friend become a priest, confided to him: "I begin the day with Mass, then it's visits to sick people in the parish; more unhappily, confessions, catechism and the offices… you know the priesthood's also a full-time job. I see a lot of people, numerous women, but they're more like clients; that doesn't replace a single woman or even wife who's waiting for you. It's nothing to do with sex..." Delaroche hastened to point out with embarrassment.

'Garnier, who reported his friend's torments to me, commented mischievously that on this last point, he didn't quite believe him. In any case he, not being a priest and not having taken vows of chastity, wasn't able to stop himself from tasting, if possible, that delicious fruit offered by God since the creation. Before finally shutting up shop, as he'd thought he was able to do, he'd realised he still needed to live in company. In other words, wisdom should have waited a little...

'I rarely deal with elderly people, but more often than one would imagine. At first they're embarrassed: "I'm not too old for this..."

'Then they set out detailed requirements, like all those who've lived long enough to know what they want. Oh, Garnier wouldn't want to remarry... he wasn't hoping to relive his life, it was already lived; he just wanted to end it agreeably, with a sufficiently attractive woman, who would share whatever remaining years were left to him. Moreover, he didn't want to deprive his children of their inheritance. I objected that, like all serious agencies, we didn't provide that kind of service; we only dealt with marriages made in good faith; we were already accused of immorality often enough. He assured me that his intentions were honourable, that his future companion, if I agreed to find him one, would lack for nothing; matrimonial contract excepted, he would offer her all necessary guarantees of the duration of their relationship, even written, and an appreciable lifestyle. He spoke with so much warmth, seemed so sincere and above all seemed to need my help so much that I allowed myself to be convinced.

'To help people, it's not enough to show them an often touched-up photograph, to proudly go through a curriculum vitae, to organise a date... then to collect one's honorarium; you first have to listen, divine the secret desires that they daren't always immediately express, in short to help them understand themselves. Still, one can never be sure of the result, the relationship between a woman and a man is so mysterious; that's why I've often obtained success when everything seemed to go against it, and lamented unexpected failures.

'So I undertook, without any illusions, to organise some interviews with candidates whom I thought might suit him, a little younger, but not excessively. But to my surprise, he refused all of them, one after the other, until almost impatiently, I asked him to clarify what he expected of me. He hesitatingly replied, while we were at it, he preferred a much younger woman. An elderly woman reminds you of your own age; her white hair warns you that you're also getting older, which is exactly what he wanted to forget, at least as much as he could. I wasn't overly surprised; I'd often been faced with that kind of demand, principally from men, but I knew equally well that those liaisons scarcely lasted, assuming I could lay my hands on that rare bird: a young person who agrees to live with an old fogy. I explained, tactfully in order not to wound him, that youngsters almost always ended up being tempted by another partner of their own age, then taking flight, leaving the old man to his regrets. However he held fast, accepting the risks of the enterprise in advance, assuring me that he wouldn't hold me responsible.

'It was then that Ghislaine Ripois introduced herself, a very young woman who was looking for a companion, without making any particular demands. I wouldn't know whether to say she was pretty, she was surprising. A tiny mouth, almost round, made even rounder by her lipstick, a small inexplicably pointed nose in the middle of a flat face like many Asians (Garnier would call her his "little moon", sometimes his "winter sun"), very naturally white, made even whiter by powder, high cheekbones, she would have brought to mind a Chinese theatrical mask, a heroine from a Japanese film, if she'd had slanting eyes. On the other hand, there was nothing exotic about her body; it belonged to the solid provincial type, frequently seen in Normandy where she came from, with large shoulders, big breasts, heavy hips and thighs, without her youth suffering from those natural exuberances. At first sight, her clothes revealed her modest background; her unevenly dyed auburn hair was held back by a cheap, brown, plastic headband ornamented with gold motifs. She moved slowly, spoke little; not that she was unsure of what she had to say, but the natural flow of her speech was quietly assured without apparent emotion. I tried my luck, or more exactly, that of my client. To my relief, she asked scarcely any questions about her possible future companion. Although I warned her from the outset he was no longer a young man, she agreed to meet him, then to see him again, to get to know him better. A fortnight later, Garnier sent me a basket of dried fruit and Ghislaine a cheque for my honorarium.

'I hadn't heard from the couple I'd brought together for several months, when Garnier telephoned my secretary to make a new appointment. I was immediately persuaded that according to my predictions, their relationship having broken up, he wanted to call upon my services once again. Such big age difference, I repeated to myself, was decidedly impossible to bridge; I promised myself, in order to avoid future disappointments, to be even more dissuasive this time. Perhaps he'd already learnt his lesson and given up his unnatural stipulation.

'Well! I couldn't have been more wrong, in any case it wasn't what I expected! It sometimes happens, I'd say, that one fails when one believes the conjunction to have been altogether favourable and one succeeds when the outcome had seemed the opposite. But I've rarely seen partners apparently so well matched as the unlikely couple of Jean Garnier-Ghislaine Ripois, who were coming to see me in my office. Put it down to experience: I guessed it before they'd even opened their mouths, so much was evident in their manner, the looks they bestowed on each other, those scarcely perceptible gestures which indicate tenderness and peace of mind in a couple. Far from coming to tell me they weren't getting on, they wanted to thank me; they were coming to confide the news that Ghislaine was pregnant (it wasn't by chance but a decision taken together), and to show their gratitude, would like me to be the godfather of their future child, which I naturally accepted.

'Garnier had changed to such an extent that I nearly didn't recognise him. He was always a fine-looking man, tall and well built, on whom age hadn't weighed heavily, and whose already white but plentiful hair seemed almost an ornament; due to his height, a discreet bald patch on the top of his head wasn't visible when he was standing up. But, unconcerned about his appearance, he used to wear the same austere navy blue uniform all year round, understated tie on a white shirt with blue pinstripes, office clothes. Now he was dressed in a light-coloured fancy suit, Italian or English cut, overlaid with green and red check. Where his tie would have been, straightjacket of all bourgeois outfits, a silk scarf to match his suit; instead of a strict razor haircut, sideburns and some curls falling freely on his temples and neck. He no longer had that concentrated, if not worried look, which I remembered. He had slimmed down; having got rid of the excess fat accumulated during business lunches, he'd gained some wrinkles on his skin, become thinner, he seemed rejuvenated; he was now nearer in age to his partner.

'Especially as Ghislaine, on the contrary, had put on weight, storing reserves for her future baby. She was beginning to thicken out on those weak spots for women, her chin and waist, but had acquired a new fullness. Become loquacious, she talked to me about herself for the first time without any embarrassment, in front of Garnier, to whom she'd already confided. Having lost both father and mother, she'd left the province where she was born and moved to Paris, avoiding with great difficulty the pimps and hoodlums who prey on naive young girls at the exit to

Montparnasse Station. She'd tried various jobs, being regularly dismissed, as much for her lack of interest in the necessary tasks as for her slowness. "I think, if I hadn't met Jean, I'd have ended up badly," she courageously confessed. "To be honest," she added laughingly, "I might have been living in a harem, I have a weakness for that, I'm a kind of kept woman."

'On the advice of a friend, she'd decided to reply to one of my announcements, to look for a partner and a support. Being unable to take herself in hand, she was grateful to her friend for having done so. "He's become my whole family."

'Something she'd never had. For Garnier it was a lucky chance; at her age, Ghislaine could have been his daughter, and she became one, just as much as his lover; moreover an unrebellious daughter already out of adolescence! In short, despite the age difference, they presented the picture of an old couple solidly united.

'Afterwards, they occasionally came back to see me. Wasn't I the godfather of their son? From what I could make out, it wasn't even certain that they made love very often; Garnier could no longer perform so gloriously, and Ghislaine, not being very fond of it by temperament, almost never initiated contact. Moreover, it was mutually agreed that they didn't always share the same bedroom; they even had the luck to possess two bathrooms in Garnier's large apartment, which avoided the inevitable risks of too intimate a promiscuity. Later on, Garnier told me, he'd had to resort to some medical aid, when the need arose. So was Ghislaine cheating on him after all, as I'd feared beforehand for ill-matched couples? Garnier preferred not to think about it; he was happy for the moment with what good fortune was offering him. Even if he suspected his companion wasn't completely satisfied with the arrangement, she wasn't about to wander off. And, if it did happen, he would have earned some reprieve from the inevitable decline that awaits us all. "In short, I'd have had two lives!" Garnier said jubilantly.

'"Me, I haven't had two lives," Ghislaine affirmed, "as I only really began to live with Jean…"

'As she doesn't read the papers, Garnier is for her, the inexhaustible conveyor of the world's news. He guides her in the realm of culture, where truth and falsehood are intimately mingled; he chooses the films, he introduces her to the theatre and even opera. Some women know how to say "you're right" to their companions in a tone which signifies: "you're wrong, but I'm saying it in order to avoid scenes". Ghislaine has no need of such ruses; she listens to Garnier with sincere admiration. In exchange, he lets nearly everything go by, never reproaches her. When she comes out with naiveties or excessive prejudice, he limits himself to gently correcting her, with the indulgence and tenderness that age inspires. Moreover she's far from being stupid. He, who used to be in the habit of impatiently getting things done, has learnt to respect the dreamy distraction of his partner, persuaded that what he owes her is far more important than the consequences of her limits and shortcomings: the irreplaceable presence of a woman in his house. Ghislaine is always there and that's what matters. She even became indispensable to him. One day, he found a kind of hard spot behind his ear, probably a result of his glasses rubbing. The doctor advised immediate surgical removal, which he agreed to, and afterwards he had to submit to various post-operative follow-ups which went on for several weeks. Ghislaine, normally not very active, cared for him with attentiveness and efficiency, which surprised and moved him. He saw it as the sum and symbol of his new situation: what would he have done without her? He wouldn't have been able to look behind his ear!

'The young woman wakes up late, breakfasts in bed on a tray which Garnier prepares, who, being used to getting up early for so many years, can't bear to hang about in pyjamas. Then he leaves her to go and sort out the innumerable little administrative tasks that nobody escapes today, even in retirement. Ghislaine stays stretched out half the morning reading some sentimental novel, while, on Garnier's advice, she doesn't try the more elevated literature to be found on the bookshelves in the apartment. When the cleaner arrives, to whom she's delegated the entire household maintenance, she gets dressed and goes out to make some purchases for meals, which have become very easy today with frozen and pre-cooked dishes. Garnier comes back around one o'clock; they eat lunch together, and, after a short siesta, he leaves again for his famous leisure time activities, none of which he's renounced; boule, visits to the Louvre, courses at the Collège de France; even a game of Jaquet has been added, with an old colleague become merchant, whom he meets twice a week in his shop. She never asks him where he's going or where he's come from; he could cheat on her, he takes care not to do so, he doesn't want to, he's too cognisant of his good luck to put it in peril. Ghislaine, for her part, goes out to prepare the trousseau for the future baby, and makes use of the time to do some window shopping and buy some trinkets for herself which women are fond of, and which she was deprived of before she knew Garnier. Unlike her partner, she doesn't seem to need anything or anybody else. Her only outside activity, recently discovered, is a fortnightly meeting of a Buddhist circle where she cherishes the idea that love is a kind of reincarnation; after all aren't she and Garnier living another life? In the evenings if they don't go out for dinner, and they go out less and less, they snack on trays in front of the television, full of good things with which Ghislaine has filled the refrigerator; even television is more fun to watch with two.

'From time to time, they go on a trip. Garnier, who's travelled a lot professionally, now worries about getting tired on long journeys; without telling Ghislaine, whose mere presence satisfies him, he's given up the idea of going to China and India which he'd previously nursed. In this regard, his companion's youth is a great advantage: everything is new to her, she didn't know Venice or even the Châteaux de la Loire, which suffice to give her a change of scenery. Like many ex-directors in retirement, Garnier's advice as an expert is sometimes solicited by provincial companies in difficulty, or even those abroad. So Ghislaine accompanies him and they take advantage of the time to visit local monuments and places of interest. Initially, during professional engagements, embarrassed by their difference in age, he used to ask her to wait for him in the hotel with one of her railway station novels. Then he noticed that, far from condemning or mocking him, his colleagues were envious; thereafter he decided to introduce her as his collaborator, which no one found fault with.

'This has been going on for five years; the baby, happily arrived, is now a strapping little boy who looks like his mother. Garnier has made provision in his will for Ghislaine and his son, so that when he's gone they won't be in need, and his last child will have the same rights as the others. As my agency is situated on the way to the Louvre, he occasionally drops in to see me; I offer him a coffee with pleasure and he talks to me with gratitude about his happiness. However, he's still just as surprised by what happened to him; he only wanted to put an end to his solitude and there you go, at his age, a new father! It was Ghislaine, he confessed, who really wanted it. So I remind him of the old dictum, Chinese I think, which asserts that a good can come from something bad, and when he tells me that he still sometimes feels ashamed of the difference in age between himself and his partner and that he must be "a dirty old man", we laugh together complicitly due to our similar ages. I even admit that I envy him; true wisdom doesn't lie in renunciation but in living life to the full in the present. He'd had the courage to overcome prejudice, and he'd been rightly rewarded. Then, exchanging roles, I plead in defence; I remind him once again about my neighbour's dog.

'My neighbour has an old dog – a Saint Bernard or Deutsch-Drahthaar or a cross between the two, I don't know which – that she cares for and exercises with devotion. I meet them regularly on Saturdays and Sundays during my own walks. He's grown to such an extent that one's amazed his paws can still support that heavy body; he moves forward painfully, stops, and then reluctantly continues. Like all old men, he looks down at the ground, as if nothing else interests him, as if he were now attracted by the earth into which he will soon escape, or maybe just because he fears bumping into an obstacle. I ask my neighbour for her news, and that's how I learn that he has asthma, difficulty in breathing, and problems with his digestion. "In the old days, he used to get excited every time he saw me put on my coat, now I have to force him to go out. The worst," his mistress told me, "is that torpor which comes over him more and more often, as if he wanted to sleep all the time. Except," she adds with a smile, "when we meet a young bitch, when he seems to be reborn, he lifts up his head and I have to pull on his lead to stop him going towards her."

'Aren't we like old dogs? I said to Garnier. Don't we wake up every time we see a young or even not so young woman? Don't we want to go up to her? We stop ourselves from doing so only because we're held back by the leash of convention. On finding a female of the species the dog discovers that he's not facing sickness, old age and death, alone; doesn't the Bible say that it isn't good for man to be alone? As for the difference in age, it's also a prejudice peculiar to our civilisation, which stops us from allowing it; the ancients sought out the company of young people without shame, even if they were their own sex. To have younger partners is a privilege accorded by nature to men, but it's also a necessity: they become protectors and providers. Ghislaine, I added, doesn't she need you? Hasn't she found a protector for her children and for herself? The only time she ever cried, you told me, is when you made allusion to your death.'

A Kurdish passion

'Again on the subject of solitude,' Laurent Bastide went on, 'why did Jocelyne Trichet (naturally it's not her real name), a senior executive in a merchant bank, successively refuse five hopefuls, break with the sixth and the seventh, to the point when I gave up helping her, and she ended up living alone? If not because solitude is rarely the fruit of chance. Even if it's not openly sought after, it is, perhaps, the fruit of temperament rather than circumstances. What did she expect? What was she hoping for? Separated from her husband for six years, she got regular news of him through her son; she knew he'd remarried, that he had two children with his new wife, that he seemed to be happy. But this man was still present in her life; there are solitudes so populated with a single being that they bring to mind chests stuffed so full of old clothes that you couldn't slip a ribbon in.

'Here's another case: Joan Strike, a tall, beautiful, Australian, a real Aussie, several generations of kangaroos, an abundance of red hair, naturally blue eyes, a hockey champion in her own country. She's finishing a doctorate on Indian untouchables at the University of Nanterre, and she's looking for a husband; which is why she came to see me. After two years living in Paris, she still doesn't know anyone. As usual, after having chatted with her, I give her a list of possible candidates. Why did I slip in the name of a future Indian doctor, a Hindu, who was also finishing a thesis at CHU de Bobigny, that's to say, he explained to me, the Central University Hospital? He wanted to marry a European "an emancipated young woman", willing to accept an Indian husband, who'd agree to later follow him to Bombay, where he counted on setting up a medical practice. What more can I say? Perhaps because of Joan Strike's interest in Indian castes, or because of her status as a foreigner, which suggested to me that she'd accept another foreigner, or by some vague intuition, which often happens in my interviews with clients, who appear utterly dissimilar but share a common taste for the exotic.

'In any event, I'd put my finger on it, it's he who's chosen by the beautiful Australian without hesitation; while lacking in any particular charm, of middling height, not much taller than her, the skin on his face of indeterminate colour, grey overlaid with yellow and pockmarked in places, it's true it's compensated by intelligence and the dark acuity of his gaze. They both seem delighted. They marry rapidly in the Bobigny Town Hall, where the happy elite live and work. Afterwards, a cocktail party brings the agency's staff together with the husband's colleagues. They needed to finish their respective theses before taking off for Bombay.

'I heard nothing more of them for several years, until the day when she came back to see me, alone. Taking advantage of a stay in Paris, she was looking for another husband; the first, with whom she'd had a daughter, who remained in India, had been assassinated by a Muslim fanatic during one of the periodic uprisings which trouble that country. She's still just as superb. And as she lets me know she's only passing through and wants to return to Asia, I put on the list, deliberately this time, all my candidates of Asian origin. She scarcely hesitates and again chooses an Indian, an engineer, doing an internship at Villacoublay Airport, Muslim this time, like her husband's killer. There were no cocktails, but in order to get things done quickly, she asked me to be one of the witnesses. Then they left for Calcutta, where the new husband had been posted.

'Why did the Australian woman, Joan Strike, who'd never set foot in India, choose such an exotic partner for a husband on two occasions, from a list of ten candidates, and not a Protestant like herself or at least a Christian Catholic of European culture? My client not being very loquacious, I never solved that mystery. The second time she presented herself at the agency, she was wearing a yellow sari, draped over her shoulder in the manner of Indian women and priests, which caused quite a stir among the female staff. She told me in passing that she'd never finished her thesis and that she'd converted to Buddhism. Had she found an answer to her solitude there? It didn't seem so; although she engaged in social tasks, she mixed with few people, her husband and her daughter were sufficient. You could say, she'd exchanged one solitude for another, perhaps even greater. She developed a passion for painting and there was no lack of subjects in India, she was entirely taken up with her art. She'd didn't return to Australia, which I noted she never talked about. My secretary ironically remarked that "if marriage is complicated, there are some who search for even more complications", but I don't think that's a sufficient explanation.

'Why,' Laurent Bastide continued, 'did Christine Brochier – nicknamed Christou by her friends and Tounette by her parents, daughter of a distinguished Parisian lawyer and a famous pianist of Hungarian origin, from a liberal background, comfortably off, apparently spoiled by life, vaguely working for a degree in literature at Jussieu University, volunteering in a philanthropic organisation from boredom as much as generosity – decide to respond favourably to one of my announcements concerning Osman Rahmad-Ogli, a Turk, or more precisely a Kurd, which isn't quite the same thing. If Kurds are considered to be Turks because they've been conquered and dominated by the Ottomans, they've never been resigned to it, so being a Kurd is doubly exotic. Let's admit it, for a Christine Brochier to fall in love with a Turk is surprising enough, but with a Kurd is even more astonishing. However it must be said that she'd had a previous affair with a very French kind of hoodlum, who beat her up and took her money, and another with a North African whom she met during the course of her social work, who was deeply in love with her, but insisted she convert to Islam before marriage, which she refused to do.

'In any case with Rahmad-Oglü, it was love at first sight, a question of passion. Osman was handsome, it's true: a supple, muscular athletic body, eye's like an eagles, if eagles have eyes as black as his, a superb moustache as black and shiny as his eyes. But should one marry for muscles, good looks and a moustache, without considering the whole man, his origins, his background and his future? That's what I tried in vain to explain to my client.

'A student, at least that's how he presented himself, a member of a group of young Kurdish revolutionaries, which had sections in Europe, preoccupied more with his militant activities than with his studies, Osman had ended up, following a police inquiry, being notified of the non-renewal of his residence permit. It was after a long period of illegality, and after having tried in vain to obtain the status of a political refugee, that he'd addressed himself to me and asked me to find him a French wife, which would have permitted him to regularise his situation. To cut a long story short, if he was attracted by Christine's charms and fell rapidly in love, he'd have been happy to do so with the firstcomer.

'And above all, nothing seemed to connect Osman Rahmad-Oglü (which I learnt at the time, means Osman son of Rahmad) and Christine Brochier; at first I tried to persuade the young girl of it, convinced that she was running into certain catastrophe. My secretary was right, marriage is enough of a challenge, why create more obstacles to be overcome? She'd been educated as a middle-class Christian from Paris, mildly sceptical and somewhat epicurean, like her parents. Osman, son of a little mountain peasant, professed Shiite Islam, that is to say the most austere category, if not the most intransigent in the Islamic world. He also nursed a dark romanticism for everything concerning his country and his people. Unemployed, he'd little hope of finding any, due to his poor knowledge of our language and an absence of qualifications, which condemned him to the most menial and badly paid jobs, in any case insufficient to support a wife and perhaps one day children. Lacking papers before his marriage, half clandestine, running into difficulties at every step, he'd lived in the permanent state of a hunted animal, which had left its traces on his character despite the relative laxity of the authorities whose immigration policy, if there is one, I've never understood. If he'd been sent back to his country, he would have been immediately arrested and, he claimed, tortured and probably executed by the Turkish authorities, to whom he had always demonstrated hostility. His marriage with a born and bred French woman was going to allow him to live in France legally, but supposing all his administrative and economic difficulties to be sorted out, how would such an incongruous couple bridge the abyss in culture and religion which separated them so profoundly? In what tradition would they raise their children? How to reconcile two so dissimilar cultures in each of them? Or would it be necessary to choose one to the exclusion of the other, at risk of causing regrets if not resentments. How would Christine, for example, overcome the challenge of circumcision for boys? And later the wearing of the veil imposed on girls?

'But the young woman seemed ready for everything, nothing deterred her: "I want him! I want Osman and nobody else! Otherwise I'll remain an old maid!" she told her friends in an almost distracted way.

'When she announced her decision to her father, he, like me, put to her the risks of such a union, suggested that she at least think about it for a while; he offered her anything she wanted, for example taking a long trip with a female friend, why not a luxury cruise... she let him go on, obstinately staring at the end of her shoes. She nearly reproached him for not having paid enough attention to her during her solitary childhood, which was true, both parents having been mainly preoccupied with their careers, he with his lawyer's office, her mother with her concerts. But what's the point, she thought? He certainly wouldn't understand; he'd tell her she'd been spoiled rotten, brought up in luxury, that she'd always had everything a young girl could desire. She interrupted him just to say disdainfully that "money wasn't everything", that there were other things in life apart from making money, as her father was happy to do. And when, at the end of reasonable arguments, the lawyer, taking an unusually commanding tone, said: "And if I forbid you to do it, will that change your mind?", she didn't even bother to reply. It only remained for him to desperately repeat: "But why? Why that choice?"

'She was no longer replying; what could she say? She didn't exactly know herself; she just felt that her life depended on it and that she couldn't do anything else.

'Osman's family being situated several thousand kilometres away and the young woman's separated by prejudices more constraining than geographical distance, they got married without their respective parents being present, with only two friends as witnesses, as law dictates, in the town hall of the 20th *arrondissement* where a number of Middle Eastern people reside. From then on she shared her husband's proscribed existence; she kept him company during interminable waits at the Préfecture de Police, in order to definitively regularise his situation, perpetually ending up in a sardonic staff member's office, a bit sadistic, who told them that a document was still missing because one already on file had become obsolete, due to the administration's slowness. French by birth, sure of her rights, more affronted than her husband who'd learned to be resigned, she protested indignantly, without any other result than a quasi scornful smile cast on what the civil servant considered to be a kind of betrayal, or at least a lapse.

'She made unending calls on people she knew to try and obtain their help. And so she came back to see me, believing I might have some influence through the intermediary of my clientele. She had tears in her eyes, shining with anger, while letting me know that she was also pregnant, and that her parents in order to punish her, she insisted, were only sending her derisory subsidies. Her father would have refused to intervene with the authorities, which would have been easy for him to do as a lawyer, because he didn't want it to be known that it was a question of his own Kurdish son-in-law. "You see," he kept repeating to her sadly, "as you make your bed so must you lie on it!"

'But none of that got her down; on the contrary the young girl, until then rather passive in nature, was transformed into an unexpectedly energetic woman. Perhaps it was an effect of my imagination, but it seemed to me that she'd even changed physically; previously rather pudgy with a tendency toward roundness, she'd become more refined, with a firmness in her features, in her body and in her manner of carrying herself. She attends meetings of the Associations of Kurds in France, where she often speaks, exciting the admiration of all the delegates, very grateful that a European by birth is taking their side so energetically. Hugely taken up with her new creed, like all neophytes, she pays attention to everything that affects her husband and more generally her adopted people. Following the example of Osman and his companions, she who was previously so chic, now only wears jeans and faded leather jackets bought in charity shops; she would have dressed like a Turk, chador included, perhaps even converted to Shiism, if Osman, more reasonable, perhaps embarrassed by her excesses, wasn't opposed to it. Out of solidarity with women of the third world she had her luxuriant hair trimmed and curled into multiple plaits, which transformed her into a blonde Negress, albeit that Turkey being a great power had no need of those tokens. She makes rare visits to her parents, which irritate her, mainly in order to leave the baby with her mother. They socialise more comfortably with mixed couples, increasingly numerous among immigrants. She, who never put a foot outside the smart areas of the capital, assiduously frequents the Middle Eastern quarter of the Gare du Nord; she helps Kurdish women being abused by men, she's organised a workshop for new arrivals – which she takes advantage of to familiarise herself with their customs – and a conversation course for men, sometimes so bad at expressing themselves in French that they're practically incomprehensible. It's as if she'd adopted the totality of things contrary to her background, which also frequently happens in mixed couples. As well as fighting European law and jurisdictions represented by her father, in the name of all the disinherited and excluded of the earth, she's given up on European music which she used to enjoy, but which reminds her of her mother. Now she favours reggae and rap, syncopated speech obviously an echo of African griots; she goes into ecstasies over hip-hop, half dance half acrobatics, where dancers, at first using their hands to help, end up spinning round on themselves like tops, with only their head as a pivot. And tags, those stammers which are increasingly taking over the city's buildings, and in which she sees the expression of revolutionary art and imaginary revenge for oppression. She goes out to eat strongly spiced kebabs made from meat pummelled by sweaty hands in smoke-filled greasy spoons, together with Osman and his friends, who happily wear trousers that hang down on their shoes and buttocks like sheep's tails, obliging them to continually pull on their belts. When her friends, whom she sees less and less, tell her to be careful, not being used to that type of food she risks picking up some kind of intestinal problem, she retorts aggressively that in wine-making, grapes were not so long ago crushed by the naked feet of the grape pickers, and in bread-making, dough was kneaded with the naked hand.

'Don't ask me to explain why Christine Brochier married all the dispossessed of the world in the form of Osman Rahmad-

Oglü, homeless and impoverished, from a civilisation so different to her own, from a far-off country whose location on the globe she couldn't exactly find, I wouldn't know how to reply. Why did a young carefree and apparently happy girl, so privileged by fate, decide to renounce a comfortable existence for the life of a pariah, already with child, to embark on that hulk? Because she's pink and blonde and Osman is brown, burned by the sun for generations, and as one says a bit facilely, opposites attract? Perhaps because somewhere in that little Parisian Christian, already attracted to charity, was a hidden aspiration to sainthood? Because often there's something to be admired in the way women marry, together with a husband, the whole of his people? Or, as my secretary archly suggested, because Osman must make love wonderfully? I'm more inclined to believe, quite simply, that she found a warmth in her new milieu which she'd never known with her parents, preoccupied as they were by their work and social life; an only child as well, she hadn't even benefitted from the instinctive solidarity that exists between brothers and sisters. In essence, this is what I think; if there are various forms of solitude, and if the way of dealing with them depends on each individual, the emptiness which they expose is the same for everyone.

'In any case to finish, I have to confess that this time I was once again mistaken. The catastrophe that I feared never happened. After a period of ups and downs experienced by the parents, and because they loved their daughter, they ended up adapting to her new life and even welcoming their grandson with jubilation, which is the commonest outcome. While waiting for something better, they gave her a studio they owned in the 5th *arrondissement*, whose walls Christine decorated with reproductions of the Golden Horn and the Blue Mosque of Istanbul. She resumed her literary studies and planned to teach as soon as she got her degree, as she wanted to support herself independently of parental aid. Osman, who'd put water in his wine, if one can say that of a Muslim, didn't talk so much about combatting Turkish power. He repeatedly tells Christine how delighted he is that fate led him to meet the woman of his life; which is truer than he imagines. He also dreams of resuming his legal studies, seriously this time. While waiting, as he's already partly in the game, his father-in-law has succeeded in finding him a job in a colleague's office. And, when he eventually obtained that precious French identity card, he had tears in his eyes and drank champagne with his parents-in-law. Afterwards, if he identifies as both French and Kurdish at the same time, he knows very well that he'll be more and more French and less and less Kurdish.

'And finally, up to the present time, it doesn't seem the couple is in peril, on the contrary.'

The swing of the pendulum

To begin with, the story's almost banal.
Rose-Marie Dupin, the happy wife of Marcel Dupin, chief executive of a chain of supermarkets, employs a young girl to help the children with their homework, and also to keep her company during her husband's frequent professional absences, and as Dupin's often away, Rose-Marie, a rather reclusive character, spends her evenings alone when the children are asleep, either reading or in front of the television.

Roselyne, the young girl, originally from the Netherlands, has a transparent complexion, often seen in that country due to the permanent humidity in the maritime air, fine features, perhaps too much so, overly light hair which accentuates her evanescent dreaminess, like a pale copy, lacking ink, of a Vermeer character.

Dupin, accustomed to unexciting conquests over the obsequious pool of his own staff, couldn't remain insensible to that exotic femininity; he made urgent advances to which she rapidly gave way, more out of passivity than enthusiasm.

At first the lovers took precautions. In the presence of the wife, they affected a polite indifference. They met in hotels on the outskirts of town, the Novotel de la Porte de Bagnolet or the Sofitel de Montreuil. So their secret was preserved until the day when a friend of the family took it upon himself to expose it. Under the guise of rendering a legitimate service to the couple, he set about destroying them (he did indeed succeed but he didn't reap the expected benefit; probably he was hoping to take over the wife whom he didn't quite realise he was in love with). He used to telephone Rose-Marie anonymously to let her know that her husband had been seen in the company of Roselyne, in a certain restaurant, a certain cafe. However, Rose-Marie, upset, refused to take her informant seriously until eventually he was able to furnish her with decisive proof: he'd just, himself, followed the two of them to the threshold of a charming hotel, Le Home, at La Porte de Vincenne, where she could find them if she hurried, and whose address, Rue Eugène-Gérardand exact position in relation to the Château, he could supply her with.

So she takes a taxi, and this time has to accept the facts.

On her husband's return, Rose-Marie, who was a strong woman, didn't explode, didn't burst into tears; she simply demanded that the guilty parties immediately broke up; as for her, from now on she'd do without a female companion: the traitress must leave the conjugal apartment immediately; otherwise, she threatened, it's she who'd be going. It's a mistake not to be made, which is often made: "it's her or me!", "it's him or me!". This challenge is most often answered: "then it's her!", "then it's him!". To her surprise, far from apologising and retreating, Dupin flatly refused the two injunctions. Son of a small shopkeeper, proud of his success, he'd begun as a simple buyer for the business whose whole network he now directed; given to anger and impulsiveness, red-headed, full-blooded, enriched by generations of wine drinkers and maintained by business lunches, he replied with the same bluntness he employed to close down stores, which had made him notorious amongst his colleagues, who'd nicknamed him, with derision nuanced by admiration, "The Supermarkets' Napoléon". He simply declared that he was keeping his mistress, and her presence in the home, that he wasn't used to being told what to do, that she should resign herself to it, or if she couldn't bear it, she should get out.

She did indeed leave. The next day she packed her bags and having told the children and her sister, she took a train for Avignon where her other sister lived. But when she reached Orléans, she got off and made the journey in reverse. "What'll become of me?" she asked herself; she hadn't any profession, no connections other than those of her husband, whom she admired in spite of everything, and for whom she still cherished some affection, and then, there were the children… in short, she resigned herself.

As usual, Dupin thought he'd triumphed; he even saw it as an added bonus: now his liaison was out in the open, there was no need to hide. He openly slept with Roselyne in her bedroom, took her to restaurants and shows, gave her presents, and took her with him in the ski season.

It was hell for Rose-Marie. She was accustomed to being on her own, but not really, because she used to wait for her husband who always eventually arrived home. Now she was experiencing true solitude, that of indifference.

However all hells, or nearly all, eventually die down. After a period of cold war with her rival, then simply peace, she discovered some fellow feeling for the young girl, as women in harems seem to do, which is a great comfort to them and also a connivance against the male. One winter evening, a week when the children were on holiday in the mountains and Dupin was on a business trip, and when it was particularly cold, she invited her rival to drink a grog in her bedroom, which was the best heated room in the place, then, since they were alone in the apartment, to share the double bed.

Soon, even in fine weather, the moment that Dupin left, after having put the children to bed, they continued to sleep together, chatting agreeably, watching television, nibbling chocolate, and caressing each other in all sorts of ways.

Was it the revenge of a scorned wife? One can't be sure. More probably the affair was a matter of self-discovery and she was only obeying a kind of "swing of the pendulum", where the injured party is no longer happy to return to the point of balance but exceeds it in the other direction.

Dupin finally came to suspect the true relationship between the two women. He created a violent scene with Rose-Marie, this time himself demanding Rose's departure. His wife replied with the same brutal candour that he'd employed with her: she refused to give up the presence of the young girl. The new situation suited her better than the old one. She didn't wish it, but he could leave if he couldn't bear it. And when her husband threatened to cut off support, she replied that she was prepared to work, if necessary, to meet the needs of her new living arrangements.

Why didn't Dupin go? Although he swore that one day he'd make time to find an apartment, and that he wasn't a man to let anything be imposed on him, he never put his threat into practice. Perhaps he really had fallen in love with Roselyne as soon as she became unattainable? Perhaps he'd discovered that he harboured more tenderness for his wife than he'd believed? Perhaps he feared the loss of his children's affection? Perhaps, perhaps… in any case, he continued to undertake everybody's maintenance, and to live in the apartment, where he now occupied the young girl's bedroom.

Nothing appeared to have changed, even in the eyes of their parents and closest friends; those who had any doubts dared not express their suspicions of what they considered to be a disturbing scandal. However the new permutation of roles had profoundly altered the behaviour of each of the characters. Roselyne took on part of the housework and devoted herself more to the education of the children, who were very fond of her; they told their little friends that they were lucky to have two mummies instead of one. The young girl lost a little of her translucent complexion, but she gained some colour. Rose-Marie put on weight, accentuating her appearance as a tall, strong-willed woman standing squarely on her feet. She guides her friend and protégée through the arcana of Parisian fashion, the young Dutch girl, previously provincial in her dress and bearing, has become more elegant and attractive. The two friends scour the department stores for bargains, for jewellery and for the most attractive lingerie, as lovers who want to please each other must do. But if in such relationships, there has to be a masculine and a feminine role, doubtless it's the tall, beautiful Rose-Marie who plays the part of the man and the frail Roselyne that of the woman. They're even less inclined to hide it from Dupin now, and indulge in demonstrations of tenderness, sweet nothings, stolen kisses and quick caresses, in front of him.

As for Marcel Dupin, the Supermarket's Napoléon, after having haughtily refused to do so, every now and then he has to beg for a night, sometimes with one of the women, sometimes with the other. Generally he relies on his usual hunting ground, the female personnel of his businesses, but, surrounded by so many women, he nonetheless feels alone, because he doesn't have what he wanted, and nothing can truly replace an object of desire. Thus, after Austerlitz, comes Waterloo.

The carnivorous rabbit

Like everyone, Nathalie Flesch had chucked flagstones into shop windows on the Boulevard Saint-Michel, set fire to a few cars, helped uproot trees to make barricades against a regrouped police force, insulted the unfortunate Republican Guards with ridiculous cries of "CRS! SS!", joined in meetings where students dumbfounded workers by urging them to demonstrate: "everyone, get out there now!", because "there's a beach under the pavement". But the wind of May '68's pseudo-revolution having completely subsided, the middle class would return to its easy life, the students to their privileges, and the poor to their poverty, only retaining long hair as a benefit.

Nathalie had to agree that, for her, there was no need to dig up the pavement in order to find a beach, she already had one, and even sea and fish, since one of her uncles possessed a flotilla of fishing boats at Saint Malo, and another was a banker like her father. She rediscovered that she was an heiress, quite an attractive one at that, if she took the trouble, which she now wanted to do. By applying henna, she gave character to her hair's somewhat pale redness, and she reconciled with her father. Distraught at the idea of his daughter committing herself to the leftists, he'd threatened to cut her off; she'd countered by threatening to prostitute herself to make a living. Terrified by the prospect of such a dreadful scandal, he'd continued to supply her with a monthly allowance, but he'd broken off with her. The reconciliation allowed Nathalie to obtain an important loan from him, to set herself up.

She was looking for an agreeable and lucrative thing to do. At first she was torn between an art gallery, which was tempting to cosmopolitan women (one became part of "the art world" and one made money), and an estate agents, which paid more but would have been embarrassing for an old May '68 activist. Then she told herself she needed "creativity" more than money. Having educated taste, since schooling is no more forgotten than how to ride a bicycle, she decided to resume her career as a "fashion designer", in other words a chic milliner, which had been interrupted by "the events". In order to do this, she needed to refurbish the vast apartment on the Rue Jouffroy, handed over to her by an aunt who'd moved to Menton, which she'd allowed that braying shameless horde, her "comrades", to sack. They'd used it to discuss the future of "The Revolution", as a convenient place to make love, and to empty the aunt's wine cellar.

While waiting for the end of works on the Rue Jouffroy, Nathalie went to live in Bièvre in another family property, to be honest a very dilapidated house, since nobody had been living there. Fortunately she'd brought Miguel with her, from her days in "The Community", a Chilean whose natural elegance and intellectual gifts had earned him the nickname of King Miguel, which flattered Nathalie. Among Miguel's other gifts was that of DIY; nothing deterred him, nothing was too much for him, neither wood nor stone, nor metal nor cement; nor structural work nor the most advanced finishes.

He built a single flight of stairs in the middle of the living room joining two floors, which gave it an unexpected sense of space. Going down in the other direction, he extended the staircase into the basement where he installed a dining room, adjoining a kitchen dominated by steel and equipped with all the electrical marvels. Patiently collecting similarly coloured shells with which he lined the walls of the bathrooms, he created minuscule aquatic grottoes which brought to mind Facteur Cheval's dreamscapes. Being an advocate of plant-based food, he took time between two projects to scour the countryside for herbs, which he dried for next winter's tisanes… in any event, when the work was completely finished, he couldn't have been more wrong to think that having shared the bed of the mistress of the house, he could speak of marriage; scandalised by that ridiculous bourgeois institution, Nathalie kicked him out.

Next came the turn of the apartment in the Rue Jouffroy. It was then that she met Ludovic Flesch, an architect specialising in renovations. The homonym occurred by chance; Flesch wasn't even a distant relative; he belonged to an Alsatian family who had also emigrated to Paris during the fall of the Second Empire. He'd published an article on "The New Architecture" which gained him a certain notoriety. But in a second article, he'd committed the imprudence of wondering whether the inhabitants of Le Corbusier's "Cité Radieuse", radiant but a bit schizophrenic, were really happy. The human animal loves the street, its smells and noises, the hubbub of his fellow humans reassures him. The Swiss Master had conceived a closed universe, aseptic like his native country, which would be sufficient unto itself, and would contain everything, except life. Flesch concluded by suggesting that a utopia, even a generous one, always ended up making people's lives miserable. From then on he was refused publication and even shunned by all the avant-garde journals. Moreover that dispute, familiar to people in the profession, deprived him of a single new referral.

The architect had been recommended to Nathalie by some friends who'd praised his work. On top of that he was, after all, "a comrade", having also taken part in May '68, without believing in it all that much, it's true. By temperament and philosophy he wasn't inclined to extremes, which according to him could only lead to failure, if not worse. He didn't see why "The Revolution" required the sawing down of trees on the Boulevard Saint-

Michel, the architect in him was sickened by it; nor why votes should be taken by a show of hands, which was anti-democratic and terrorised the moderates, nor why professors getting on in years had to be locked up in the WCs, sometimes reduced to tears from exhaustion and humiliation. One day, all the equipment had been thrown out of the windows of the Jussieu University, to the great joy of the local inhabitants, who shamelessly looted it. In Nanterre, a very expensive and irreplaceable language laboratory was ransacked.

Crowds made him feel vaguely frightened, and for fear of being ridiculed, he'd more often watched others march than joined in himself. He'd been present at numerous meetings of his fellow students, all enthusiastic disciples of "Corbu", Le Corbusier, and of his "machine for living", where it was proclaimed that the "New Society", issuing from "The Revolution", would need a huge amount of adequate living accommodation, so many new architects would be required. Alas, it came to nothing, society remained old, "La Cité Radieuse" a dream, and architecture a profession in crisis. Young architects, already too numerous for the market, had to content themselves with changing a window, removing a partition or enlarging the size of a garage door.

So Nathalie's commission was providential for Flesch. While waiting for better days, highly hypothetical, he had wisely turned towards "interior architecture", which is to say, decoration. But this too, hadn't been a thundering success. It was one of the doubtful benefits of "The Revolution", to have encouraged the belief that everyone's taste was of equal value, in choice of clothes, hairstyles or even house building. So one could bypass the masters and the experts, scorn the professors and the architects, and treat oneself with "Natural Medicines".

The large apartment on the Rue Jouffroy required the construction of a veritable worksite, which Nathalie had the wisdom to realise exceeded her own capacity. Everything there had been laid waste by "The Comrades", broken tiles, curtains torn or disappeared, electric wires ripped out for no apparent reason, rugs burnt by fag ends, carpets spotted with grease or wine stains. The space also needed reorganising; one section for private living, another for a studio, a third for the reception of possible clients.

The encounter with Nathalie was doubly happy for the architect, who apart from his professional difficulties, was going through a painful marital crisis. His young wife, Hélène, was coming to terms with, or rather suffering, an unwanted pregnancy which had made her temporarily give up her job as a trainee pharmacist. She was impatient of, if not disgusted, as much by the inconveniences of her condition (increased by her own negative attitude), as by what she called her husband's egotistical, typically male lack of understanding.

'Men, you'd rather not know; we live side by side and you live in another world. You don't even want to imagine what we're going through, what condition we're in…'

Then, without fear of contradiction, since if Flesch was incapable of understanding, why accuse him of it?

'Then it's pregnancy! We're hit with incapacity, we have to give up work, we're swollen with water, ugly, deformed… then its the delivery, what a horror! We're like animals!'

She'd almost screamed, her eyes filled with tears. Flesch noticed once again how afraid she was; a more common fear than you'd imagine, masked by the prodigious attention given to expectant mothers. Once again, the young woman went over the story of her own mother's first delivery, which was very difficult. She'd been told about it many times, each time her mother's eyes filled with tears, her intolerable suffering ("Why did God make us so narrow, He who's all powerful?" that convinced Catholic complained). She could hardly speak, she remained so terrified of the horrible never-ending nightmare into which she'd been plunged, only ameliorated by the anaesthetic the doctor finally administered. The following births were less painful, but she could have done without them, if her husband, with men's egoism... to say nothing of the miscarriages, in an era when there was no birth control, where all married women were permanently either pregnant or nursing a baby, which procured some respite for them before the next pregnancy, the next delivery, or the next miscarriage. Once, as a child, Hélène was woken up in the middle of the night by the comings and goings of women, who were carrying bowls full of bloody linen. Her father, who seemed to be running around like a headless chicken, was repeating to general consternation: "If she dies, I'll kill you!", without Hélène ever knowing whether he was addressing his remarks to everyone, children included. But that night when the customary drama had almost turned to tragedy, she'd also jubilantly discovered how much her father loved her mother, whom he used to scold on a daily basis. The implication: look, that's how a man ought to love his wife!

Did Flesch love his wife that way? He loved her tenderly, he was happy to be having a child with her, but he wasn't sure that he'd be running around like a headless chicken when she gave birth. What does it mean, to love? He saw what an abyss there was in this regard, which separated men from women, and probably always would separate them. Almost all women want a loving man around them. Perhaps they have that need to be loved in order to accept what's in store for them. One day when she let him put his head on her stomach to feel the infant moving, and he'd questioned his wife about what she was feeling, she'd replied that she felt "inhabited". He felt a kind of anxiety; the only image which came to his mind was that of a solitary worm which he'd picked up during military service in Algeria. He certainly couldn't have borne to be "inhabited".

He wanted to take her in his arms; she thought he was trying to make up for having been the cause of her condition, which was partially true, but mostly he wanted to reassure her. She pushed him away.

'Leave me alone! Please, that's too easy...'

Why do they have to give birth in such torment! What can one say about the scandalous suffering of woman, which has always made men uneasy, even theologians? The editor of the Bible must have invented original sin in order to excuse God! Sickened by his impotence, crushed by guilt, without knowing exactly what for, he had recourse to the usual masculine alibi:

'*My work*... I need to get going... I have to be at Rue Jouffroy...'

He ran off to find Nathalie who was, in fact, expecting him. When she asked about his down in the dumps look, he let himself go, and told her all about the scene he'd just endured, vaguely hoping for some comfort. To his surprise, Nathalie took Hélène's side, whom she wasn't usually slow to put down.

'Your wife's right: it's a horror, the feminine condition... to be a woman, it's humiliating, it's disgusting!'

He regretted having let himself indulge in the untimely outburst, but it was too late, nothing could stop Nathalie once she'd started.

'Look, blood, you know nothing about it, you look in the other direction when you see a drop; we, we live with it, all the time! We begin our lives as women with it, with that bleeding, which only stops when we're no longer women! Periods, every month, several days per month, one's whole life long, from puberty onwards! Sanitary towels! You talk about hygiene! Absorbent underwear, tampons, as if one's a baby in nappies! Who needs wiping!'

She smiled disdainfully, curling her upper lip over two incisors more prominent than the others, which suddenly made her seem childlike, made her look like a rabbit, on reflection not so reassuring, one who wouldn't limit itself to nibbling carrots; a carnivorous rabbit. While she was talking, Flesch eventually realised what she reminded him of: she brought to mind that strange rabbit in *Alice in Wonderland*.

'Your wife's right, but she isn't logical, she shouldn't be having a child.'

Nathalie, herself, didn't want children, because, on top of all that:

'Children, it's crap, endless bawling, you can't sleep in peace, they're shitty all the time, they're always hungry, you no longer have a life of your own, and of course, you can't hope to have a career in the same way as men! A child is a trap for women, I don't want to get my feet stuck in it!'

Later on she told him she'd had two abortions. How come? Flesch asked her in astonishment; why, given her philosophy, had she let herself become pregnant? Out of carelessness, she claimed! She'd been sick after having eaten something that was off, forgetting that she'd just taken her pill, she'd vomited it up. But the second occasion astonished the architect even more. 'Idem,' she replied bitterly.

She too was now talking with so much vehemence that Flesch wondered if the same angst as Hélène's wasn't hidden behind Nathalie's violence and bravado, each of them expressing it in their own way. To put it in a nutshell, both would have liked to suppress their biology.

'Me,' Nathalie proudly declared, 'I take precautions, I don't bother my partners with that! If a woman falls pregnant today, it's she who's really wanted to… it's to keep hold of a man.'

Which pleased the architect who, like most men, didn't know what attitude to adopt when confronted by that unforeseen and monstrous female. "As soon as we touch them they begin to sprout…" He didn't know how to reply to the permanent accusation: "he made me pregnant!", as if they'd been raped after having been chloroformed! Nathalie had the honesty to recognise her share of responsibility in the upset, and to take steps to prevent the consequences.

'All the same they've taken off their knickers!' She laughed. 'Opened their thighs!'

However he was puzzled: how could Nathalie not want a child, not even one, just to see, to find out what it was like? He, himself, was happy to soon be having one; even if he didn't know what to do about Hélène's likely suffering. He preferred to doubt Nathalie's sincerity and to put her violent response down to provocation, for which she had an obvious taste.

Moreover, Nathalie wasn't an easy client; she had strong preferences and the will to impose them. But Flesch preferred her firmness, which obliged him to question his own ideas, to the tyrannical capriciousness of his usual employers, who, often disagreeing with one another, even when spouses drove the architect up the wall, endlessly obliging him to change his plans. From the outset Nathalie had a good sense of space, of matching colours, and moreover only had to convince Flesch, who gladly agreed with her. A pleasant and productive collaboration ensued.

They got together, with pleasure, every afternoon, and could be found leaning over the kitchen table, promoted to a drawing board, or taking measurements in one of the rooms, or even good humouredly sharing some more workmanlike task. With her practical sense, Nathalie had persuaded the architect that they could do a number of small jobs themselves, which would normally have been allocated to different tradesmen and lengthened the time taken to complete the work, as well as increasing the cost. His emoluments, she made it clear, would thus, of course, be augmented. At least, she ironised, his self-respect as an architect didn't prohibit him from taking on the work. Flesch wondered, in fact, if he wasn't in the process of replacing Miguel as an all-round handyman; he reassured himself by saying that, unlike the Chilean, he was being paid, and he wasn't sleeping with Nathalie. He replied gallantly that it was in any case a pleasure to work with such an attractive and intelligent woman. Nathalie, who refused to be outdone by a compliment, retorted:

'You're not bad either.'

She'd used *tu* but he scarcely noticed, all the old '68ers used that kind of familiar language.

While they were working together, sitting side by side, standing up or bending down, Nathalie's lush hair trailed over Ludovic's shoulder. One day, during a coffee break, they got to talking about other things than carpets and curtains.

'Do you know,' Nathalie suddenly said to him, 'most of my friends think we're lovers?'

Surprised and flattered, the architect saw it as an invitation; it was one. He didn't know what to reply, but when several days later his hand brushed against Nathalie's, which she didn't withdraw, he kissed his client, who gladly responded. In order to lie down, they had to get rid of a mountain of tracing paper full of Flesch's designs, which were piled up on the aunt's large four-poster bed. Flesch would always remember that day. Penetrating the foliage of the plane tree veiling the window, the sun fragmented into moving stars, making the old cherry wood of the aunt's furniture sparkle.

Soon they would be making love in the rubble, just as often as they worked in it.

From then on, out of tactfulness, Flesch refrained as much as possible from mentioning his married life in front of his mistress, as already, instinctively, he'd talked about Nathalie as little as possible with his wife. When he was obliged to, he invented things as he went along, navigating between the lies which he forced himself, with difficulty, to make coherent. For example he had to eat dinner twice, picking at his food on each table, or he had to modify his caresses according to the different desires of his two women. But if Hélène, self-absorbed by her pregnancy, only complained in fits and starts about those long afternoons spent in the Rue Jouffroy, accepting with an absent-minded air the same ever-repeated explanation, "it's lucky to have work nowadays!", Nathalie needed no special encouragement to express herself and wasn't so easily reduced to silence. When he visited her, still visibly upset by some conjugal exchange, she accosted him with:

'So, she's still making life difficult?'

And even if on the way over, he'd succeeded in erasing all traces of domestic worry, she interrogated him.

'How's your little bourgeois lady getting on? Does she still have the vapours?'

One day when, despite his resolutions, he let himself speak about the expected baby, Nathalie quipped:

'Are you sure it's yours?'

Struck by his dismay and realising that she'd gone too far, she continued:

'I'm joking. On the contrary, I'm sure it's yours. That idiot would never have had another man…'

As if it was decisive proof of Hélène's foolishness, or worse, a kind of betrayal of the feminine species, which having at last acquired liberty, not to take advantage of it constituted connivance with "the guys". Another time:

'I'm going to tell you something: sooner or later, you're going to leave that idiot, so why not now?'

'You're mad,' he stammered, angry with himself for not answering more brutally, blaming himself for even answering at all. What would become of Hélène? And the child?

'She only has to dump it! If she wants to keep it, that's her business.'

Poor Hélène! He couldn't even imagine her agreeing to terminate the pregnancy. In any case, he'd never abandon her in that condition. Even if she was using the child to hold onto him, it rather flattered him. However Nathalie's vehemence also flattered him, even if she scandalised him by believing him capable of exposing his wife, any woman, to an abortion.

'Anyhow, it's too late,' he said like a coward.

'It's never too late to take your life into your own hands,' Nathalie declared emphatically.

Did Nathalie care about him to the point of wanting to destroy her rival? Or was it simply another challenge that she'd given herself – to conquer the architect – and being used to getting what she wanted, it would be unbearable for her to lose? She'd actually said: "It's crazy! As soon as you touch me, I wet my pants!", which excited his manhood, in spite of his embarrassment at her crude speech, which he generously attributed, in part, to Nathalie's constant provocation. Even more surprising coming from her mouth, she said to him in a moment of abandon:

'We're the most extraordinary couple in Paris: Flesch and Flesch! And we're both redheads! You'd think we were twins, incestuous! Perhaps we'll be suspected by the cops, that would be really funny! It's truly an omen of fate! With you, I wouldn't even have to change my name...'

With that evocation she clapped her hands. Flesch didn't really regard himself as a redhead, more light brown, and he didn't believe in omens; he didn't see how it'd be amusing to be pursued by the police. He smiled politely at her excitement.

'Perhaps we're both redheads, but certainly not from the same father.'

He was mainly thinking of the allusion to one of the feminist demands of the day which declared: I shouldn't have to fight to keep my name. But that also implied: if we were to get married. That idea, even in hypothetical form, surprised the architect, touched him, but also struck home; it suggested Nathalie's attachment, but once again, "she was totting up the bill without the restaurant owner", as is said in their common place of origin, she hadn't asked her lover for his opinion.

They were working without let-up, nearly every day, interrupted only by occasional visits from old friends, always Nathalie's. Although she'd warned that the apartment wasn't ready and there was still lots left to do, they always arrived without notice, which irritated the architect. That's how he met Sylberstein, a Jewish philosopher, perhaps one of Nathalie's old lovers, who went on and on about his politico-metaphysical ideas, and Joséphine, a small swarthy girl, tough and dry as a shrivelled chestnut, Nathalie's best friend it seemed, who in that capacity made scarcely welcome remarks about the works; Ludovic was surprised by Nathalie's friendship with that mean-spirited person, for whom she made every allowance; doubtless she used her as a foil. Miguel, always impeccably dressed, also seemed to inspect everything, but had the good grace to keep quiet. Nathalie fully indulged her "comrades in arms", however she ended up showing them the door with the same affectionate firmness.

But if Nathalie was willing to expend a few minutes on these visits, she nevertheless seemed untiring, and wanting to get things finished as quickly as possible, she kept the architect very late.

'I stocked up the fridge this morning, we can have a bite, then carry on...'

He demurred and sometimes accepted. Once or twice he even stayed the night, after telling Hélène that he was going to discuss a possible job in the provinces. They'd make love all night long. But the guilt he felt for leaving Hélène on her own, out of pure egoism, spoiled his pleasure. He blamed his mistress every time, suspecting her of trying to go further than the terms of their tacit agreement, of forcing him to have to defend himself with Hélène.

The day of his birthday, carefully noted by Nathalie, but which he himself had forgotten, he found a single candle on the table, placed in the middle of a superb chocolate cake from Laporte's. In response to his surprise:

'It's for your first birthday with me,' Nathalie declared peremptorily. 'It's the only one which counts from now on.' Then with a little smile, 'It's as if you've been born a second time.'

That touched him, and irritated him.

'And you, do you love me?'

He wanted to reply yes, I love you, but in the way we agreed; not otherwise. But was that really love?

'To celebrate, we ought to go on a trip together, that'd be great!'

'We decided we had to finish the work first...'

'You mean you don't want to leave your good wife alone!'

'There's that... we'll see later.'

He no longer knew if Nathalie really loved him, with what is commonly called love. Perhaps she'd simply decided to have him for herself, and was in the process of succeeding, like everything she undertook. She seemed to play with love, as with all other things, but with passion ruling the game, sometimes holding back for no reason, just to enrage her lover, sometimes provoking him, leaping on him, but then, in exchange, giving herself unconditionally, "wildly", he noted with pleasure and gratitude; she satisfied her lover, who obtained everything he wouldn't have ever dared ask his wife. That frenzy, which left her almost inanimate, sweating on the pillow, her face exsanguinated, her reddish pallor accentuated to the point of being disturbing, had to be enough for both of them.

They saw each other every day, and it was no longer for work alone that he couldn't wait to get to the Rue Jouffroy. They enjoyed themselves, they laughed a lot together. Nathalie was a redoubtable gossipmonger, good at picking up on others' shortcomings; that superabundance of energy also transmuted into generosity, which made her willing to do anything anybody asked of her, or even didn't ask. Like most artists, Ludovic was only mildly interested in politics, he took little interest in the press, preferring to daydream. Nathalie scoured numerous papers avidly and regularly listened to the radio. The architect often found articles or information concerning his profession that she'd saved for him, carefully cut out and underlined in red pencil. She spontaneously distributed presents to those around her, usually well chosen and suited to the beneficiaries, something which Flesch admired. He, like Hélène, was more reserved and more economical. Coming from a petit bourgeois family, like Hélène, where father was a government official and mother a housewife who didn't contribute to the household costs, for whom thrift was necessity become a virtue, he was fascinated, and frightened, by Nathalie's profligacy with regard to money. A bit envious as well, he'd have liked to be more generous, like her, to scatter money like confetti; he did sometimes, but on the other hand more often he hesitated over a tip, or conversely, was unnecessarily lavish. He made himself leave the small change he was given in all his pockets, but it was a game he played with himself. For her part, Nathalie quite naturally offered her lover designer clothes from luxury labels, costly trinkets, that he'd never have dared pay for himself even if he'd been able to, which Hélène would never have thought of, because she judged them unnecessary. For "nibbles", she went to specialised delicatessens, Chez Flo or places where one could get the rarest and most expensive stuff. Flesch thus got to know those exotic foods better, which he only usually enjoyed in receptions, but eating too much, too quickly, almost without chewing, and standing up, he got stuffed to the point where he couldn't dine in the evenings. He discovered that to eat well, you needed to eat little, and casually, but to do that, you needed to accord less importance to food than he'd learned to do in his childhood. Along with Nathalie's unrestricted largesse, an almost amusing leitmotif regularly recurred, unaccompanied by any particular anxiety: "I'm broke!", always short despite the comfortable paternal monthly payments.

'I don't know how *we* are going to get to the end of the month my poor dear, you're going to have to content yourself with kisses!'

Hélène, who calculated every expense in advance, would never have said:

"I'm broke".

But he no longer knew if he felt more at ease in the security organised by his wife or Nathalie's insouciance.

Even Nathalie's unpredictable bursts of laughter, her sudden explosions, the cries she let out in paroxysms, which ended in a strange kind of whistling, which at first he'd found vulgar, suspecting them to be some kind of theatrical performance, to the point where he'd put his ear to the walls to find out if the neighbours were obliged to hear their lovemaking, now amused him and seemed to be the manifestations of a superior feminine exuberance. Her sneers, which gave birth to a network of pale creases on her forehead and cheeks, that made her look ugly, also reflected the extraordinary mobility of her features. Then he thought of Hélène's beautifully smooth face, almost expressionless, even if it was only a mask, in the way a world full of life is hidden beneath the surface of still water. In her family they were taught not to "make grimaces", supposedly because they'd end up being engraved on one's face.

'If an angel passes over just at that moment, you'll stay that way all your life.'

But Flesch no longer knew what gave him the greatest happiness.

He was happy with Nathalie, he had to admit it, even if it was on her terms. He would have been more completely happy if she'd kept to the contract that she herself had imposed. He decided not to ask himself any more questions that he neither could, nor wished, to answer. But Nathalie didn't understand things that way; she did ask questions and responded to them in a sarcastic manner often unfavourable to her lover.

'Me, I'm not like your wife,' she threw at him, without him having asked her (he'd have been well advised not to), 'I've lived like a man and I certainly count on continuing to do so!'

When a woman says that she wants to live like a man, it's not principally a question of money or power, but of sex; it means she wants to make love with whomever she pleases.

Flesch could have guessed as much; he knew that Nathalie had spent time in a "community", where the principal aim was to have sexual partners in common, that's to say free choice of the men by the women, since the men already enjoyed that freedom.

May '68 was above all women's revenge. She told Flesch about it in detail, which he'd have preferred not to hear, that she'd even created a kind of calendar: on Mondays she'd receive so-and-so in her bed; Tuesdays someone else; Wednesday, etc. There was even a day of rest devoted to her masseur, with whom sometimes… true or false, she wanted to tell him all about the way she'd organised her love life. In principle he wasn't opposed to that new freedom for women, even if his heart was reluctant to follow his reason. Why should it only be men who had the right to go from one bed to another without too many scruples? So if Nathalie wanted to shock him, it failed. He simply didn't want to debate the matter with her. By his impassiveness, he'd avoid giving her the occasion for sarcastic comments on "his hopeless prejudices". However, Nathalie was too acute not to see, behind that feigned indifference, not a veritable acquiescence but a kind of flight. Flesch was, it's true, one of those people one would call a hypocrite, who prefer not to name things for fear of increasing their reality. In his family and with his parents' friends, one never spoke openly of the details of anyone's love life. But Nathalie, on the contrary, needed to provoke Flesch, to force him to acknowledge his defeat in order to be sure of her own total victory. Just now, she neither had the time nor probably even the desire to make love with anyone else, but she had to make clear to her lover that she could do so if she chose to. Even that, Flesch went along with, though he wasn't immediately happy, and preferred not to think about it. But she also wanted to make him feel uncomfortable.

'In other words, you're deciding not to know,' she insisted ironically.

He hesitated.

'There's nothing to know, I know. But I don't want to have to think about you sleeping with someone else every day, that it might have already happened…'

For several weeks they'd hardly left each other's side, sitting by the kitchen table or working with their hands, they often ate together, sometimes slept together, made love when they felt inspired, which was always marvellous. The old apartment's heating, which they hadn't yet been able to deal with, dispensed a capricious amount of warmth, but they only noticed it later, when they were frozen. But, why does a woman who wishes to behave like a man, think it's necessary to treat men the way that *some* men (of which the architect wasn't one) treat women, that's to say in an execrable manner? Why when a woman has gained her liberty, does she feel obliged to exercise it unceasingly in relation to all men, including her companion, even if he sincerely accedes to her new prerogatives? This argument demonstrated some naiveté if not injustice, for in relation to whom could this new freedom be exercised, other than men? With whom did she need to confirm it if not the man closest to her, that's to say her husband or her lover?

In fact, beyond their entente in bed, hostilities between Flesch and Nathalie had never ceased. At first tempered by politeness, curiosity, the spontaneous attraction between the sexes, and the effort Nathalie made not to interfere too much with the architect's exercise of his profession. As soon as they became lovers, those elementary precautions were pointless and Nathalie was able to give free rein to her true philosophy. Once their intimacy was established, she suggested to him as a kind of game that they fight with each other, physically, asserting that she'd win, because she'd learnt to defend herself against rapists. After the surprise of that extraordinary hand-to-hand encounter, he was only moderately satisfied. Especially since having been a rugby player and being a lot heavier, he quickly triumphed and pinned his adversary to the floor, and Nathalie, bad sport that she was, almost furious, then bit and scratched him, which annoyed Flesch because of the marks which risked being noticed by Hélène.

After making love, both Flesch and Nathalie liked to lie in bed, smoking, dreaming, drinking coffee when they had the energy to make it. On one particular day, in order to drink more easily, he'd gone to find another pillow in a next-door bedroom and propped himself up comfortably.

'That's it, guys,' Nathalie acidly threw at him, 'one pillow for the chick, two for them!'

The architect, his mind still foggy, stammered that he didn't know she wanted one… that she usually slept without any at all… that he hadn't realised she now wanted two…

'That's exactly what I was saying,' she cut in, 'guys, you only think about yourself.'

Finally snapping back, for once he became angry, all the more so because he wasn't sure he was in the right.

'I'm not all men, I'm Ludovic, your lover, I refuse to engage in this permanent, generalised battle with you…'

'I'm only defending myself.'

'But I'm not attacking you!'

'But yes! But yes! All the time… because you're a man, that's how you're made.'

'So, whether I like it or not, I'm your enemy, and you treat me as such.'

'Yes, it's a bit like that.'

'Listen, Nathalie, I admit there are, or rather there were, serious problems between "guys and chicks", as you put it,' on pronouncing those words, he noticed that he hated that way of referring to men and women, 'we have tyrannised, exploited, and humiliated you for centuries, it's true, but we've equally well desired, loved and dreamed of you! And moreover we've proclaimed that from now on, we must "make love, not war", so it no longer applies!'

'No, because the oppression of women by men has never ceased.'

'Perhaps,' but then he threatened her, 'one can't make love and war at the same time!'

'Basically, you want to fuck us, protect us, even support us, on condition that we remain submissive. If we defend ourselves, then nothing works, then no more kisses, no more love! Well so be it, no more love... or at least another kind.'

Flesch didn't know what to add; he never had the last word, he thought ruefully. Probably she wasn't altogether wrong, but nor was he. Or worse, they were both wrong; perhaps paradise was forever lost? Perhaps it had never really existed between men and women? How could it have been otherwise? To what kind of love was she alluding? He didn't have time to ask; in a sudden about-face, she changed the subject.

'Good, let's leave all that,' she continued. 'When are you going to take me out to dinner?'

It seemed to be an offer of a truce, it wasn't; on the contrary she was pressing on another sensitive point. Moreover she was smiling, curling her carnivorous rabbit's upper lip. Because of Hélène, Flesch restricted going out and being seen together as much as possible, which would have revealed their intimacy. As he didn't respond quickly enough, she repeated:

'So?'

'Whenever you like... next week?'

'Why not this week?'

'If you like... except Thursday, of course.' (The day he devoted to Hélène.)

'I know about Thursdays,' she said dryly. 'So, tomorrow.'

'Tomorrow.'

'8 o'clock at Lipp's?'

'Why Lipp's? Good OK, at Lipp's.'

One couldn't have chosen a more public place.

She arrived very late as usual, dressed as Barbarella, the famous comic book heroine, black leather and plastic, chains and silver-plated costume, her breasts visible under transparent black gauze, and above all a skirt so short and tight that one was amazed she could move, and which allowed one to make out the most intimate details of her anatomy.

'Hello!'

She greeted him at the door in a very loud voice, as if she was simultaneously addressing everyone present. She immediately became the centre of attention for all the regulars, and judging by the obvious body language of a woman who feels looked at, she was visibly enjoying it. Like most men, Flesch was flattered by the interest his companion excited and at the same time ill at ease, almost threatened by the effervescence of the males and the ironic hostility of the females, infuriated by Nathalie's monopolisation of masculine regard. He couldn't stop himself from showing his dissatisfaction, reacting in spite of himself to Nathalie's provocation, aimed more at her lover than the others.

'Don't you think your skirt is too… exotic?'

He succeeded in not saying too short or too provocative; he'd be met with a quick riposte on his prejudices, his hypocritical puritanism, etc. But Nathalie obviously wasn't fooled.

'I'll dress how I like, I couldn't give a damn what others think,' which was clearly contradicted by her outfit. And since Flesch refrained from replying, knowing that when it came to the question of freedom, he couldn't win, she pushed her provocation even further.

'I sometimes go out with no knickers.'

'Why do that?' he asked in a voice which he forced himself to keep steady.

'Because it feels good, that's it! Have you never gone swimming naked? It's delicious, no? Because of the direct contact with the water; without knickers, one can feel the air circulating between one's thighs.'

'That's true, but in the water there's no risk of a gust of wind…'

'Exactly, that increases the pleasure. You see,' she continued, 'how hypocritical you are: you know perfectly well that, under our skirts, actually we're naked! We're not in any way protected by that little bit of spider's web called knickers! And that's the way you like to see us! You foolishly resisted when we began to wear trousers! Women were sacked from businesses for that, they were forbidden in administrative offices. We want to be able to choose to wear skirts, trousers, or nothing at all!'

Carried away by that wicked demon that got into her on certain evenings, she didn't spare him a thing. A freelance photographer was offering his services to diners; she made a sign to him without consulting her companion, who showed his displeasure.

'You're scared we'll be seen together in the photo? It's because of your wife?'

As he wasn't replying:

'There are times, I wonder if you really love me, if you dare to love me...'

Then, raising her voice, as if playing a part:

'Do you love me?'

'Yes... of course, but please, there's no need to take the whole room into confidence!'

'I couldn't care!'

'I could.'

Flesch concentrated on his plate; they ate for a moment in silence.

'Good, I'm fed up, I've had enough,' Nathalie declared. 'I want to go home.'

'Straight away? Let's finish our meal first...'

'I'm not hungry anymore.'

She left enough to feed a family on her plate, which annoyed Flesch, having always been told to "finish what's on your plate!", an injunction which Hélène continued.

They went back to Nathalie's little English car, left in the car park on Boulevard Saint-Germain. He accompanied her to Rue Jouffroy, intending to stop there and not go up to the apartment. As if she'd read his mind, she stopped alongside the pavement of an adjacent road.

'We can say goodbye here, kiss me.'

He kissed her lightly.

'Not like that, a real kiss.'

He gave her a real one, following which she demanded "a cuddle".

'Here?'

'Yes, here.'

'Let's go up to your place.'

'No, it's more fun here.'

Looking round for passers-by, luckily rare at that time of night, he slipped his hand under Nathalie's short skirt, who thankfully came very quickly. She wanted to do the same for him, he held back her hand.

'Tomorrow.'

'Whatever,' she said, suddenly dreamily, 'I wouldn't have believed you'd dare.'

'I did dare,' he replied unhappily. 'What does that prove?'

It's true that he didn't dare to fully love Nathalie, for both good and bad reasons. How could he, with his moribund business, meet the extravagant tastes of his mistress? As for being supported by her, that idea scandalised him. But those weren't the real reasons; Nathalie frightened him as an unpredictable unknown.

She placed a quick kiss on the architect's cheek, as if they'd spent an unclouded lovers' evening.

'I'm leaving the car with you; I can't be bothered to take it home. See you tomorrow.'

She left him, skipping along like a goat.

Why that unending way of putting him to the test? Hadn't they explored every aspect of themselves? Didn't they each know the requirements and limits of the other. How often had she repeated:

'I'm warning you! Making love twice a week on the same day, à la mummy-daddy, is too little for me. That doesn't interest me, I have a right to pleasure! To the real thing!'

Silence being Flesch's usual manner, he didn't generally reply to that kind of proclamation. Moreover, he didn't really understand what she was talking about. So was he stopping her from taking her pleasure? In what did this "real" pleasure consist? In fact, like all women, she demanded that he provide it. Women don't just want to reach orgasm, they expect men to deliver it. Apart from the fact that she was assuming a mastery that he didn't always possess, she didn't see that she was contradicting herself: she proclaimed her total liberty yet she continued to expect care and support from the man, including sexual fulfilment. With whom, against what, was she really arguing? Against the male sex or against her own?

The baby not being very well established, Hélène had to be admitted for observation. As he seemed upset, perhaps to console him or ironically, she said:

'But you have Nathalie.'

So she knew? She'd said it in a detached tone. Even though he'd lived intimately with his wife, he didn't know whether he really understood her. Did he know Nathalie any better? However, deep down, he was sure that the relationship with a wife was the most important thing in the world. For example he was angry with "The Chestnut", and with Nathalie, for having belittled it.

This fantasy, this madness of Nathalie's, which pained him and made his visits difficult, wasn't completely displeasing to the architect. Without doubt, driven by the frustration that Hélène's pregnancy had caused, it was that which had first thrown him into Nathalie's open arms. Then he'd been taken up by a whirlwind, which disturbed him but carried him giddily along to undreamed-of happiness. Nathalie loved everything, wanted everything ("Everything, straight away!" Perhaps it wasn't such a stupid idea). With her, he learnt to love in a completely new way; there were other happinesses than the creation of a really good design!

But Hélène's inchoate appetites reassured him. Daughter of a pharmacist from Larzac, where Flesch had in the past gone to stir up the population, she had nothing of a Bovary. Until that untimely pregnancy, she was happy with her fate, with her husband and with herself. To conform with current trends, thinking it would give her pleasure, he'd suggested that she keep her maiden name on official documents. She mildly said yes, all the same, signed "Flesch" on her first application for a chequebook as a married woman. It was Flesch who always suggested where to go and what trips to take, most of which she refused. Ah, it wasn't she who'd take risks just to test him and herself! He'd wondered if Hélène hadn't suspected his affair with Nathalie, despite his explanations; if yes, he was persuaded that with a wife's confidence, she was capable of not showing it, while waiting for better days.

Nathalie demanded that he choose. Passion is decidedly unviable, because of its exclusivity. Why the devil did he have to choose between the two women? Can't one love two women at the same time? Yes, yes! One can! That question, which surprised him, made him smile with pleasure. Until then he'd refused to put it clearly, but his efforts to stop thinking about it proved that it had to be answered. Must he choose between love without passion, Hélène, and passion without love, Nathalie? Must he give up Hélène's slightly cold, classical beauty, the almost translucid perfect oval of her face, always underlined by a band around her jet-black hair, which had immediately excited his admiration. He'd fallen in love with Hélène, as one does with the Parthénon, as an architect does; he'd asked for her hand almost without knowing her, the way an art lover buys a painting on a whim. Then he'd discovered her patience, her kindness towards everybody, even those who scarcely merited it, which sometimes annoyed her husband but ultimately appeased him, inclined him to a more ironic view of things and people. And above all there was his quasi-certainty, perhaps absurd, as Nathalie had slyly suggested, that she'd be incapable of betraying him.

Then there was Nathalie, permanently at war, carried away, provocative, curious, indiscreet, unfaithful on principle, who one day would slip through his fingers; Nathalie, her vitality, her sudden crazy laughter, which for a moment restored her childlike face and which drew in her companion, ravished him. Why did he have to renounce one or the other, when he needed both? But how to convince each of them that both were indispensable in their own way?

He went to see Hélène, who was patiently waiting for him. She'd entered into that blissful languor which precedes giving birth, where the future mother, her anxieties assuaged, seems to be looking inside herself, her features swollen, her whole body transformed in order to prepare itself for nourishing the future baby. Flesch was moved by the trusting smile with which she welcomed him. She was tired but happy with her day. Carrying her bump in front of her, she'd searched the specialised shops to complete the baby's trousseau. The future father looked with amused curiosity at those lilliputian clothes. He filled a tiny bootie with one finger; Hélène took it back and carefully tidied it away in a shoebox. Then she seized his hand and placed it on her enormous abdomen, on the point of bursting like an overripe pomegranate.

'My darling,' she murmured, without Flesch knowing whether she was addressing him or the child who happened to move at that moment.

How do they, the architect marvelled, transform a spoonful of slightly salty seminal fluid into a complete living being, who'll soon develop into a man or woman? If I was a woman, I'd be immensely proud of that prodigious power, of that miracle of miracles, and I think, deep down, they are so proud. One only has to see their triumphant air when they carry their full belly in front of them, then later the infant's pushchair, up to the feet of passers-by. And now they no longer want to make babies! How could Nathalie deny herself that prowess of nature!

'Nothing's more like a pregnant ewe than an expectant mother,' she'd declared disdainfully one day, obviously targeting Hélène.

'Of course,' she quickly added, 'a man's erection is no different from a ram's.'

Albeit that ewes also give birth to new beings, and even plants do, it's no less fascinating a mystery. Why is it necessary to go against biology? To the point of disdaining it? Must the act of love and its consequences be refused, because we share it in common with animals? In which case we should stop eating, breathing and all the rest… to accept one's animality is to get closer to nature, or to God if one prefers; in any case whoever loves love, loves life.

The next day, he telephoned Nathalie to tell her that he couldn't come. He preferred to avoid talking about the evening at Lipp's. He made the excuse that he had to go to Lochacq's, the director of a gallery specialising in African art, for a possible small assignment. In fact, he had to accompany his wife to the gynaecologist. Nathalie put the phone down on him.

Moreover, the work in Rue Jouffroy was coming to an end. It had been slowed down a bit by a new idea that Nathalie had: a guest bedroom! She wanted a guest bedroom to put up possible stray cats amongst her friends, of whom Flesch disapproved. She turned once more to her father for supplementary funds. He refused; she coldly declared that her father was a shit, to Ludovic's indignation, scandalised by her ingratitude. Even in May '68 he was astonished to hear his co-disciples in the school insult their parents… while at the same time continuing to rely on them for support. For his comrades, born with a silver spoon in their mouth, it was simply their entitlement; for him, nothing was due by right.

Nathalie decided to organise a house-warming party. She sometimes threw parties in memory of old times, to try to have a bash again. Flesch didn't like those occasions. When Nathalie reconnected with old solidarities, she seemed alien to him. He was being unfair, and he was angry with himself for being so. He remained silent or let himself make a few uncalled-for remarks, inevitably followed by Natalie's remonstrances.

'You were odious with my mates!'

That evening, however, was to be special; because of the importance of the event, he decided to be more cooperative than usual.

'Does Tuesday the fifteenth suit you?'

'Yes, yes… as long as it's not Thursday…'

'I know,' she said dryly.

Nathalie wasn't there when the first guests arrived; she was still at the hairdressers. It fell upon him to play the role of host with bad grace. He'd often taken up Nathalie on her systematic latenesses. She denied that they were intentional; she had things to do, time passed, she thought she could just do this and that, etc. Flesch strongly suspected that it was one of the means she utilised, more or less consciously, to exercise control over others.

When Nathalie finally arrived, there were "ohs!" and "ahs!". She'd had her hair buffed into an impressive gold crown; once again he admired what women were able to do with their hair. It was only then that "The Chestnut", rivalling Nathalie with her lateness, made her appearance. She trumpeted all around:

'Ah, I nearly didn't come! My period hasn't finished.'

All the women had made real efforts to glam up, often successful, sometimes grotesque, the usual feminine carnival, that Flesch didn't hate but just about tolerated. In celebration of the new freedoms they'd allowed themselves unprecedented extravagances: Mexican ponchos, Spanish stoles, Sahelian gandouras and, to Flesch's horror, all sorts of caps, from train mechanics' to Canadian trappers'. A stall of exotic dolls from all over the world. Most had naked shoulders down to their breasts (how is it they never get cold, with naked legs and naked chests!). Some having got rid of their hair, resembled male transvestites with overgrown hips, which the architect deplored. He admired femininity and didn't like the lack of distinction, which perhaps disturbed him; he preferred a woman to be a woman and man to be a man. There was even a "judge" (how does one say it correctly: madame *la* juge or madame *le* juge?) who was wearing enormous earrings, and to whom all the ladies spoke with deference, despite her profession despised by the leftists (she probably practises her profession very well, Flesch thought, but, despite myself, I can't take a judge wearing earrings seriously!), she irresistibly brought to mind *La Vache-qui-rit*. On the masculine side, it was less striking. Still some long hair, longer than the women's, because that again was one of the doubtful benefits of May '68 (which they were wrong to take up, washing it less often than women, it always seemed dirty), jeans, torn of course or fake labels, trainers, in case there was a police raid, you had to be ready to run, but most were wearing suits and ties, the bourgeois elite's uniform, which they were now part of, having inherited, according to the usual fate of students, the privileges that they previously denounced. Flesch, who'd changed his calculated architect's casualness (large cashmere pullover and elephant leg trousers) for a classic suit that he hated and a tie which constricted his neck, regretted his efforts at grooming.

Nathalie had refrained from adding to the invitation cards, as in the past, "feel free to fuck"; she had even taken care, he noted with amusement, to lock the bedrooms and to put ash trays out everywhere. On the other hand she'd kept the portrait of Che Guevara in a beret with a red star.

Without a glance in Ludovic's direction, Nathalie danced the whole evening very obviously with Miguel, looking superb in his black velvet suit. When tiredness, alcohol and the "joints" ("have a joint, it's cool") knackered the dancers' legs, a circle formed to discuss and review the usual subjects, as if nothing had changed.

Sylberstein, in espadrilles, long hair on a roll-neck sweater, concertina trousers, expounded; he denounced the revival of the Clerical Reaction, although this time it was really the end.

'Religions are nothing more than old fairy tales that hinder humanity's march toward progress.'

Flesch wasn't far from thinking the same about the setback caused by religions, without agreeing that they were going to disappear any time soon, but he had a bone to pick with the philosopher, since Nathalie, who didn't know how to keep quiet, had perfidiously told him a nasty comment made by Sylberstein. The philosopher had decided that the architect was "not very bright", and for him, that was all that mattered: "being bright".

'All utopias end up being fairy tales, indeed,' Flesch said, 'leftism included...'

Sylberstein contented himself with a shrug of his shoulders. However the reply would have been obvious: "we all need utopias, to exorcise our demons", but that would have been to confess that he too went along with the believers. If a certain number of leftists had returned to the religious tradition of their fathers, even to the point of mysticism, it wasn't by chance. Sylberstein, who like most Jewish intellectuals believed himself obliged to be more universalist, more humanist, more socialist, more pacifist than his *confrères*, which made them feel guilty and annoyed, was now explaining seriously that, anyway, only violence could bring peace on earth. (Jews, Flesch thought, it's always the same intellectual arrogance; even the most secular take themselves to be the chosen people...) Flesch immediately blamed himself for that xenophobic idea. All the same what is it that keeps pushing them forward? Why are they involved in all the uprisings: the Bolshevik Revolution, the Spanish Civil War? They often lose their lives, Jesus already...

'I've thought a lot about whether I should have gone undercover and joined the Red Brigades. By philosophy, I share the opinions of the comrades who voted no. But I'll regret to the end of my days not having been "part of the action".'

Flesch noted with irritation the vagueness of the formulation, when what it meant was "killing"; because in the end, to throw a bomb into a crowd, is that anything other than murder? And the contradiction of all terrorism: killing people whom one claims to be fighting for. But he went quiet again, he knew that the discussion would be short-lived. Sylberstein would have dogmatically explained to him that it really was necessary "to break eggs in order to make an omelette", an argument that Flesch abhorred due to its cruel idiocy; the eggs in question being human lives, it's not certain the omelette would be edible.

'You did the right thing,' Flesch said to him half-jokingly, 'you'd have been in prison by now, and we wouldn't have had the pleasure of your company.'

An ecologist explained that one could perfectly well do without nuclear energy: all that would be necessary was to install solar panels on all the roofs (so much for aesthetics). Far from applauding him for this important information, Joséphine sneered nastily:

'Guys, they snore and they know it all.'

'You're too easy on them,' added a beauty in a poncho, whom Flesch had never seen before, 'you're forgetting their other noises.'

The most incongruous figure in the party was a young baby-faced Catholic priest, whose thin blond hair made him look almost bald, his eyes were drowned behind the thick lenses of his glasses, which enhanced his exotic appearance. He'd been taken away in a CRS van, where the police, even more furious at the involvement of a priest (their usual ally) with the agitators, beat him up and broke his glasses. He came out of the Panthéon police station, an atheist. Meeting his future wife in the corridors of the Sorbonne ended up converting him back to the faith: like many Christians on the left, he devoted himself from then on to the third world.

'I gather millions to Christ there,' he said.

He was warmly congratulated for having finally discovered the truth. An exactly opposite case was scornfully cited, a notorious communist ex-director of the CP, a Stalinist, "ugh!", known for the number of exclusions he'd overseen, who'd himself reconverted to religion, bringing with him the same exclusive zeal.

Flesch, however, couldn't see the difference between the two histories.

Naturally, sex was talked about a lot, while at the same time affecting an indifferent attitude to the subject. If it was so unimportant, why talk about it so much? The women presented a perfectly united and offensive front.

'All guys are potential rapists,' the journalist stated.

Why do they have to exaggerate so much? Flesch wondered… although, had he been a woman…

The men clumsily tried to defend themselves, joking or outdoing each other. The ladies, while saying the opposite, because everything American was scorned, were visibly nostalgic for those New York marches where demonstrators solemnly burnt their bras, demanding that rapists have their balls cut off. They wouldn't want to become "sexual objects" again, for anything in the world! What did they want to be? Flesch wondered perplexed, who was pained at the mention of burning bras. If they no longer wished to be sexual objects, why so much effort to capture the attention of men? Aren't those exposed areas of skin an invitation, as in food sampling, have a taste, the rest is of the same quality. What about those naked shoulders, those half unveiled breasts, those minuscule skirts. Since they acquired their vestimentary freedom, hadn't there been an unprecedented surge in lingerie, make-up, scent, everything capable of attracting, trapping, and keeping hold of men! If one adds the shelves devoted to beauty, the various jewels and trinkets, a good half of department stores is devoted to feminine glamour! Have they ever stopped their affectations, their alluring postures? Are women's magazines anything other than seduction manuals? So what! All living beings caress and dance with each other! Men too, we have our own displays in front of them. Why this hypocrisy? They proclaim that they no longer want to be women. As if that depended on them! As if one could go so far against nature! It's not enough to wear "unisex" clothes and mess up their hair…

However they like to congratulate themselves on being natural, all things pagan, which the new young girls live by.

'Me, I admire them,' declared a journalist who, glass in one hand, cigarette in the corner of her mouth, which made her constantly blink, succeeded in smoking, drinking and eating simultaneously and continuously the whole night long.

'They're spontaneously freer than us, they're proud of their bodies and they show it.'

(Are they actually so sure of themselves? This insistence on their form, isn't it rather a sign of insecurity, just as much as in their elders?)

'They mainly like to show their asses!' one of the males chuckled, whose alcohol level had made him imprudent.

'If you go on like that, your eyes'll be torn out,' Joséphine calmly said to him.

'Women,' the journalist added (she pronounced the word emphatically), 'we've been too soft with guys. That's all over, we've found our marbles… and we're going to use them! Nobody's going to grope our backsides with impunity!'

"Angry does," Flesch tried to reassure himself. But he thought he could see so much resentment, almost hatred, that he felt sorry, above all for them. Several thousand years of servitude aren't erased by a semi-revolution! This is the worst time for the pendulum to swing back. Where would they and we be going, if the deer were to make a furious charge?

Out of masculine solidarity, he couldn't resist the desire to help the downtrodden. He described, with restrained pleasure, how one of the young female consultants who happened to be working in his agency, where she was obliged to adopt a strictly rigorous dress code, went home at the end of the day to take off her long skirt and Claudine collared blouse, and went back out wearing a micro-skirt for a walk on the Boulevard Montparnasse. It was she who'd told him that, with an air of naïve triumph.

'So what?' Joséphine continued. 'She's affirming her freedom by getting rid of her straightjacket, what's so astonishing? It's the most natural thing in the world.'

'Sure,' conceded the architect, 'but is it necessary to exhibit one's thighs to affirm one's freedom?'

However he knew the response. She wants to say to men: "You've tormented us enough for centuries: 'Hide your breasts! Hide your bums! Hide your bodies!' So now that we're free, we're showing it all! Our sex has been the place, the excuse for our repression, it will become the banner of our liberty!" Like children who've been forbidden to pronounce swear words and who, because of that, delight in repeating them. He remembered an English woman, seen in Soho in London, sporting an enormous butterfly made of multicoloured material in the exact position of her vulva. But perhaps she was just a bit more exhibitionist than average for her generation, who were already pretty well endowed?

He thought he'd said enough, he preferred to keep quiet as usual.

'All the same, what gets me about them, are the sanitary towels,' said another professor timidly.

(It's unbelievable what some professors in those circles are like, Flesch noted; it's understandable though: they rebelled against their masters only to succeed them; the way bourgeois kids rebel against their parents and then go on to be senior administrators and bosses of businesses, often family run. The May '68 revolution was about students as well as women.)

Flesch had difficulty in understanding what sanitary towels had to do with the discussion. The professor explained that, in his lecture theatre, the skirts were so short that – although those ladies kept pulling them down to their knees – he could see their knickers, which didn't displease him, not particularly… but not the sanitary towels!

'And have you asked them why they wear such short skirts?' Flesch asked slyly.

'Yes, of course, to every class; it's always the same reply or rather refusal to reply: my question is an old man's issue; the mere fact that I ask it proves that I'm past my sell-by date; friends of their own age find it completely normal.'

'And is that really true?' Flesch insisted ironically, who didn't remember having been any the less stirred when he was an adolescent, by an exposed breast or a glimpse of thigh.

'Perhaps… I haven't asked them, although, the students sitting next to them, their comrades, can't have the same plunging view that I have.'

However everyone agreed that the essential thing was freedom, of speech and action. All the rest followed. They were often all talking at the same time, cutting across each other, talking over one another; supposedly because they'd "taken the floor", they never let go.

'You see,' Athanase Angélopoulos explained to Flesch – he was a Greek who bore an astonishing resemblance to a film pirate, dark and bony, pockmarked face, and who let it be understood that he'd been a general with the partisans in his country – 'the Revolution is above all this: if I want to fuck your wife, I do it… and I tell you about it.'

Flesch had to make a big effort not to show his displeasure at this outburst. He raised his voice to ask his interlocutor:

'And me, I can fuck yours too?'

'Of course,' Athanase quickly replied, who wasn't married.

Dancing and drinking resumed, a lot of cigarettes and "joints" were smoked, all the more furiously by the women than the men, which made Flesch, who had a sensitive throat, uncomfortable. Before the "Revolution" a man who dared to smoke without having asked the women present for permission, would have been taken for a boor. Which of today's women would worry about knowing whether she risked putting anyone out? The party-goers rejoiced again in rehashing, with jubilation and boastfulness, common memories of the combatants of the Rue Gay-Lussac and the Boulevard Saint-Michel.

'You remember when the CRS… we thought that… it was fun!'

All the big problems were brought up: nuclear energy, ecology, the consumer society (which these nouveau riche spat upon), ignoring the fact that the vast majority of men still weren't benefitting from it.

Of course, save for the solemnly reaffirmed grand principles against common enemies, people didn't agree about anything. In view of their supposed fundamental fraternity and under the guise of openness, or even being helpful, they gave voice to all the nasty remarks and horrible things they wanted to say to each other. They accused each other of dark machinations in the interests of obscure groups in which one or other of them were "Trotskyite Submarines", "Stalinist Commies", "Nostalgic Talas". The vegan végétal*iens* bitterly reproached the plain végétar*iens*, or the reverse, Flesch wasn't sure he understood the difference.

The party wore off around 4am, it was about time. Flesch was suffocating in a thick cloud of smoke, not daring to say anything, even trying not to cough for fear of seeming to undermine the freedom of the guests, as "it's forbidden to forbid", even if the freedom of others is infringed.

When the last of the company withdrew, including Miguel, the architect indicated that he was also ready to leave.

'Stay a bit longer,' Nathalie asked, 'besides, I've got something to say to you.'

She sat down comfortably in an armchair, right opposite him, as if she was just beginning a second party, and to Flesch's displeasure who was falling asleep, she lit another cigarette.

'You've heard the news,' she said quickly as if she was savouring it, 'Miguel's done very well: he's just been appointed Financial Attaché to the Chilean Embassy, he's in charge of economic relations with French businesses.'

She had a knowing smile.

'He's making lots of money.'

And as Flesch wasn't saying anything:

'Can you believe it,' she added with apparent detachment, but watching the architect's face, 'he suggested I go and live with him in Chile.'

'And what did you reply? What do you think about it?'

'Nothing... I don't know.'

Then, after a silence:

'I'm going to tell you something,' she murmured with a sudden frown, as often happened with her, passing from broad sunlight to a sky obscured by clouds, 'you're never going to leave your wife.'

'I never said I was going to leave her.'

'I'm speaking for myself.'

He refused to spend the night in the Rue Jouffroy despite the late hour.

Luckily, Hélène didn't wake up when he slipped into the conjugal bed.

Nathalie had additional plans for the newly renovated apartment: other than parties for old friends, there were going to be Penguin Parties, named that way because everybody, men and women, had to dress up smartly, in black, including Nathalie who would provisionally renounce her vestimentary fantasies. On the insistence of his mistress, Flesch also attended them, at least the first one.

'They're useful,' Nathalie said to him peremptorily, 'for you too,' she added.

He was bored to death. He didn't know anybody. There was an art dealer there, a "gallerist", as one says nowadays, dealer being a bit vulgar, a film producer, the director of a fashion house, an importer of agricultural machinery, several others whose names and occupations he couldn't remember, but he guessed why Nathalie had chosen them: she was expecting something from each one of them. The gallerist, a fat, apparently stupid gentleman, who invariably replied to every question about a painting, "ah, I like it, I like it" but who owned, according to Nathalie, a huge house in the Midi with a park containing open-air sculptures from all the best contemporary artists, and he could buy drawings she'd got from her family; the director of the fashion house could order clothing "creations" for her; the producer, perhaps a sugar daddy, in any case nearly deaf, into whose ear a ravishing young woman was transmitting what the other guests were saying, might be interested in a film project on fashion. The only one that Flesch didn't seem to mind was the agricultural machines importer, perhaps because he didn't know why he was there. "He's a billionaire!" Nathalie whispered in passing by Ludovic. Nearly all of them, except those who were alone or with their gay gigolos, were accompanied by very attractive young women. In Saint-Tropez trendy young things turn up at the weekends looking for a meal and a bed for the night, and some manage to settle down in one bed for a bit longer.

No one addressed a word to him. Just at the beginning of the party, the director of the fashion house had exclaimed when Nathalie introduced him:

'Ah! You're also part of the Flesch family!' thinking he belonged to that powerful tribe.

As he said he wasn't, she lost interest in him. That first party was enough for Flesch; to Nathalie's displeasure, he decided not to repeat the experience. He was no more part of that world than he was part of the revolutionaries'. Moreover the two milieux were beginning to diffuse into one another; the children, adolescents in May '68, were becoming bankers, distinguished doctors, university professors. He admired his mistress's perfect adaptation to that world, which had never ceased to be hers. He would have liked to be amiable, pretend to admire them, but it was beyond his ability. All those people had made a business out of culture; they were at best, if one wanted to be indulgent, cultural promoters, carnivorous promoters. Too bad. He wouldn't get those big commissions that an architect needs to become famous. Perhaps, deep down, he didn't want them at that price.

He no longer knew where he stood with Nathalie. He wondered if, immersed in her old interests, she wasn't incontrovertibly distancing herself from him, but one afternoon, while he was trying to sort out the accounts for their project, which was really finished, Nathalie suggested a coffee break. Then, seeming to forget their recent disagreements, she announced to his stupefaction, as if it were a logical consequence, almost a present he'd been waiting for and which he deserved:

'Look: I've decided that from now on you'll spend three nights with me and four with your wife.'

He was more irritated than surprised. Once again she'd decided without consulting him; what he wanted was, as usual, of no consequence.

The following day he didn't go to the Rue Jouffroy; he didn't telephone. It was Nathalie who called him at the end of the afternoon.

'Are you angry?'

'No… but perhaps it's better if we don't see each other so often, and we don't have a lot to do now… I need to find another project.'

Of course he went back there the next day, irritated with himself.

But it was his body that made the decision, denying him the wholehearted ardour which had led him into the affair and which carries lovers away in spite of themselves.

Nathalie didn't immediately understand the significance of Flesch's repeated failure. As usual, choosing the offensive, she mocked him:

'So you've run out of fuel! Short of juice! A flat battery! Well, too bad for you!' she concluded.

'No,' he said, 'it's all the better.'

She didn't understand, or didn't want to understand. He didn't seem to be humiliated, as men usually are when their cock doesn't work. However, she had the intuition that events were escaping her.

'You're joking,' she said, disturbed.

'No, it's better that way. I can't do it, that's all.'

'Good, it's not serious, we'll see tomorrow.'

'No, we won't see.'

'And why, if you please?' she asked in a slightly trembly voice.

'Because I can't do it anymore.'

They had a bit of extra work to do in the apartment; Nathalie seemed to have agreed to their abstinence. From time to time she asked, with a newly indulgent smile:

'So, are you still having a crisis?'

He didn't reply, also smiling.

One afternoon, arriving late, he found the door to which he possessed a key, already open. He discovered Nathalie, a bottle of whisky in her hand, sitting on the kitchen floor, back against the wall, naked under her dressing gown. She was crying. The garment having slipped down her raised knees, her red-haired vulva was plainly visible, obscenely so.

Flesch pulled her up, gently carried her to the bed and got undressed. But although Nathalie tried all the passes which usually succeeded so well, nothing, nothing happened; the bull remained apathetic.

It was the last time that they would try to make love. They'd finish their work in a kind of polite truce.

Nathalie, however, wouldn't have been Nathalie if she'd taken herself to have been unquestionably beaten.

The architect had created a servant's room, above the conjugal apartment, designed like a small studio, into which he withdrew more and more often, especially since he was no longer going to the Rue Jouffroy. He was making sketches for Lochacq, when there was knock at the door. He thought it was some canvasser or Jehovah's Witness, who never let themselves be discouraged by his bad humour. He found a small gentleman, a kind of tramp with a trapper's cap with earflaps, pulled down to his eyebrows, and an old military coat. The tramp joyfully declared:

'Hi!'

It was Nathalie, exactly in her usual manner: when faced with an obstacle, instead of retreating, she accelerated.

He reluctantly invited her in. She'd violated one of their agreements, imposed by the architect at the beginning of their affair, not to do anything that would disturb Hélène, above all never to arrive unannounced at his place. She reassured him:

'There was nobody,' which meant Hélène, 'on the stairs.'

He only saw Nathalie once more, by chance (was it really by chance?), at an opening at Lochacq's, also an old May '68 comrade. The old faithfuls were all there, stuck to the buffet, and, in the middle, he spotted Nathalie attractively dressed, well made-up, her head surmounted by an extraordinary hairdo. She came towards him, smiling.

'Let's go outside,' she suggested straight away, her tone still just as assured, 'I've something to say to you.'

He was suspicious.

'I can't now, I have to see Lochacq.'

She turned her back on him without replying and left the gallery.

When, much later, tired of the general brouhaha, he also left the reception, he found Nathalie sitting in the courtyard on top of the dustbin store. She'd obviously been crying; the tears had left furrows in her make-up. He sat down next to her. He'd often asked himself if Nathalie loved him; he had his response: she loved him in her own way, love and war mingled indissolubly.

'You know,' she murmured, 'I never cheated on you a single time, even with Miguel.'

Then, in the same breath:

'Do you want us to have a child?'

Hélène was going to give birth in three weeks, so he'd have a child, whose future would occupy him sufficiently. Even according to Nathalie's own demands he had to choose, he would choose against her: who would ever have the sacrifice of a wife on his conscience?

'I mean, what did I ever do to you?' she begged.

'Nothing... I just couldn't go on.'

It was the simple truth.

He had chosen peace and security, even if he was slightly ashamed, even if conjugal life led inexorably to boredom or guile. Perhaps he'd also feared Nathalie's sexuality, for him excessively free? He couldn't have borne to live with a woman whom he risked losing at any moment, even if today, all women risk being lost, even if nobody can ever be sure of anybody.

'For you, the ideal woman,' Nathalie'd said scornfully, 'is the Virgin, who succeeded in the tour de force of making a baby without using her vagina, since, according to that male chauvinist, Saint Augustin, she remained a virgin "before, during and after" giving birth!'

Perhaps Nathalie was right. Perhaps that was it, actually, every man's secret wish? Perhaps all men were frightened of that gaping sexual organ, greedy, bloody and capable of engendering life? In order to say something, he interjected:

'And Miguel?'

'I wanted to make you jealous,' she replied pitifully.

He almost put his arm around her shoulders when she asked him, in that voice which women have, unbearable to men:

'Is that why you've abandoned me!'

Nathalie, abandoned! "Seduced and abandoned!" as in melodramas. Always the ultimate feminine blackmail, which they're scarcely conscious of, and which always works, because of men's permanent guilt. Suddenly, he felt immense pity for her. Why did she have to quickly add:

'You'll see, I'll get you commissions through my family...'

He stiffened. Clearly there weren't leftists in one camp and the well-off in the other; there were the privileged who'd played at being leftists for a moment.

'Come on, be reasonable,' he said pathetically.

It was all he could find to say to this poor chicken, plucked alive! For sure, Nathalie beaten down, was no longer Nathalie; he could scarcely recognise her. He vaguely regretted the triumphant Nathalie. He kissed her on the cheek and went off.

He never saw her again.

Much later on, he learnt from one of the old frequenters of the Rue Jouffroy that Miguel, having become ambassador for his country, had married her; they had two children, and Nathalie having inherited from her father, they'd taken their place among the great and the good, and were living… probably… happily.

The marvellous night

'As you can imagine,' declared the *abbé*, 'I don't have stories about women to tell you, other than those of my parishioners, but I'm bound by the secrets of the confession.

'Permit me to say that I've found you very harsh on your companions.

'You'd like them to be perfect: are you? If they've become less gracious, it's regrettable, but isn't it your own fault? You reproach them for being devious: isn't it because they daren't ever stand up to you? If they're flirtatious: isn't it because despite everything, they're trying to please you? Would you prefer them to always dress in grey and to smell bad?

'Instead of a story, here's an apologue I found in an old book; it'll be my contribution and I hope the conclusion to the evening.

'*Having arrived too late at his stopover, a traveller wasn't able to find a bed for the night. After having looked all over town, exhausted, he ended up collapsing onto the wooden bench of a run-down tavern, resigned to spending the night in discomfort.*

'A poor woman with a scarred cheek, dressed in rags and covered in dust, seeing his plight and perhaps finding him to her taste, took pity on him. "Come back to my place," she suggested, "you can use my dead husband's bed."

'He accepted, in spite of his repulsion and the jeers of the other guests. "In the company of such a beauty," they cried, "you're going to think you're in paradise."

'The woman's lodgings, dark and untidy, befitted their proprietor, who apologised for only being able to offer him a little tea. "Lie down," she suggested. "While you're waiting I'm going to prepare something to eat; if you go to sleep, I'll wake you up."

'Indeed, as soon as his head touched the dreadful straw bed, he fell asleep.

'But when his hostess tapped him on the shoulder, he couldn't believe his eyes; he could scarcely recognise the slut from the tavern in that stunning vision. In a flowing brocade and gold gown, her neck ornamented by a diamond and emerald necklace, her hair freshly washed and so carefully combed that it seemed to light up the shadows of the room, she had the air of a queen. He looked for the scar on her cheek; it was there, but whether he'd overestimated its importance, or thanks to some secret preparation which women know about, it seemed minuscule.

'She helped him get up, then taking his hand, she conducted him toward an open door that he hadn't at first seen. In the middle of a large room was a table laden with rare dishes, flagons of wine, opulent fruits and extraordinary flowers, amongst which was enthroned, wings outspread, a whole peacock. The walls were covered in fine tapestries and ornately framed mirrors reflected dancing light from a number of vermilion and gold candlesticks on the immense mantlepiece. Sweet smells and music coming from one knows not where pervaded the scene, covering it with heavenly grace.

'The traveller, dumbstruck, didn't know how to express his ravishment and his gratitude. They took their places in front of the feast, ate, drank and enjoyed the music and the sweetness of the perfumes. Carving the meat into small pieces, she brought it to his mouth; she filled his glass as soon as he emptied it. Then she sang, more melodiously than the instrument with which she accompanied herself. To the point when, satiated with food and caresses, dizzy with alcohol and the smoke from incense, they found a large bed, covered in silk drapes, occupying one of the corners of the room.

'The next morning, the traveller woke up late, still moved and happy with the memory of his marvellous night.

'But scarcely had he come to his senses, when he discovered he was not in the canopied bed, but on the awful straw where he'd gone to sleep in the first place.

'The woman, who'd returned to her rags, was preparing some drink on an old stove. He looked around, searching for the door to the large room; all he found was an ugly shelf cluttered with chipped cooking utensils.

'Disturbed, disappointed, not knowing if he'd been the victim of some sorcery, he rudely confronted his hostess. "Female spell caster! Witch! Confess that you tricked me! What did you put in my tea?"

'"Nothing that I don't normally put in my own," she calmly replied… "I don't know what you're talking about. The moment you lay down, you went to sleep. I did what any woman would do: seeing as you were so tired, I thought it better not to wake you. You haven't moved until morning… perhaps you were dreaming?"

'"Perhaps I did dream," he admitted ruefully… "It was a marvellous night!"

'"So, now you tell me," the woman asked maliciously, "if I'd given you the choice between last night's dream and my dead husband's hard straw bed, which would you have chosen?"'

Translator's Acknowledgements

I owe many thanks to my wife, Kate, eagle-eyed reader, and to my friend, Anne Desmichellechardon, for advice on French usage.